Jennie Sherborne's  days of World Wa than many. Her fatι test pilot for Vickers Mitchell and Jeffrey Q ᴗcvelop the most iconic airplane of ᴗιe Battle of Britain, the Spitfire. He recorded more than 1,000 test flights, survived two crashes and met his death in a tragic accident in a Bren gun carrier. Jennie tells his story in her acclaimed family history – When the Clouds Roll By. She also records how her mother coped with the loss and how with help from Vickers she and her sister Ann attended the Godolphin School in Salisbury where Jilly Cooper was her friend. Her research and subsequent magazine articles on that period gave her the inspiration for this novel. In addition to her many interests, Jennie founded the Rockbourne Fair which has raised more than £700,000 for charity for she was awarded the MBE. Jennie is also a trustee of Leukaemia Busters.

# GIVE US THIS DAY

*Life, death and romance in World War II*

**By Jennie Sherborne**

First published in Great Britain in 2013
by Rockbourne Publications.

Copyright © Jennie Sherborne 2013

The right of Jennie Sherborne to be identified as
the author of this work has been asserted by her
in accordance with the Copyright, Designs and
Patent Act 1988.

All rights reserved. No part of this publication may
be reproduced, stored in a retrieval system or
transmitted by any means without the prior
permission of the author in writing.

All  characters in this book are purely fictional.

ISBN: 978-0-9573310-5-1

Edited by John Jenkins. Designed by Alan Cooper.

Printed in the UK by Biddles, part of the MPG Books Group,
Bodmin and King's Lynn.

*So many gods, so many creeds.*
*So many paths that wind and wind*
*While just the art of being kind*
*Is all the sad world needs.*

Ella Wheeler Wilcox

I dedicate this book to darling Ian, my late husband, who gave so much and took so little. Also my thanks go to my lovely family and friends whose love and support have encouraged me to write. And a special 'thank you' to John Jenkins without whose editing and guidance I would never have put pen to paper. **J.S.**

# CHAPTER 1

The All Clear siren had sounded. Wearily, Johnnie Kershaw clambered into the cockpit of Spitfire K9926 cleared for his last test flight of the day. Seeing Mike Pinkerton standing on the tarmac he called out, "How about a drink later Pinkie, what's your programme?"

"I shall be here for a while, how long will you be?"

"I'll see you in the bar in about forty five minutes. There seems to be another bloody problem with the ailerons. I wish we could get to the bottom of it."

The familiar sound of the Rolls Royce Merlin engine thundered as the aircraft taxied along the rustic runway and then suddenly, just at lift off, there was silence. Mike turned in time to see the Spitfire's nose embedded into the grass at 45 degrees. Mike, a fire engine and ambulance, bells ringing and lights flashing sped to the scene. Johnnie, still in the cockpit and clasping his head in his hands, did not look up.

"Are you OK Johnnie, what the hell are you playing at?" Johnnie's eyes appeared through the cracks of his fingers, followed by a series of expletives, and then as he climbed out of the cockpit "Why the bloody hell did she do that (always a she when there was a fault!) - completely cut out on take off." Johnnie leaned over the shoulder of the aircraft mechanic asking for an explanation when Pinkie impatiently interrupted.

"Oh come on Johnnie, you'll find out soon enough. We've both done our bit for today – last one to the bar buys the drinks." With that they sprinted towards the Hampshire Aeroplane Club only to be waylaid by the agitated work's manager, Len Levison.

"We've just heard that the Woolston Factory has been bombed. We have lost all communication with them but believe there is absolute carnage. Those German bastards . . .."

There was no hanging around, not even a quick drink. Mike jumped into Johnnie's Riley and followed the ambulance as it sped out of the main gates with its bells shattering the ominous peace of the neighbourhood. Not a word was spoken as they drove through the back streets of war-stricken Southampton, just a dreaded fear of what they may encounter. They could see clouds of black smoke billowing into the late afternoon sky and then the full impact of the disaster lay before them.

Complete chaos. The dead and wounded were being stretchered to the waiting ambulances, firemen attempting to dowse the leaping flames while pulling victims from the burning buildings. The intensity of the heat, the acrid smoke and the wailing and screams made any kind of order impossible.

While Johnnie and Mike were deciding where they could best be of use they heard desperate screams from a woman. "Help, help my darling babies are buried, I can't find them."

Silhouetted against the smoke stood a young woman, her soot-blackened face streaked with tears, clutching a baby. "God, God, where are you, I need you," she implored. The two men hurriedly went to her aid. She was hysterical. Her twin daughters aged two were buried among the blitzed ruins. Johnnie gripped her firmly. Rubble and shards of glass crunched beneath his feet.

"We are here and will do everything possible to find your children. Please, calm down and answer a few questions." The hysteria continued. Johnnie shook her. "I'm sorry, we cannot help you unless you cooperate with us. Every moment is vital so STOP screaming."

She stopped and when she had regained her breath she said her twins, Annie and Biddy, were playing in the front room when the bomb fell. She had been in the kitchen, feeding baby Paddy. She then pointed vaguely to where she thought they must be buried.

Mike took her arm. "Come my dear now, it's vital that you sit down out of the smoke and keep very, very quiet so that we can listen for any cries or movement." With that he guided her to a broken wall and removing his sweater laid it down for her to sit on.

Mary O'Reilly, with baby Paddy nestled into her breast, sat motionless staring into space trying to recall what had happened. Apart from an ear-shattering explosion, she remembered nothing, not even how she had come out unscathed. 'Brendan, where is Brendan?' This thought suddenly flashed through her mind. "Oh no! My husband Brendan, how can I find out if he's safe? He works on the assembly line at the factory."

"Please bear with us, nobody can do any more than they are doing already and it will, I am sure, be many hours before we know the fate of so many people. Try to be brave. Your name again?"

"Mary," she meekly answered.

Johnnie continued, "I know this is an horrendous ordeal for you and so many others. Mike and I realise the urgency of the situation but we have to work slowly to prevent any more debris caving in on top of your little ones. It would really be a good idea if you and little Paddy could find a safe haven in someone's home. This awful smoke cannot be doing him any good." Mary was not to be moved. She felt a complete sense of helplessness.

Paddy, her rosary beads and her deep religious belief were now her only solace. While deep in silent prayer, sitting on that bombed site, memories of her childhood in Ireland came flooding back. For the first time she questioned her faith.

# CHAPTER 2

Mary's thoughts switched back to Limerick, her mother, drunken father, and her remaining siblings. Terrible days of a poverty-stricken childhood in Ireland. What had she done to deserve all this? According to the 'Faith' those who were not true believers would be doomed or burned in hell or some other indescribable horror. She tried to recall a reason why God should be punishing her in this way. Maybe she should not have married Brendan O'Reilly and deserted her family - "but that had been Mammy's wish" she muttered quietly.

Life in the O'Shea household in the late 1930's had reached breaking point. After centuries of discontent, Southern Ireland won home rule from Britain in 1920, only to be followed by a bitter conflict leading to unemployment, poverty and a struggle for survival. The Catholic Church had always been a powerful institution and the Irish turned to religion in the belief that God would help them to improve their lives.

Home Rule became Rome Rule and penetrated every element of cultural life.

In slum conditions Jimmy and Molly O'Shea tried to raise seven children. Desperate with neither work nor money Jimmy found solace in alcohol. And Molly, almost always pregnant, shouldered the family responsibilities.

But come what may, mass was attended daily, prayers were said morning and evening and grace before each meal. Anything less was the road to hell.

As she sat on the smouldering bombsite, she remembered the shenanigans of bath night at St. Thomas Street. The copious jugs the family, with the exception of Jimmy, had to carry backwards and forwards to fill up the old zinc bath in front of the fire. If at home, Jimmy would take the first plunge, followed in pecking order down the family – Mammy, unselfishly, would wait to last by which time the water was cold and grey. It was always while Jimmy O'Shea was taking his bath that the rows would erupt. Jimmy's naked vulnerability gave the otherwise timid Molly a vestige of confidence.

"Jimmy, you've got to do something. Look at our children – they have no food, no shoes, they are cold, and you show them no love. You come home drunk. Where do you find money to buy drink? I have to send Seamus out on to the streets begging, otherwise we would starve." The more Molly O'Shea pleaded with her husband the worse he became. He would swear, shout, lose his temper and storm out of the house leaving his children huddled terrified on the staircase.

Widower Brendan O'Reilly who ran a stall nearby would often bring them eggs and left over vegetables after the market closed. And the warmth and friendliness that he brought into the home was something they all cherished. Some of the happiest evenings that Mary could recall were when Brendan would join them for an evening meal.

To Molly's delight, she could detect a strengthening bond between Mary, still only eighteen, and Brendan, who was twenty years her senior. Mary, over the months had certainly grown to respect and maybe even love Brendan, but in no way considered him a long-term suitor.

Molly thought differently, and probably, without fully realising, put so much pressure on the couple that it was not long after their first meeting they were married. Mary moved into Brendan's flat giving the O'Shea's a little more space, and one less mouth to feed.

Brendan had at long last brought some relief into the lives of the O'Shea family, and the arrival of Mary's twins, Biddy and Annie, were heralded as a gift from God.

With this added responsibility, Brendan realised that the profits from his market stall were insufficient to keep a family of four, and believing Ireland offered little scope, secretly applied for jobs in England.

"Mary, I have wonderful news," he announced one morning. "I have been offered a job working on the assembly line for a new aeroplane called the Spitfire in Southampton, England. I cannot believe the wage they have offered. Beyond my wildest dreams."

Mary looked dumbfounded. "Why haven't you told me about this Brendan? What does it mean? Are you going to leave me and the twins to work in England? In England? You know what we think of the English. Dear God! Whatever next, what are you . . ."

"Please listen, and just try to understand. We now have our two lovely babies. Surely, you want to give them a better life than the one we've known. What has life to offer here? Nothing. Let's start a new life together. We will be able to send parcels and money home to your Mammy and in this way help her. Come on Mary, this is a chance of a lifetime."

She realised that it made sense, but what would Mammy think. She would be gutted. Mary remembered taking Biddy and Annie with her to break the news. She felt a traitor. The ominous threat of war also preyed on her mind.

"I can't believe it," was Molly's first reaction but in her naturally unselfish manner, added:

"Of course, my child, there is no question, you must go. I would hate to think of you having to bring up your children as I have had to. You must think of Biddy and Annie. I am happy for you. God bless you both."

Mary and Brendan had three months before embarking on what they hoped would be a better life. Brendan went ahead to find a home, and settle into his new job and Mary and the twins followed a few weeks later. Brendan left on July 1st 1939, and Mary and the children booked their passage for August 13th. Mary remembered thinking, 'there would now be no going back'.

14b, Paynes Road,

Woolston

Southampton

20<sup>th</sup> July

*My dearest Mary*

*Well I've made it! I have found us a little two-bedroomed house about three minutes walk from the factory, and you'll never guess, it's got electricity and a lavatory inside the house. I have to work long hours but already have lots of good mates who are showing me the ropes.*

*I am longing to see you all again. I miss you so much. I will be at the dockside to meet you. All my love my darling Mary, a big kiss for the twins. God be with you.*

*Brendan x x x*

Mary had just finished reading the letter, when there was a loud knock on the door. Molly in tears was on the doorstep.

"Oh Mammy what's up? What's happened, come and sit down."

"I hardly dare tell you my child, but I have just discovered your sister Bryony has got herself pregnant, and the baby could arrive at any time. Oh Mary, what are we to do?" Mary had noticed that for the last few months Bryony had kept apart from the rest of the family – but pregnant surely not? She has never seemed in the least bit interested in boys and she didn't seem at all fat.

"Who's the father Mammy?"

"You tell me Mary, she refuses to tell me. She is very frightened.

Nobody must know about this or her whole life will be finished. Can I bring her here?"

In Mary's mind, there was only one man who could be responsible for taking advantage of Bryony. She had already lost all respect for her father, Jimmy, but now she despised him.

Mary recollected the stressful time that followed. Bryony, still only fifteen, the wretched child had been carrying this burden for months, too frightened to tell anyone; the traumatic birth administered by Molly and Mary, and then before Mary had fully realised she was breastfeeding this tiny baby as well her eighteen-month old twins. There was no time to be lost. Baby Paddy must be included on her passport and Mary would take him to England with her.

She recalled the voyage to England with three babies. The rough seas, the nervous tension of never having been abroad, the homesickness and hardly a moment went by without wondering what Brendan's reaction would be when he saw baby Paddy.

Suddenly, something jolted her thoughts and brought her back to reality. She could detect a slight air of optimism.

# CHAPTER 3

"Did you hear that Johnnie? Shush. Keep quiet, I am sure I heard a little whimper."

"Yes, I heard it too." With infinite care, Mike and Johnnie moved brick by brick, plank by plank, and then handfuls of rubble with their bare hands which were now bleeding.

"Annie, Biddy can you hear us?" Although unsure whether the twins would understand him, Johnnie continued. "You must not move, keep very still and we will get you out and take you to Mummy. Don't be frightened, it's all over now." Mike quickly went over to the expectant Mary.

"Mary, I think we have found them. We just want to be sure and make certain everything is safe and when we give you the OK, will you come over and speak to them. Your voice will give them comfort. Hopefully, it shouldn't take us too long now."

The only contribution that Mary felt she had been able to make thus far was to pray, and that she certainly did. Now with renewed hope and with baby Paddy still snuggled into her breast, she joined the two men and felt at last she was doing something constructive.

"Biddy, Annie, it's Mammy, can you hear me darlings, I'm right here and two lovely friends will soon bring you back to me." Within seconds a cry was clearly audible. Only one of the twins was responding. They tried not to entertain negative thoughts.

Johnnie, with infinite care, eased himself into the opening they had prepared, and disappeared for what seemed an age. Mike and Mary listened intently.

Then, "Come on little one, you're quite safe now." Within five minutes Johnnie emerged with Biddy in his arms. As Mary handed Paddy over to Mike, and she opened her arms to Biddy, the tears from them both were inconsolable. All seemed ominously quiet from below.

"Here Johnnie, you take Paddy and I will go down this time and find the other one." Tension again took over from the momentary relief, as they waited in the smoky twilight. Minutes seemed like hours.

"I've found her, she's OK," Mike's voice forced the glint of a smile on the waiting faces. Mike soon emerged after extricating Annie from a beam that had fallen across her. She was fully conscious, her wide eyes prominent against her dirty and bloodstained face.

"My darling, darling little girl. Annie, you'll be all right now." Annie showed no emotion whatsoever, but Mary thought she detected a little recognition on her face.

Suddenly from behind came a voice with wavering southern Irish accent "I've come home Mary." Mary quickly turned to see Brendan, hardly recognizable in the dark gloom of the evening. He was alive. Oh Brendan! Thanks be to God you're alive. We're all alive. Thank you, thank you God."

"Mary, what have I done to you? Can I ever forgive myself for bringing you here to this hell?"

To Mary's surprise, Brendan, her pillar of strength, broke down. It was all too much. The long embrace was interrupted by Johnnie's insistence that he got them all to the casualty department of South Hants Hospital. Annie was cause for concern.

Another long haul awaited them. The hospital was heaving and the medical staff unable to cope. At 2am they finally saw a doctor. Mike had conjured some food, nappies and a few basic requirements to tide them over. As dawn was breaking, Brendan, Mary, Biddy and Paddy were discharged, but Annie, completely traumatised had to remain for further investigations. Mike offered them refuge in his home in Hamble for the remainder of the night, promising he would find them transport to visit Annie the next day.

The O'Reilly family's trauma was a tiny part of the overall catastrophe. More than 90 people had been killed and 40 injured in and around the Woolston Supermarine factory. Mary and Brendan did not realise that they were the lucky ones.

# CHAPTER 4

The exasperated and hostile look on Virginia Pinkerton's face said it all as she opened the front door of Creek House to Mike and his four mentally and physically exhausted refugees. It was 4am.

Mike, anticipated her reaction: "I will explain everything to you later Virginia, but this family has been to hell and back and desperately needs food and a wash. Can you find them some towels, show them the bathroom, and I will see what I can rustle up in the kitchen."

Not waiting for a response, Mike made his way to the kitchen. Confronted by an empty refrigerator he checked the larder for inspiration. As he emerged with a couple of tins of spam and some eggs, the kitchen door opened.

"What on earth are you playing at Mike? Did you really have to bring all those people back here to our home at this ungodly hour?" Mike tried to explain the traumatic events. That the family were bombed out, had nowhere to go and that their other little girl Annie was in hospital. He had offered them a temporary roof over their heads.

"Sorry Mike, this is just not on. Although Len phoned me to tell me where you were, I have been worrying about you all night, and now this. We're finding it hard enough to feed our own children without you bringing in more off the street. I suppose you think I am going to look after them."

Exhaustion was now showing on Mike's face. "Yes, Virginia I do. If you had seen what I have tonight, maybe you would hold a different view. In case you don't realise it, there is a war on. I think it's about time you accept this fact and perhaps share your privileged lifestyle with others."

She had heard enough and strutted out of the room, her eau de nil satin dressing gown swirling above her velvet mules.

Mike did not let the matter rest. He called after her: "Will you make sure their baby has a supply of Phoebe's nappies to tide them over, and then will you go and collect the eggs from the hen house as I have only four here and that won't be enough. And could you please see if there are any spare blankets and pillows so they can bed down on the floor in the drawing room."

Realising perhaps that he was being a little unreasonable and to alleviate the tension, Mike concluded, "Virginia, darling when you have done that would you help me cook the spam, eggs and baked beans...I love you!"

Almost unaware of the nightmare that had beset them, Biddy and Paddy having been bathed and fed could stay awake no longer, Biddy curled up in pillows and blankets and Paddy was tightly tucked up in Phoebe's pram. Fortunately Mike and Virginia's daughters, Kate and Phoebe had not been disturbed. They slept through it all. Mike reassured Mary and Brendan that he would make sure they would get to the hospital, but it was vital that they all got some sleep.

"Things won't look so bad after a good sleep" were his last words before he fell into bed utterly and completely exhausted.

Kate and Phoebe were the first to stir, and although Virginia had tried to keep them quiet, the excitement of finding so many unexpected visitors was too much for them. By 10am, to Virginia's disgust, the house was in chaos, with Paddy being exceptionally noisy. Mrs. Honeywell, the Pinkertons' daily cum mother's help seemed to cast a magical spell and in her quiet way took charge of the four children while Mike, Brendan and Mary planned their day, keeping Virginia in the picture.

Mrs. Honeywell volunteered to work extra time and offered not only to look after Kate and Phoebe, but also Biddy and Paddy, and if necessary take them home with her until their parents returned.

Mike telephoned Eastleigh Aerodrome, explained the situation and told them he hoped to be in soon after midday. The lines were still down at the Woolston Supermarine Factory so he was unable to report that Brendan was alive but would not be reporting for duty that day.

He then contacted the hospital who said that Annie was comfortable but advised that she should have no visitors for at least forty-eight hours. But Mary insisted she would not rest until she had seen Annie, so her anxiety and tetchiness was only matched by the hostility of Virginia who made it clear that they were not welcome. The friction in the Pinkerton household that day was something they could all have done without and revealed Virginia in her true colours. Her lack of compassion riled Mike.

Mike had first met the stunningly beautiful Virginia Bellingham-Smythe at Henley in 1935. Wearing an alluring Molyneux cream outfit, her tall statuesque figure, brown glistening hair, smouldering eyes and perfect olive skin had instantly made Mike feel weak at the knees. She was surrounded by drooling young men, all vying to make the greatest impression. Mike summed up the competition. So far as he was concerned they were only gormless public schoolboys. Quietly confident he eased himself into the group. Thus began a whirlwind romance and within three months, much to the dismay of both families, they were married.

To Mike she was beauty personified and because of his overwhelming love he was blind to any flaws lurking in her character. The children came along in quick succession and as long as Virginia had everything she wanted the marriage had run smoothly. He even accepted her vanity, never wanting to go on his boat because it would spoil her 'hairdo'. This shallowness he found irritating, but her dismissive attitude towards the O'Reillys had stunned him. Mike found this unforgivable.

'How could she be so callous?'

Mary had a problem, albeit in retrospect a small one. Not only had she never left the children in the care of someone else, but she was still breast feeding Paddy, although she had felt that morning the supply appeared to be drying up; probably a reaction to her shock. Mrs. Honeywell told her not to worry, as she was a retired maternity nurse. Paddy would be in good hands; She also advised that perhaps it was a good time to start to wean him.

Mike duly dropped Brendan and Mary off at South Hants Hospital, and hand in hand, they approached the intensive care ward. Annie was not there. Seeing the consternation on their faces, the ward sister introduced herself and asked them whether they were looking for little Annie O'Reilly because she was now out of intensive care and had been moved to the Children's Ward. Dr. Todd, the paediatrician, would like to see them.

Annie was sitting up looking out of the window when they arrived. She turned as Mary and Brendan approached her bedside. A broad smile lit up her bruised face and tearful eyes when she saw them. There was no question she recognised them.

"Annie, Annie, my little Annie what a relief you're OK, Dadda and I have been so worried. Oh, thanks be to God." Hugs, kisses and more hugs followed, and tears of joy rolled down their faces.

"I take it you are Mr. and Mrs. O'Reilly," came a gentle voice from behind, interrupting the joyous reunion. "It is good to meet you, I am Dr. Todd. I wonder if you could come to my consulting room so I can tell you about the examinations we have carried out on Annie so far". He turned to Annie and slowly and clearly pronouncing every word said "Mummy and Daddy will be back to see you in a few minutes."

A quietly spoken man, Dr. Todd began, "I am pleased to report that physically, apart from bruising, Annie appears not to have suffered from any broken bones or internal injury. There also appears to be no brain damage. However, we are concerned about her apparent loss of hearing. She appears not to hear anything. She is still in a state of shock, so this may improve. I have referred her to an Ear, Nose and Throat Specialist who will give her a thorough assessment and we will be able to give you a clearer picture shortly.

"We would like to keep her here under observation for the time being. Please rest assured she's in good hands. Try not to excite her too much. She must be kept calm. I would like to see you again in about three days." He stood up, shook their hands, and with "please try not to worry too much" politely showed them the door.

It was only when Mary and Brendan returned to Annie's bedside that the realisation came to them that maybe Annie was unable to hear what they were saying. Mary's ingrained religious belief once again came to the fore – she dismissed from her mind that her darling Annie may be afflicted for the rest of her life; God in his wondrous way had saved her, and the rest of the family, and they must now waste no time to visit St. Bride's Church, where they had been worshipping since their arrival in England, to give thanks.

Tears swelled up in Annie's eyes as she watched them disappearing down the corridor, her little hand continued waving, and the tears rolled down her cheeks, long after they were out of sight. Mary just hoped that they had made her understand the reason she was to stay in hospital and that they would be back every day to see her.

St. Bride's was no longer there. Just a bombed out shell awaited them. To Mary it was bad enough to lose her home and all her belongings, but then to lose her haven, her church, was just too much. Brendan, noticing the sheer panic on her face gently put his arm around her.

"Come on now Mary, be brave, the church may not be there but God is." With that Mary, got down on her knees and prayed, giving thanks to God, completely uninhibited by those around her.

Helping her back to her feet, Brendan realising he must be strong, sympathetically but fairly sternly announced, "Mary, both of us now must have courage and be sensible. We have many problems ahead. Our lovely children we must protect, and at the moment our lives are in shreds. Let's see if we can find Father O'Sullivan and perhaps get some clothes, and then we must go back and see whether Mike has any ideas where we go from here.

"You'll see Mary, to be sure, we'll win through and everything will be all right. We cannot only rely on God. We must have faith in ourselves."

Armed with a bag full of clothes and some basic food Mary and Brendan took a bus to the Bugle Inn, at Hamble just a ten minute walk from the Pinkerton's house. After a strenuous day and both feeling emotionally drained, they fell into almost instant sleep.

The terrifying sound of the air raid siren woke them. Recollections of two days before came flooding back. Their stomachs churned and Mary complained of feeling nauseous. "Oh Brendan, this is all too much, do you think Annie is safe?"

"Don't even think about it, even the Germans would not want to bomb a hospital. She will be all right," reassured Brendan.

# CHAPTER 5

As Mary and Brendan staggered along the pathway to Creek House they were greeted at the door with "Oh, so you're back! Your children are with Mrs. Honeywell, so I suggest you go straight up there so you can sort them out."

Virginia's aggressive attitude towards them had not diminished - she could not even bring herself to enquire after Annie.

So with a polite "thank you," the weary couple dragged themselves to Mrs. Honeywell's enchanting, but neglected little cottage.

"I've just made a pot of tea, my dears, come and put your feet up. Your children have been angels. Kate, Biddy's Mummy and Daddy are here," Mrs. Honeywell called. The children came running in, Biddy's arm stretched to give Mary a big hug.

"Where's Paddy?" Mary asked. "He's asleep, and Phoebe is with my Mummy" a bright-eyed little Kate replied.

Mrs. Honeywell's convivial manner, her natural and confident way with children and the cosiness of her home brought an immediate feeling of tranquillity to Mary and Brendan. Perhaps all was not lost. Mary's nausea, triggered by the air raid siren, however, had not abated, and following tea, and a piece of Mrs. Honeywell's homemade cake, she was violently sick.

"It's all been too much for you my dear. You need to have a complete rest, and I would like to suggest that you Biddy and Paddy stay here and let me look after you. I am sure Brendan will be happy to stay at Creek House." Mrs. Honeywell had already felt vibes from Virginia that the family were not welcome there and now with Mary feeling unwell she was convinced this would be the answer.

Brendan immediately replied, "Mrs. Honeywell, I don't know how we'll ever be able to repay you, but this is a wonderful idea, thank you so very much." Mary just nodded in appreciation.

It was nearly eight o'clock before Mike arrived home. Brendan, having struggled to make conversation with Virginia, found the comfort of an armchair more appealing and was soon oblivious to the world.

"How about a beer old chap?" Through his heavy eyelids Brendan could see a hazy Mike towering above him passing him a glass of beer. "Come on let's go into the snug where we can talk."

Having enquired after Annie and asked Brendan how their day had gone, Mike was brimming over with news. "The bad news is those German bastards have again bombed the Itchen works. There was a direct hit on an air raid shelter and nearly a hundred people were inside. Thank God you weren't there." Brendan recalled hearing the air raid siren when they were in the bus.

Mike continued, "We've been concentrating on removing as many Spitfires and other aircraft from Southampton and hiding them in various parts of Hampshire and nearby counties. We received these urgent instructions directly from Lord Beaverbrook, so you can imagine this has been quite a hectic operation in itself. My goodness, what a terrible catastrophe it would have been if we hadn't acted immediately. As it is, the production of the Spitfire has been brought to a halt. Fortunately, this shouldn't be for long. For everyone's sake let's hope not anyway."

Drawing breath to gulp a long swig of beer Mike went on, "Brendan, looking at things optimistically, this will give you time to get back on your feet. I've made enquiries about getting you all new ration books and identity cards and that is under way. Meanwhile, an old mate of mine is coming in to clear out my boathouse and the old annexe to make it into living accommodation for all of you. I don't know what your building skills are like but it would be good if you could help him.

It shouldn't take long as the annexe already has two rooms, a kitchen and a bathroom, as the previous owners employed a couple that lived there for many years.

"It's just filled up with all my clutter now, so if I get that all removed up into the attic, and then a good lick of paint it will look like a palace. Oh, and Johnnie, who helped rescue you, says he has some furniture to help out. They have a lot in store down in the docks in Southampton."

Brendan couldn't wait to tell Mary the great news. He was sure this would be the incentive she needed and would help her rebuild her mental and physical strength.

The Spitfire's testing programme at Eastleigh Aerodrome continued virtually unhindered by the two devastating raids at the Supermarine factory, and Mike and Johnnie were relentlessly testing up to forty Spits each a month to keep the RAF fighter squadrons replenished. The production rate of the German Messerschmitt 109 was an unknown factor, and there was always the ongoing fear that the production of this awesome fighter might outstrip the Spitfire and the Hurricane. To win the battle against German air supremacy was vital, and the urgency to all working in the aircraft industry was apparent. Although Mike and Johnnie wanted to help the O'Reilly family, in no way would they jeopardize this priority. Brendan's work on the assembly line was vital and it was imperative that he reported back as soon as the factory recovered.

These were desperate times. Churchill had earlier in the year replaced Neville Chamberlain as prime minister and had immediately instilled confidence in the British people. Germany, though, had already invaded Denmark and Norway, and on the very day Churchill took office, Western Europe encountered the Blitzkrieg when Germany invaded France, Belgium and Holland. British troops had to retreat in haste, and then followed the miraculous story of Dunkirk.

An armada of ships and boats, ranging from Navy destroyers, fishing boats, pleasure boats and other small craft from the south crossed the channel and rescued 226,000 British and 110,000 French troops from Dunkirk. The free-spirited Mike had desperately wanted to take his boat for this exciting venture but knew it was out of the question. Instead, he and Virginia stood outside their boathouse and in the silent darkness could detect the figures of many of those brave men preparing for their epic voyage.

One by one they slipped their moorings and stealthily chugged down the river Hamble to the Solent and an unknown fate. It was a weird feeling watching them and shivers ran down Mike's spine while Virginia seemed completely unmoved. As they turned to walk back to the house, Mike muttered under his breath "Good luck boys, you're going to need it."

Hitler's next target was Britain. Fortunately, due to the intensive production of Spitfires and Hurricanes, Britain, although short of pilots, maintained air supremacy. This of, course was not known, and although morale was high, Britain stood alone. No commitment from the United States and none from the Soviet Union. These were gloomy days.

\* \* \* \* \*

Unfortunately, confirmation of Annie's hearing problem was explained to Mary and Brendan by Dr. Benson, the ear, nose and throat Specialist. As a result of the explosion he feared that she had been left almost totally deaf. This would impair her speech. To all and sundry she would appear deaf and dumb, and would always need a great deal of patience and understanding from her family to help her to communicate. He explained the importance of always facing her when talking, and to mouth every sentence slowly and in an exaggerated way. It might also help to let her hold the throat of anybody talking to her, because she would pick up the vibrations.

He then tried to explain the situation to Annie and although she did not fully understand what was happening there was a big smile when she realised she could go home. Dr. Benson concluded that he would like to reassess Annie in three months' time. He would have a clearer picture and be able to recommend a way forward.

Mary's joy that the family were now all reunited, and with the added excitement that, due to Mike's amazing generosity, they would shortly have a roof over their heads, gave her the strength to be positive over Annie's disability, and put her own sickness to one side. She gave her thanks to God over and over again. Although a Catholic himself, Brendan found it a little galling.

Mrs. Honeywell's cottage was now bursting at the seams. A line of nappies, clothes, sheets and blankets, stretching the width of the garden, flapped in the breeze. She had found two old camp beds from the annexe which she had scrubbed up so all her visitors had a bed. She was not to be daunted, and with her affectionate warm manner, it was only a matter of minutes before she had taken Annie under her wing.

A rabbit stew was simmering away on the old range, and vast quantities of potatoes were baking in the oven. Mrs. Honeywell's finger pointed to each one of them, counting, "I reckon, that with the two babies, there are eight of us. I found a whole lot of plates, mugs and cutlery in the annexe while I was down there, so we are now well set up."

Just before their high tea, Brendan took Annie for a walk along by the old salterns by the side of the Hamble river while Mary explained Annie's problem to all gathered around, Kate, being that bit older, seemed to grasp the situation immediately, but Biddy was unable to understand that her twin sister would never be able to hear or even speak again. She looked bewildered. After a noisy but jovial meal, Mrs. Honeywell picked up Phoebe from a high chair and said, "I will take these two back to their home and get them to bed. That will give us a little peace and more room. Come on Kate, say 'good night'." A disgruntled look came over little Kate's face as she pleaded to stay. "All right Kate, you stay here while I put Phoebe to bed, then I will come and get you."

Kate quickly ran to the corner of the garden where she found a big ball which for a minute or two she kicked around before beckoning to Biddy and Annie to come and join her. Soon the three of them were picking up the ball and throwing it over the washing line while one or the other tried to catch it. When they got bored with that they ran in and out of the washing chasing one another. Mary and Brendan watched through the kitchen window while washing the dishes. Their eyes met. Affectionately, Brendan put his arm around Mary and with a big squeeze and kiss he said, "Hold tight Mary, you'll see everything will be all right." Mary smiled. She was feeling much better but her nausea still prevailed.

# CHAPTER 6

The weekend that followed was a hive of industry at Creek House. Herbert, a retired builder, was pleased to lend a hand to get the boathouse habitable for its new guests. Mike's beloved boat, Sexy Susie was moved out to the slipway, made secure and covered in a large tarpaulin. His precious Norton motorbike was squeezed alongside his car in the garage, and once he had had a good clear out of what can only be described as junk there was room to manoeuvre. As Mike was working all weekend he was unable to oversee the operation, but he left instructions for "Sniffy Herbert" as he had cruelly nicknamed him, and Brendan, to put in a communicating door between the annexe and the boathouse, divide the boathouse into two rooms, and for each one to have a window facing the river.

"Have you got the gist of what we are trying to do?" Mike asked. "I know Sherbert you are an expert on this kind of thing and with Brendan's practical help the two of you will soon have it all up and running. I'll see to finding the doors, windows and wood, so good luck chaps."

That done, he strode off – he had more important challenges to overcome.

There appeared to be a conspiracy between Mrs. Honeywell and Mary. Mrs. Honeywell announced to Annie and Biddy "Your poor Mammy is not well and must have complete rest for a few days. I'll take you to see her every morning and to say 'goodnight' to her but I would like you to be very good children and not to go in and disturb her."

Mrs. Honeywell also conveyed the same message to Brendan, so Mary was left for two days to recuperate.

Time alone gave Mary an opportunity to wonder about her family

# Jennie Sherborne

Coutts Cottage Rockbourne Hampshire SP6 3NF

Tel: 01725 518333

Email: jen.sherborne@btinternet.com

With many thanks – I hope you enjoy it.

Jennie

With Compliments

in Limerick. There had been little contact since Mary arrived in England over a year ago. Messages had been relayed back through some of Brendan's family who were able to read and write, but due to the O'Reilly's extreme circumstances, no food parcels, as promised, had been sent. Mary just hoped that they were unaware of the dangers they had all been subjected to, but she knew that Mammy in particular would be worried. Bryony on two occasions, had written letters, devoid of much news, and omitting to mention little Paddy.

Mary assumed she was suffering from depression and was careful in replying for fear of upsetting her even more. How was Bryony coping now, she wondered, and had Jimmy, her father, sobered up to make a little effort to provide for his family? Above all she prayed that he was not verbally or sexually abusing any of them. Was her wonderful Mammy being able to manage without her?

Before making a conscious effort to dismiss these thoughts from her deeply stressed mind, she could not help but wonder when, if ever, she would see her family in Ireland again.

Mary was amazed at the progress that had been made to the boathouse in just two days. She could not help but notice the euphoric atmosphere as Brendan and 'Sherbert' worked and joked together, and Kate, Biddy and Annie played excitedly nearby.

The men briefly downed tools when Mrs. Honeywell came down with a tray of teas, and milk for the children. "My word, I can't get over what you've done already, you must have been working non-stop" were Mary's welcoming words. Both men preened with pride.

"Well, I'm back to work tomorrow Mary, so we want to get as much done today as possible. My poor old mate Sherbs here is going to have to work on his own for the rest of the week." After the jovial tea break Brendan suddenly remembered, "Oh, by the way, Johnnie, the test pilot who helped rescue us, and his wife Maisie, have invited you and the children to go and stay for a few days at their cottage in the country."

This came as a  shock to Mary. She really couldn't face going anywhere at the moment. She reckoned she had been pushed from pillar to post enough, and certainly did not relish going to stay with someone she didn't know, and definitely not without Brendan. Not wanting to seem ungrateful she stood there in silence, not knowing what to say. The expression on her face said it all, so Brendan did not pursue the matter.

Back at Mrs. Honeywell's cottage, Mary sat at the kitchen table feeding Paddy, contemplating how she could politely get out of going off to the country, when Mrs. Honeywell came in with an arm full of ironing.

"How'ya feeling my dear," she enquired. This was just the cue for Mary.

" I'm all right Mrs. Honeywell but we've been invited to stay in the country for a few days with Johnnie – I don't know his other name – the test pilot, and his family. Oh, to be sure, I don't know what to do because I just don't want to go. I don't know them, and I couldn't cope with it all. What can I say to them?"

"Don't you worry about it Mary, if you really don't want to go I'll speak to Mr. Pinkerton and tell him you are not well enough. You would, though, love it there. I often take Kate and Phoebe there to stay when Mrs. Pinkerton goes away, and Mrs. Kershaw always treats me like one of her family. How about if I mention to Mr. Pinkerton that I go too, I know they have already asked Kate, and they may be pleased to have another pair of hands?

"I'm due to some time off and I'm sure Mrs. Pinkerton will take care of Phoebe.  Leave it to me dearie, and don't you worry about it. Will you go if I come too?" Feeling a little more reassured but still uncertain Mary gave a half smile and nodded.

They all squashed into Johnnie Kershaw's Riley, but it was over an hour's journey before they all peeled out at Rose Cottage and were greeted by a laughing Maisie wondering how many more would fall out of the car. "What a party!" she exclaimed as she gave Johnnie an affectionate kiss and ushered them all into their big farmhouse kitchen. "Well now, I know Mrs. Honeywell, and of course, Kate. You must be Mary and little Paddy and then the twins – which is Annie and which is Biddy?" After all the introductions were duly completed, Maisie and Johnnie's two little daughters came running in. "Now this is Lucy, and this is Tilly."

Maisie went all round again repeating everyone's name. "Lucy and Tilly will take you to meet all the animals when we've had tea."

Johnnie had not been home since the two raids on the Supermarine factory, so after boiled eggs with soldiers, bread and dripping and cake, Lucy and Tilly, under Mrs. Honeywell's supervision took the children to meet the three cats, Jet the Labrador, Joey the pony and Norah the parrot, while Mary went upstairs to unpack.

During the past few hectic weeks Maisie had seen little of Johnnie and they had only been able to keep in touch by the occasional telephone call. There was so much news to catch up on and so little time, as Johnnie had to report back to the airfield early the next morning. With six children bustling in and out, these precious moments weren't' exactly quality time, but the indefatigable Mrs. Honeywell managed to keep the children at bay.

Johnnie, still a schoolboy at heart, found time to play some boisterous bedtime games with the five girls. It was quite touching to notice how Kate had taken Annie under her wing; the two of them had really bonded and Kate had found a way by speaking slowly and in an exaggerated way which Annie seemed to understand and prevented her from feeling left out. No therapist could have done a better job.

Johnnie Kershaw was another free spirit, more so than his friend and fellow test pilot 'Pinkie'. It was probably just as well that Maisie did not see too much of him and was unaware of the mad and daring exploits he got up to. He had admitted to her confidentially that evening, that he had flown a Spitfire under a bridge near Winchester, and someone had reported the incident.

There had been a temporary furore, but due to the desperate plight of Britain's air defence the matter had been dropped.

"You know Maisie, it's a pretty intense job, especially at present, and sometimes we need some light relief. We can't be expected to work under such pressure without having some fun, so . . ." Mary interjected "For goodness sake, don't you live with enough danger, without going out looking for more. Surely you can find other ways of relaxing without continuously living life on the cusp, or for that matter getting drunk. I love you so much Johnnie and I don't want to lose you. You know you owe it to me and the children not to take unnecessary risks. Please bear that in mind."

With a twinkle in his eye, smiling, he put his arms round her and gave her a passionate kiss. "My darling, darling Maisie, I too love you with all my heart, you are a wonderful woman, a wonderful wife and a wonderful mother. I can ask for no more and I listen to what you say. I know I cause you a lot of worry, but please don't try to change me."

Maisie and Johnnie had been childhood sweethearts, living in neighbouring villages in the Chilterns. They lost touch when Johnnie joined the RAF and was posted to Malta. When he came home on leave a few years' later they met again and fell deeply in love. He was incorrigible then, and that trait was obviously there to stay. It was the nature of the beast, and it was that, with his sense of humour and strikingly good looks that had attracted Maisie. Did she really want him any other way?

Autumn had now well and truly established itself, leaves were falling fast and the end of November had become dreary, damp and cold. You would think miserable enough to keep the five girls in their warm snug beds in the morning. Johnnie had got up quietly so as not to wake them, but when Maisie came back from saying goodbye to him shortly after six, all the girls were sitting round the kitchen table rolling a ping pong ball one to the other.

"What's for breakfast Mummy?" asked Tilly. "That, I might say Tilly, is a very good question. I haven't even thought, and even if I had, there isn't much to feed five hungry mouths. How about porridge and an eggy toast?"

Heads nodded all round. While Maisie was preparing this sumptuous meal, Mary, with Paddy in her arms, shortly followed by Mrs. Honeywell were soon all sitting round the table with great expectancy. With only four eggs, but plenty of milk, Maisie managed to eke out enough porridge and 'eggy toast' for everyone.

"Now, what would you all like to do today?" That certainly stimulated the chatter and after ten minutes of lively discussion it was decided that they wanted to take Jet, go for a walk across the water meadows and catch minnows.

About an hour later they had finally sorted themselves out. The normally cluttered boot room was in chaos as they tried to find gum boots that fitted; warm windcheaters and scarves, and then finding five jam jars and tying pieces of string on to each one. As they all set off, Jet in tow, Maisie gave a sigh of relief. She hoped that Paddy would sleep in his pram most of the morning giving her time to prepare for the onslaught of their return.

Rabbit pie, mashed potato and leeks followed by blancmange were her aim to satisfy what she knew would be seven hungry people.

Rabbit, rabbit, rabbit, if Maisie never saw another rabbit she would not be sorry. It had certainly become their staple diet, her neighbours were always bringing her one or two, the milkman would often put one on the table as he filled up her milk jugs from his large churn, and then to crown it all, Johnnie and Mike laid snares all around the airfield, and after the last flight of the day would collect all their bounty which they would proudly take home for their wives.

At least at this time of year their diet was more varied with the addition of pheasants, partridge and the occasional joint of venison. Maisie knew well that she should not decry the rabbit, because most people were on such meagre rations that a rabbit to many would be considered a feast.

Five days later Johnnie returned, laden with more rabbits. Again, he was only able to stay the one night and then leave early the following morning, this time laden with Mrs. Honeywell, Kate and the O'Reilly family, as well as an extra large suitcase crammed into the boot. Maisie had been all through the wardrobes and done a severe cull on the family's clothes.

"I thought Mary some of this would tie you over, there will be more to come if you need it." Tearfully Mary replied, "Oh, thank you, thank you Maisie, it will help us no end, and thank for letting us come to stay in your lovely home, it's been wonderful." The children waved until Maisie, Lucy and Tilly were out of sight. The children were ecstatic and the noisy chatter was ceaseless. Firm friends had been forged and to Mary's relief Annie had been taken unconditionally into the fold, induced by the empathetic Kate.

As they drew up outside Creek House, Mary had felt a tremor of fear. She was excited to see the progress that had been made with the boathouse, but she had become fearful of the future even with God by her side.

# CHAPTER 7

Sherbert welcomed them back with a cheery smile. "Won't be long now m' dears, you should be able to move in very shortly now. It's beginning to look real good." Some of Johnnie and Maisie's furniture, including rugs, taken out of store, lay scattered on the lawn. A man was anxiously and trying to fit linoleum in the annexe as storm clouds formed overhead and a heavy downpour was imminent. He wanted to get the furniture under cover before the heavens opened.

Mary was overwhelmed, her prejudice against the British fast disappearing. She would never forget the support the family had received in their distress, and now with so many people rallying round to provide them with a home, she could not help but be amazed at their united spirit. Everyone was in this treacherous war together. Germany was the only enemy, and it would appear the British people were pulling together defiantly to prevent Hitler from conquering their beloved country.

That evening, with the children tucked into their beds, Mary and Mrs Honeywell were sitting chatting, huddled in front of the kitchen range, with mugs of cocoa, when the fearful sound of an air raid siren shattered their peace. "Oh dear God, not again" Mrs. Honeywell exclaimed getting out of her chair, "I'll see to Paddy, Mary dear, and you dress the twins – make sure they wrap up warm, it's really parky out there, and we must take plenty of blankets - oh, and don't forget the gas masks." Just as they were opening the front door, the air raid siren went off again, and they saw Mike running hurriedly towards them.

"There's no need to worry, just follow me and I will lead you to our air raid shelter. My family and Brendan are already down there." Although Mike seemed to instil calm, it was obvious there was urgency in his step. Just as they were clambering down the steps they heard the sound of shooting and then explosions and the sky light up above them. Hurriedly, they all squashed into the pitch dark air raid shelter.

"Where are you Mary?" Brendan's soft Irish accent then continued, "Come and sit over here and put the twins between us." Mary followed Brendan's voice and within a few minutes they had sorted themselves out; Kate had wriggled her way in to sit next to Annie and hold her hand. Mike, as only Mike would, told them to keep calm, they were quite safe and he would stand watch just outside the shelter, but would be there if anyone needed him. The air raid sirens sounding twice was a double warning, or red alarm, denoting a major raid was imminent. A major raid it was, the noise of explosions all around was terrifying. Considering the trauma the O'Reilly family had already endured, they remained completely silent, rooted with fear.

The silence inside the shelter was broken by Mike coming to tell them what he had seen from his vantage point and what he thought was happening. "German fighter planes led the raid by coming in and shooting out our barrage balloons to make it easier for their bombers to raid Southampton. I think the loud explosions you can hear are their JU 88 Bombers dropping bombs, probably on the Docks. The whole of Southampton seems to be ablaze. We are safe here, and it will all be over soon now, then we can go back to our beds."

It seemed an eternity until the all clear siren and they emerged from the damp and cold air raid shelter. They stopped for a brief moment to look at the angry red and orange sky with clouds of smoke billowing into the night. It was quite a spectacle.

"Mary, we must now stop feeling sorry for ourselves, we are so lucky, just imagine how many will be suffering tonight. We're all alive and together." With that he gave Mary, Paddy and the twins a kiss, and thanked Mrs. Honeywell for looking after everyone. Mike, and even

Virginia who had remained silent throughout the evening managed to utter a 'Goodnight'.

"See you tomorrow, Annie and Biddy, night night" said Kate.

As they climbed into their beds that night, they did not realise it was only a dress rehearsal. For the following night, about the same time there was another red alarm, a repeat of the previous night. Fortunately, Hamble was untouched but Southampton was devastated. Two nights of intensive bombing had severely damaged the docks, and virtually wiped out the High Street. In all, more than 2000 high explosives and 3000 incendiary bombs had killed around 650 people. An incendiary bomb had hit the house where Johnnie was staying but fortunately he was unharmed. He phoned Mike to tell him that all his furniture that was in store had been lost. Evidently, a bomb had landed on a nearby butter factory causing a complete furnace and wiping out many nearby buildings.

One Saturday morning; Mrs. Honeywell was busy putting the newly-washed clothes through the mangle as Mary hung them on the line, when a smiling Brendan, holding Kate by the hand, walked up the path. "Mike has asked me to invite you to Creek House at half past twelve." By the glint in their eyes, Mary realised it was good rather than bad news. She assumed it was to see the latest progress on the boathouse. Brendan only stayed a few minutes as he said he had to get back to help Mike, while Kate stayed to play with Annie and Biddy. There was excited anticipation all morning, and it became obvious that Mrs. Honeywell was in on the secret, especially when she suddenly disappeared.

At 12.30pm, Mary holding Paddy who was now nearly walking, Kate, Annie and Biddy arrived at Creek House and as they looked down the garden towards the boathouse, they could not help but see the Irish flag and the Union Jack each side of the little porch leading into the annexe. Across the door was a red ribbon, and grouped around was Mike, Virginia and Phoebe, Johnnie Kershaw, Brendan, Mrs. Honeywell, Sniffy Herbert, Dave the carpet layer and one or two others who had helped with the project.

"Brendan, Mary, Annie, Biddy and little Paddy, we hope this little home will be a big step to help you get back on your feet, and will be a haven away from all the traumas you have endured. Virginia darling will you please cut the tape." Mike gave her the scissors and she cut the ribbon and wished them every happiness. She performed this duty rather begrudgingly. It was difficult to detect any sign of a smile.

Mary and Paddy led the way into the annexe followed by Annie, Kate and Biddy. What a welcome! The little fireplace had a warm log fire crackling away, and it had all been furnished in such a homely way. It had turned out better than anyone's hopes, and Brendan and Mary were deeply moved.

Mike wasted no time in pouring out beer for the adults and lemonade for the children. Johnnie raised his glass, "Well done Mike, and here's to you Virginia. Congratulations to those who have worked so hard and so quickly to change Mike's playrooms into a home. I am told most of his toys have found another home, much, I imagine, to Virginia's delight, the rest have been dealt with in a more brutal manner. Let's toast a very brave family – the O'Reillys. Cheers!" "Cheers! Cheers! Cheers" from all around. Mrs. Honeywell bustled around with mugs of hot soup and plates full of sandwiches, adding to the homely ambience.

Brendan by this time was completely overcome by emotion. Trying to quell his tears, he managed in his soft Irish drawl "What can I say? If it hadn't been for these two gentlemen standing here, I don't think we'd be alive, certainly not our lovely twins."

That finished him. Mike went over and gave him a pat on the back

"Don't worry, old boy, please say no more, we know what you're trying to say." Mary came to the rescue, also with tears rolling down her cheeks. "I just want to say thank you, thank you, thank you, I love you all. Thanks be to God."

Although emotions had rather taken over Mike's surprise ceremony, Mary and Brendan were so grateful for the lifeline.

"This," he said to Mary "will be the turning point of our lives."

It took them an hour to move into 'The Boathouse' as it was now officially named. Annie and Biddy were so excited about their new bedroom that they wanted to go to bed in the middle of the afternoon. Tilly Kershaw's old cot stood proudly in the tiny bedroom in the old annexe, and after a good feed, and without a whimper, Paddy was put down for an afternoon's sleep while Brendan and Mary attended to the final touches. Their double-bedded room, although sparsely furnished had magnificent views down the river Hamble. Mrs. Honeywell seemed as excited as they were as she bustled around, and bringing in the odd snippet that she thought would make them more comfortable. She had returned the crockery and cutlery she had borrowed, had unpacked, washed up, and neatly put away all the kitchen items that had been lying around for years.

"These, my dears, will probably come in really useful" she said, pointing to three big stone hot water bottles. "The bedrooms will get really cold. If you like Mary I'll help you cut down those velvet curtains that came in the van from the store. Those blackout blinds won't keep Jack Frost out, and you must all keep warm.

"Mr. Pinkerton has bought you a small supply of coal, but I think as soon as you can afford it you should order some more, because there's a back boiler behind the fireplace and that will not only heat the water, but make the whole place feel warmer. You'll also find lots of twigs and branches lying around, which perhaps Biddy and Annie might enjoy collecting and put in that shed over there." All this advice was an added bonus.

Next, came the opening of the large suitcase that Maisie had given them. There was quite an air of expectancy as to what it contained. They were not to be disappointed. - Trousers, shirts and jumpers for Brendan, lots of Maisie's clothes for Mary, and for Annie and Biddy - well just unbelievable. Talk about Pandora's Box! At the bottom of the case they found three teddy bears, some games and jigsaws.

Christmas was only a few weeks away, It was decided that all the toys and some of the clothes should be hidden in Mrs. Honeywell's cottage, then to be wrapped up for the children's Christmas presents. As a good Catholic Mary was already going to confession regularly, as is customary during advent, to prepare her soul for the wonder of the birth of Jesus, and through him God coming to earth.

"Mary, we're going to make certain this will be the best Christmas we've ever had." Although Mary nodded in agreement, her thoughts seemed elsewhere. As far as Brendan was aware, she had fully recovered, but there was something troubling her. Had she built up resentment towards him for their misfortunes or was she chastising herself for Annie's devastating accident? He was concerned.

# CHAPTER 8

Christmas that year more than came up to expectation. On Christmas Eve Annie, Biddy and Paddy hung up their stockings, and before going to bed left a glass of beer on the hearth for Father Christmas. Annie had been a stalwart throughout, and seemed to have taken her disability in her stride, and, strangely enough, Biddy had not even questioned why her twin sister could not hear or really speak. They were a happy and excited family with amazing resilience.

While Brendan and Mary attended Midnight Mass, Mrs. Honeywell came in to babysit, bringing with her a small Christmas tree she had potted, and some old Christmas baubles she had dug up from the past. By the time they had returned, the tree was decorated and the brightly wrapped Christmas presents lay beneath. It had already been agreed that Mrs. Honeywell would spend Christmas lunch with them for which she had volunteered to make a special Christmas pudding.

"Look, look, Father Christmas has been, Mammy, Dada wake up." It was just after 5.30 am, cold and frosty, Biddy came jumped on Mary and Brendan's bed, hugging her stocking almost screaming with excitement.

"Shush, try to let the other two sleep on a little longer."

Pulling back the bedclothes Brendan continued, "Here Biddy jump in come and cuddle up to Mammy while I go and light the fire. Promise me you won't look into your stocking until the other two are awake and then you can all open them together in front of the fire."

The expression of wonderment as the children opened their stockings – gave their doting parents a thrill, especially as they had had no money to spend on Christmas and most of it had come courtesy of the Pinkertons and the Kershaws. They each had a ball in the toe of the stocking, the twins had a yo-yo each and a skipping rope, Paddy a water pistol, and they were all topped up with some of Mrs Honeywell's home made sweets.

Annie then spotted the presents under the tree – her eyes lit up and pointing to them "For us?" she mouthed.

"Yes, Annie, they are.for.you.all..when..we..come..back..from.. church,"replied Mary obviously pleased that Annie was now making a real effort to communicate. Whether or not it was the excitement of Christmas, but in the last few days her progress had been noticeable and she was trying hard to make sentences. Kate, in particular, went out of her way to point out objects, say what they were, exaggerating the movement of her lips, and then making Annie repeat them over and over again. Biddy would join in this exercise with great enthusiasm believing it to be a game, and with an added kudos that she was more proficient than her twin sister.

For that one blissful Christmas Day the ravages of war seemed far away, and as the O'Reillys sat cosily round the fire watching Annie and Biddy doing a jigsaw, they had time to reflect on past events and to realise, in spite of the circumstances which had enveloped them, that now perhaps there was light at the end of the tunnel.

\* \* \* \*

To wake up on New Year's Day to a magical landscape of snow caused mayhem in the O'Reilly household. Kate was knocking on the door before any of them were up. "Please Mrs. O'Reilly can you ask Annie and Biddy to come and help me make a snowman."

"To be sure my dear, would you like to have some breakfast while they're getting dressed?

"No thank you. I'll go and start. Please will you tell them to hurry up."

Mary's priority was to scrape enough warm clothes together for Brendan and get him off to work. She imagined he would have a slippery walk down to the bus stop and then maybe the buses wouldn't be running. His workshop had just been evacuated to an old steel factory fairly close by so if there was no transport he planned to walk the three miles.

It was the first time that Annie and Biddy had encountered snow, so the look of wonderment and excitement when they looked out of the window and saw Kate and Phoebe, hindered by Jet, the black Labrador, making a snowman, was a thrill. They couldn't wait to join them. Piling on any clothes they could find - their wardrobe did not quite stretch to scarves and gloves - and ignoring Mary's "you must have something to eat first" they were out of the door and into the fray like startled rabbits.

A handsome snowman, supporting a tweed cap, one of Mike's best, soon stood proudly in the middle of the lawn. However, the novelty of the snow was fairly short lived as it wasn't long before the three children, came running in almost crying with cold. The Boathouse did not exactly offer a haven of warmth so they decided to go back with Kate, where they knew Mrs. Honeywell would stop what she was doing and make them all a hot cup of cocoa and they could thaw out in front of the big Esse cooker, probably at the displeasure of Virginia, who still kept her distance from the O'Reillys.

Having completed her duties at Creek House, Mrs. Honeywell, with Annie and Biddy, came shuffling through the snow with a proposition to put to Mary.

"Good morning, my dear, is there a cup of tea going as I would like to have a little chat with you?"

"Yes, by all means Mrs. Honeywell, come in, come in, come and sit down," she continued speaking slowly and clearly, "Annie and Biddy will you go and play in the sitting room, but please don't make a mess as I seem to have spent most of the morning tidying up after the two of you."

"Mary, I have a friend, Barbara Wilkins, who runs the nursery school here in Hamble, and she is looking for an assistant . I mentioned to her that perhaps you might be interested. She said she would like to meet you. If you like Mary, I will introduce you. You'll really like her. Chuckling nervously she concluded, "don't worry, I warned her you had three children!"

Mary was really taken aback. There was a long pause and then came the expected negative reply. "Oh Mrs Honeywell, I know I couldn't do it – it's as much as I can do to look after Brendan and the three . . ."

"Come on, come on Mary," Mrs. Honeywell interrupted sharply, "give it a go, it will take you out of yourself and give you a new interest. Please don't say 'no' until you have met Barbara."

The following day, somewhat reluctantly, Mary, accompanied by Mrs. Honeywell and the children, met Mrs. Wilkins in the school room attached to the village hall. There was an immediate rapport, and after tea and biscuits Mrs. Honeywell excused herself, leaving the two of them to discuss the situation.

An unusually cheerful Mary called into Forge Cottage on her way home. As Mrs. Honeywell later recalled, it was the first time she had seen her smile. "How did it go Mary?" she enquired.

"I'm going to help Mrs. Wilkins, or Barbara as she has asked me to call her, in exchange for Biddy and Annie attending the school. I can also take Paddy along with me. That's not all, Barbara, told me she has had some experience of children with speaking difficulties and was sure she would be able to help Annie. God bless you Mrs. Honeywell for making me do this – I would never ever have done it if you hadn't badgered me into it."

With a reassuring hug Mrs. Honeywell said, "This gives me such pleasure Mary dear, I am sure it will help you all."

It was almost the Mary he used to know who greeted Brendan on his return from work. "Guess what Brendan, I've got a job!"

# CHAPTER 9

In 1941 the war continued unabated. The blitz on major cities seemed to be intensifying; Southampton was again a strategic target. Brendan was told that German aircraft had actually strafed the streets with machine gun fire. During one air raid there was an exceptionally resounding explosion which felt as if their air raid shelter was about to cave in as buckets of debris fell on top of them. As Mike was not there, Brendan took over his role as a calming influence to the terrified families who lay straddled on the ground. Nine aircraft had attacked Southampton and then dropped a huge bomb in the middle of nearby Hamble Airfield. Fortunately no one was killed and no damage done.

Possibly the Germans realised that the production of the Spitfire had been dispersed to other sites, as they were now concentrating on raiding the suburbs and dropping mines from parachutes. Four fell among the storage tanks at Shell Mex which fortunately did not explode.

It did not take Mary long to settle into Mrs. Wilkins nursery school. Off she would go every morning with Kate, Annie, Biddy and Paddy in the pushchair. This was to be Kate's last two terms there, as in September she would be moving on to a prep school. What an asset she was! There was no question of Annie being left out while Kate was around. She was like a mother hen, and if any of the other children made fun of, or mimicked Annie, she was quick to defend her.

Biddy's showed enthusiasm for everything she tried. She was keen to read, loved adding up, plasticine and colouring. She outshone all the others.

The worrying aspect was her determination to do everything better than Annie. This one-sided sibling rivalry soon became so evident it affected Annie's self esteem, already at a low ebb. Mixing with other children had highlighted her handicap. To ease this problem Mrs. Wilkins gave Annie extra tuition three days a week after school.

Kate was the real star, unaware of the beneficial effect she was having. Annie had become her best friend. They seemed to communicate with no problems, playing hopscotch, skipping, and the latest craze was ping-pong. The table tennis table in the playroom at Creek House seemed to be in constant use as they became more and more proficient. The ping – pong – ping – pong rhythm backwards and forwards was a way they could communicate as a respite from lip reading.

They were inseparable, much to the chagrin of Biddy and to a lesser extent Phoebe.

The cold winter was now giving way to spring. The daffodils had faded, and at last the bare skeletal trees were beginning to show a slight hue of green as the buds showed signs of life. The clocks had gone forward and the sinister darkness of the evenings was lifting. The birds were singing from the treetops. Nature was not going to allow a war to interfere with its wondrous cycle.

As so often happened as soon as there was a lull in air raids, something, somewhere was sure to shatter the peace. Day after day families sat huddled close to the wireless as it crackled away and Alvar Liddell reported the progress and setbacks of what seemed an interminable war.

"Garmany calling, Garmany calling." That was the spine-chilling voice of William Joyce (Lord Haw-Haw) trying to demoralise the British by broadcasting exaggerated claims of allied planes being shot down, allied ships being sunk and huge casualties among allied forces.

In spite of this, and in contrast, Prime Minister Churchill with his stirring and inspiring oratory kept up the morale of the nation.

Hitler had already warned the world that mighty Germany would not only conquer Europe, but also Russia. "When the attack on Russia starts the world will hold its breath" he threatened, and sure enough on June 22nd that year, one hundred and thirty two German divisions together with a further 500,000 Axis allied troops advanced into Russia in Operation Barbarossa.

Hitler had been planning this invasion for many months. Due to the over confidence of his success in Western Europe and his impatience to conquer the East, he became so focused on this onslaught, he seemed to lose interest in the Battle of Britain. On the invasion of Russia he said: "We only have to kick in the door and the whole rotten structure will come crashing down."

There was no such attitude at home. The urgent production of the Spitfires and Hurricanes continued apace. Then, in October, came the news that Kershaw had been seriously injured while testing a Spitfire. He had been testing the ailerons, and had just come out of a nosedive at 520 mph when the aircraft disintegrated. It all happened so quickly. Of the few observers, none of them thought that the pilot could have possibly survived, so the news received by Vickers was that Kershaw was presumed dead.

Mike was devastated. "He cannot be dead, not Johnnie. Please tell me exactly where the accident happened and I'll be off to find him."

As Len Levison, the Works Manager, and some of the senior management were crowding round a map trying to locate the site where the plane had crashed, the telephone rang. After a short conversation Len replaced the receiver. "A man cutting down trees in a wood north of Winchester has found Johnnie in a tree. An ambulance is on its way and he will be taken to Winchester Hospital. Nothing was said of his condition."

"I'll go straight to the hospital and will probably be there on his arrival. Can you contact Maisie and make sure she has transport to get to the hospital, and tell her I will see her there." Mike hardly had time to finish his sentence before rushing to his car en route for Winchester.

Johnnie was being wheeled into theatre as Mike arrived. A team of doctors and nurses were already on standby. He appeared unconscious. "Johnnie, Johnnie, what the hell have you been up to this time – it's Mike." As he was rushed through to a little anteroom he added "I'll be here old chap and will come and see you later. I'll bring Maisie." There seemed no sign of recognition.

A nurse gently put her arms round his shoulders and ushered him into a waiting room. "I think you'll be more comfortable in here. As soon as we have any news we'll let you know." With that she left, closing the door behind her.

The walls were painted in a dismal dark green; Mike sat there, feeling as if he were in a condemned cell with only the torturous tick tock, tick tock of the clock . . .

During that long drawn out wait Mike recalled the friendship that he and Johnnie had developed over the last five years.

He remembered when Johnnie had first initiated him into flying seaplanes and the immediate rapport that developed. They came from similar backgrounds, both educated at public school; Mike went on to university while Johnnie at the age of seventeen went straight into the RAF. Apart from flying machines they found they had much in common – sailing, fast cars, the odd game of golf and even the odd game of snooker. With stress playing a large part in their working lives, laughter and a few beers were prominent in their leisurely pursuits.

As he sat there, he recalled the wonderful times they had spent at Brooklands for the car racing. They also belonged to the Brooklands Flying Club, and the airfield was one of the exciting parts of the circuit. The one and a quarter mile lap was a cross between road and track racing, a really tough course requiring adroit handling.

There was no rivalry between them – and with RJ Mitchell, the designer of the Spitfire, they had worked closely together, pooling their resources in a desperate effort to get the K 5054, the prototype Spitfire, off the ground before RJ finally gave up his brave fight to cancer.

With the added problems of political forces playing their role, these were difficult times.

Throughout, Mike recalled the bond between them had never wavered.

He was still reminiscing, and wondering how he would ever be able to cope without Johnnie at his side, when the door opened and a completely forlorn Maisie entered. On seeing Mike, a few tears rolled down her cheeks.

"Oh Mike it's so good to see you." After a long embrace she continued, "Well, the good news is he is still alive. I have just been in to see him, and to my amazement he's still wearing his flying jacket. The doctors said he did gain consciousness for a short while, but I don't think he recognised me. As yet, they don't know the extent of his injuries, but his left arm is badly injured and he has lost two fingers on his left hand. They are fairly optimistic that he'll pull through. If he does make it, I fear it will be a long haul."

As he replied Mike gave her another long embrace, "Maisie, Johnnie is the greatest friend I have ever had, and knowing his character and determination I am sure he'll survive. I bet it won't be long before he's back bossing us all around and laughing and joking in his usual incorrigible way. I'm here for you Maisie at any time. You must try to keep strong for the sake of Tilly and Lucy."

"Thanks Mike, I know you mean that, and I do appreciate it very much."

# CHAPTER 10

An unexpected letter dropped through the letterbox of the Boat-house. It was from Bryony.

*Darling Mary,*

*I have just realised you would not have received my last letter as I sent it to your old address. We do hope you are all OK now. What a terrible ordeal you have all been through. Poor Mammy was so upset to hear about it, that it made her ill and she took to her bed for a few days. Our thanks to God you all survived – we talk about you so much and pray that Annie gets better soon.*

*Now for our news. I have just become engaged. It is a long story Mary and I will tell you all about it some day, but my baby's father, Rory came back into my life and we are to be married in a few months' time. Mammy has got a job in a newsagents which she enjoys, Seamus is working as an errand boy with Beefy the Butcher, and Dadda, well he's just the same - still drinking, comes and goes when he wishes, but now with three of us bringing in some money, we can cope.*

*Please write and tell me how my little Paddy is – a day doesn't go by when I don't think about him. I miss him terribly.*

*All love my darling Mary, also from Mammy and Seamus –     Lots of love to Brendan, Biddy, Annie and of course Paddy.*

*Bryony* xxx

Mary felt quite sick. She had completely maligned Jimmy O'Shea, her father. How could she have made such a mistake? How could she have really thought that he had had an incestuous relationship with Bryony, his own daughter? His drunken behaviour in the past definitely had sexual connotations, but how wrong it was for her to assume that he was Paddy's father. What was she to do?

At least she hadn't made any accusations to him or to Molly, her mother, so her family in Limerick was unaware of her malicious thoughts.

Mary decided she must tell Brendan, and then as soon as possible confess to her priest. She had already committed one sin for which Father O'Sullivan had refused to give her absolution. This still haunted her, more so as she had not had the courage to tell Brendan. It lay deep in her conscience.

By the time Brendan returned from work, Mary had already poured out her woes to Mrs. Honeywell who had rather dismissed it out of hand.

"Oh don't fret about that Mary my dear. There are far more important things to concern us all at this time. From what you tell me about your father, I am not surprised you thought it was him. I know a lot of that kind of thing goes on. Why do you even have to go and tell the priest? Surely YOU have not committed a sin. Just forget it girl."

Mary wished she had Mrs. Honeywell's outlook on life, but at least her frank opinion had made it easier to confront Brendan. She decided to let him read the letter for himself.

"Well I never Mary, you didn't think that did you?" he said passing back the letter. Mary then pointed out how terrible she felt that she had despised her father for having had an incestuous relationship with her sister when it just wasn't true.

"I feel so awful Brendan and now I must go and confess to Father O'Sullivan."

"Oh, Mary Mary, sometimes I just don't understand you. Your father was, and probably still is, an absolute bastard, he treated your Mammy, brothers and sisters abominably. He abused you all throughout your childhood. No wonder you blamed him for being Paddy's father, I don't blame you. I am a Catholic Mary, I respect the religion, but I feel strongly that in Ireland 'The Faith' has become too powerful and made us feel that unless we are rigid followers we will be condemned to hell.

"This cannot be right. I know Mary you're really scared, that you believe in a religion that has almost paralysed you with fear. Please try to distance yourself a little for your own sake, the sake of your children, and if I may add, for my sake." That belief had become so ingrained, that although Mary listened with intent it was going to take more to loosen her rigid religious upbringing.

Brendan felt more concerned about Bryony's reference to Paddy in her letter, and the thought did go through his mind that perhaps now she was reunited with her seducer they would want Paddy. He was relieved that Mary had not picked up on this point, and in her present state of mind he would let the matter ride.

Brendan had heard the news of Johnnie's terrible flying accident at the factory. It had a stunning effect. He was such a popular and friendly character with his eccentric behaviour, so there was a subdued workforce that went about their work waiting for news of his progress.

Brendan and Mary were naturally upset, and after they had finished discussing Jimmy O'Shea, the conversation moved to Johnnie, Maisie, Tilly and Lucy. They were so grateful to Johnnie, and of course Mike, for rescuing them, and the kindness and generosity that Maisie had shown them, they racked their brains as to how they might be able to help. As they waited for news of his progress, they decided, now was the time to repay them.

\*    \*    \*    \*

The weeks that followed were fraught, not only for Maisie and family, but also for Mike, who was now working non-stop during daylight hours and then would insist on visiting Johnnie every evening. When eventually he arrived home at night, he was not exactly welcomed into the arms of a loving wife. Virginia's resentment to his lack of attention to her had been building up for some time, and his dismissive attitude to her complaining riled her even more.

"I've had enough Mike, I'm not here just to do your washing and ironing – you treat this house like a hotel, you're so seldom here. I think you would pass your own children in the street without recognising them."

The same old patter came out each time. Mike then reminding her that there was a war on and she was behaving like a spoilt child, and if she were bored to get off her backside and do something to help the war effort . . .and so it went on.

Johnnie was making progress, albeit slow. He was now mentally alert, laughing, joking and building up a great repartee with the nurses and those caring for him. Much of his body was in a plaster cast which already had become the butt of many jokes. Although his medical report had stated that it would be unlikely he would be able to fly again, he dismissed it as a load of rubbish. As far as he was concerned,  he would be back in the cockpit, sooner rather than later.

Vickers had supplied Maisie with a driver and a car so she visited him nearly every day. The day she took Tilly and Lucy in to see him, unfortunately, his left hand with the two missing fingers had become gangrenous and the smell was awful. What with seeing their father looking a bit like a snowman, and then seeing his injured hand with its obnoxious smell, they became frightened and wouldn't go near him. He was visibly hurt by this sense of rejection and Maisie regretted taking them to the hospital.

Johnnie had to endure three months in hospital before being allowed to go home to convalesce. It wasn't all doom and gloom for him as he had so many friends. About 6pm every evening his mates would come in with hidden bottles of beer to drink to his recovery and update him on the entire goings on at Vickers. As he couldn't be at the Hampshire Aeroplane Club, the Club came to him. Brendan and Mary saved up their food rations and on a regular basis would take him in one of Mary's steak, kidney and Guinness puddings which he considered a wonderful treat.

Maisie relished in having Johnnie home convalescing. It was the first time in their married life that they had spent any real time together. Although at times he showed frustration at not being in on the action, it was a wonderful opportunity for him to enjoy family life and really to get to know Tilly and Lucy.

Johnnie's determination to defy medical opinion was rewarded. He was back in the pilot's seat in less than a year, although his flying was restricted mainly to communication aircraft. However, because of his expertise he was brought in to assist with the 'testing' programme from the ground.

# CHAPTER 11

In spite of endless wireless bulletins, it was difficult to follow everything that was going on in the world. But the scale of the war seemed to be increasing at an alarming rate. While Germany and their allies were concentrating on the invasion of Russia, Japan occupied southern Indochina.

The United States, Britain and Holland then froze Japanese assets. This prevented Japan from buying oil, so just as Russia was on the verge of defeat, Japan made a desperate effort to seize the oil resources of South East Asia. And so it seemed to go on and on . .

How could ordinary  British people who were so slavishly doing everything to protect their own island grasp what was happening so far away?

Suddenly, on December 7th 1941 on a peaceful Sunday morning on the beautiful island of Hawaii, Japanese aircraft attacked Pearl Harbour where the US Pacific Fleet was based. There was devastation – all the eight battleships were badly damaged or sunk and more than 3,500 Americans were killed or wounded.

Germany and Italy then declared war on the United States of America. Under Roosevelt that nation was galvanized into action, not only in mobilizing millions of troops but vastly increasing its own military expansion.

American industry had not only been supporting Britain with munitions and equipment but also played an important part in mechanizing the Soviet Army.

The arrival of American troops early in 1942 certainly had a lively impact on the every day life of impoverished Britain. The Yanks seemed to be arriving in their droves with convoys rumbling their way through the country. To the male-starved women and young girls, the arrival of these young men in their smart uniforms, bearing gifts of nylon stockings, exotic rations and candies was too much for their libidos to ignore.

Integration was not a problem for these servicemen as they wasted no time in launching themselves on the social scene by frequenting pubs, going to village hops, tea dances and inveigling their way into homes. For better or for worse relationships were soon formed. Their physical exuberance and bulging wallets were an added attraction to the vulnerable lonely females. The American troops were earning seven times more than their British counterparts, often causing much resentment.

'Over sexed, over paid and over here' soon became the familiar phrase to describe the American troops in Britain. They retaliated by describing our troops as 'under-sexed, under-paid and underfed.' The GIs were however, encouraged by thousands of brazen British girls more than ready to oblige the predatory American military. It was a boom time for prostitution.

However, many solid and lasting relationships also developed out of these liaisons.

The Bugle Inn at Hamble became a popular meeting place for many of these troops billeted in the vicinity, and the first day that Kate, Annie and Biddy set eyes on a jeep piled full of American airmen driving past Creek House they were terrified. "The Germans are here, the Germans are here," Kate shrieked as they all rushed into the house and hid under the stairs. Virginia just thought they were playing one of their stupid games and completely ignored them. Eventually they emerged from the cupboard and Kate challenged "Mummy, we saw Germans, here, just outside of the house so we hid in the cupboard we were so frightened."

"What are you talking about Kate?"

"Please believe us, there were a whole lot of them, all in uniform driving past our gate." It took some time to realise who they were and then to explain they were Americans, they were on our side and had come to help win the war.

A children's party in the village hall given by the GIs soon dispersed any fear and suspicion that their sudden onslaught on the village had caused. There were games, tea with fizzy drinks, 'cookies' and as a parting gift the children were all given chewing gum and candies. The Yanks had certainly scored with the children and their mothers, if not so well with their men folk.

Virginia soon became susceptible to the charms of the American airmen. Life had become boring and she was particularly miffed by Mike's lack of attention towards her and his preoccupation with the war.

It had been a long time since Mike had told her how beautiful and wonderful she was, and then out of the blue she was suddenly being feted by handsome men who vied for the privilege of buying her a drink or taking her to the movies. At the outset she visibly flirted with these suitors in order to make Mike jealous, but to her added chagrin he ignored her dalliances. This constant attention had quelled her incessant moaning and groaning telling Mike how badly done by she was, for which he was relieved.

The sight of a jeep parked at Creek House was now becoming commonplace, and Mrs. Honeywell's baby-sitting duties on the increase. She had noticed that since the bombing incident how the Pinkertons had grown apart, and was concerned for the children. Mrs. Honeywell had always found Mrs. Pinkerton a formidable and hard woman to work for, expecting her to work far beyond her allotted hours. But at least her weekly wage came in regularly and she was able to get by. As she expressed her views to Mary:

"Mr. Pinkerton is one of the country's true gentlemen. He always asks me if I have any worries, and whether I'm finding being both a nanny and a housekeeper too much. He, and my love for Kate and Phoebe is what keep me going there. To me, Mrs. Pinkerton is a selfish woman and doesn't seem to have time for anyone, not even her own children."

Mary had been confiding in Mrs. Honeywell over the mounting antagonism between Annie and Biddy. "I just don't know what to do for the best, Mrs. Honeywell, I think Biddy is embarrassed by Annie's inability to keep up with the others and she encourages other children to make fun of her. Kate protects Annie at all times, and now I have to put up with Kate and Biddy arguing all the time. Dear God, I am finding it difficult to handle. What should I do?"

"I think someone must sit down and really talk to Biddy. She must be made to understand what is wrong with Annie and the reason for her behaviour. Maybe Brendan would talk to her, or if you like, as Kate is so close to Annie, I could have a word with Mr. Pinkerton. I'm sure he would know what to do for the best. Anyway Mary, you have a word with Brendan and then let me know what you think. I think it needs to be dealt with quickly."

Mary nodded, "Yes, thanks that's a good idea".

Brendan and Mike decided that they would talk to all three of them separately. They thought by initially talking to Kate she would perhaps enlighten them with some of the causes for the friction.

The opportunity arose a few evenings later when Brendan was having a beer with Mike, when Kate came in cuddling her newly acquired kitten Timoshenko. "Hello Kate, what are you up to."

"I have just brought Timo in to show Mr. O'Reilly."

"Why don't you come and sit down and tell us what you have been doing at school today," suggested Mike. "Well" she said as she flopped down on the sofa, "we did sums, painting, played a lovely game called 'islands' which was funny, and Mrs. Wilkins read us a story about the Flopsy Bunnies, and then . . .."

"Do you think Annie's enjoying school Kate?" Mike interrupted. Kate paused "Sometimes Daddy - not very often. Some of the girls and boys are unkind to her, and when she doesn't understand they all laugh at her – Biddy too."

"What does Mrs. Wilkins say?" Mike enquired. "She gets cross with them, but they don't stop."

Brendan then took over in his soft Irish accent "Kate my dear, thank you for all the help you are giving to little Annie, I am so pleased you have become such good friends. I think, perhaps, Biddy feels you leave her out. Maybe this is the reason she is often unkind to Annie, so I would like you to try hard to play with her as much as you do with Annie. Will you try?" Kate nodded, trying to understand.

Brendan continued, "Will you let me hold Timo – he is just adorable." As Kate passed him to Brendan she turned to Mike. "Please, please Daddy can I take him to bed with me tonight?"

"You'd better ask Mummy that one, but I don't think it a good idea as he's still young and might do a mess." Giving her a big hug and kiss he continued. "It's time you were in bed anyway Kate. Off you go; night night darling, sleep tight."

Wishing Brendan good night with Timo locked securely in her arms she trotted happily off to bed. Mike and Brendan now had to talk to Biddy, treading softly softly. It took a few more beers to sort out how best to go about this delicate situation. Mike had an idea.

The opportunity arose the following Saturday morning when Mary was helping Annie with some of the exercises that Mrs. Wilkins had given her. Biddy was in the garden riding Kate's old tricycle when Mike called out to her.

"Biddy, can you find your Daddy and bring him here I want to show you something."

Gleefully, Biddy jumped off the bike and ran into the Boathouse to fetch Brendan.

The kitchen table at Creek House was cluttered with fishing tackle, and to Biddy, most intriguing of all, a tin of live bait. "Biddy" Mike began, "I have a little surprise. Tomorrow I thought we - that is your daddy, Annie, Kate, you and I, would all going fishing and take a picnic."

Biddy's eyes lit up and without any hesitation she came out with an emphatic "Yes". This, in almost literal terms, was a 'sprat to catch a mackerel'.

Before Mike continued he took some cotton wool and a pair of airplane ear mufflers from the sideboard, and with a twinkle in his eye, and assuring her it was only a game, he asked Biddy if he could put them on her. She immediately obliged. Mike then continued to talk to Brendan, egging him on to laugh and look animated, and then almost on cue Kate came rushing in with some garbled story. There was more laughter. As the conversation progressed, Biddy's face gradually became more and more glum.

With extreme irritation, and almost in tears, she tugged at the mufflers. "I don't like this, take them off," she demanded.

Mike, after tactfully asking Kate to disappear, removed the mufflers "Sorry Biddy, I know that wasn't very kind of me, but I want you to try to understand that Annie has built-in mufflers like that all the time. You both look exactly alike; the only difference between you is she cannot hear, she has to live in a lonely world of silence. I wanted you to know what it was like for you not to hear, and not know what's going on around you. Annie loves you Biddy, and she needs you to help her. You must always speak facing her and slowly, move your lips like this."

Mike demonstrated with exaggerated lip movements but uttering no sound, then continued, "Biddy, you're such a lovely little girl and I know it is difficult for you to understand. I just ask you to be kind and helpful to Annie and ask your friends to be also. This will also help your Mummy and Daddy. O.K Biddy?" She nodded.

Brendan picked her up, gave her a big hug, swung her round, and in his lovely Irish lilt said "Right now Biddy, can you go and tell Mammy and Annie about tomorrow. See if you can find a jam jar or two and some string, it may be easier than a fishing rod. Tell Mammy I will be back in a few minutes."

She went skipping off quite happily. Only time would tell as how much she had understood.

The fishing expedition proved a great success. The sun shone, and although the picnic was a little frugal, spam sandwiches and Mary's fresh air sandwiches (no filling) and apples. It seemed to go down well with the hungry 'fishermen' - at least there were no complaints. Mike had made sure he and Brendan were stocked up with beer, so that kept their inner souls replenished while they unravelled the children's fishing lines. The jam jars came into their own, as at the end of the day their whole catch consisted of a few minnows. However, harmony reigned, which after all had been the object of the exercise.

# CHAPTER 12

The intensity of the war in Britain seemed to be easing. The first major defeat of Hitler's armies in Russia took place in February 1943 when the Germans surrendered at Stalingrad. However, the battle of the Atlantic continued unabated. It was not until later in the year that Bletchley code breakers cracked the German Enigma signals and with help from long-range American aircraft were able to counter attack German U Boats. This caused the German fleet to withdraw, thus ending the Battle of the Atlantic.

El Alamein proved a turning point in North Africa as Montgomery's Eighth Army defeated Rommel's Afrika Corps. Then Mussolini fell, followed by the surrender of the Italians.

However, German troops fought on in Southern Italy and progress through Italy was proving slow and costly.

Back at Vickers Supermarine, the testing programme continued relentlessly. Spitfires were coming off the assembly line and tested almost quicker than they could be delivered. To overcome this, free-spirited young women were recruited. They were billeted around the Hamble area adding to the intrigue of this now upbeat village. After a few hours of training they were stuck in the cockpits of different types of planes and virtually told to get on with it. How brave they were, how they revelled in the spirit and aura of it all.

Out of the blue came the most tragic news - a phone call from Maisie Kershaw to Mike telling him that Johnnie had been killed, racing somebody on a motorbike of all things. Mike had to wonder, ' what on earth was Johnnie doing on a motor bike?' He hadn't even got one. He had now heard it all.

"Maisie, I just can't believe this story, after all you have been through.

I'll come straight over and see you."

"Yes Mike, thank you," tears preventing her from saying more.

"Hold tight Maisie, I'll be with you in an hour or so."

Mike quickly phoned the Supermarine office telling them he would contact them when he knew more. He then called Virginia who was out, so left a message with Mrs. Honeywell explaining briefly what had happened and to expect him when she saw him.

The shock of Johnnie's death had numbed Mike's senses. He was devoid of any emotion as he drove across the New Forest trying to come to terms with the news. It was less than two years since Johnnie's air crash when by some miracle he had cheated death. There was still a shadow of disbelief in Mike's mind.

Although nature in its wondrous way had defied the war, on this June day it seemed to be venting its anger on the futility of it all, as the wind roared and the rain lashed against the windscreen, bringing Mike and his Talbot to a near halt. The ponies seemed unabashed as they sauntered across the road further hampering his journey.

Two subdued little girls, Lucy and Tilly, came out to meet him as he drew up at Rose Cottage.

"Hi kids," Mike said as he gave them both a hug. "Are you OK?" They just nodded as they took his hand and led him to their distraught mother who was sitting at the kitchen table looking completely forlorn. Reality had now kicked in. Mike was lost for words.

As Maisie got up from the table Mike opened his arms and she fell into them sobbing profusely. "Oh Maisie, I'm so sorry. This bloody, bloody war, . . ." He was unable to continue. He, too, broke down in tears. "Let's just have a good cry together – you have lost a wonderful husband, and a loving father to your children. I have lost my greatest friend, my soul mate."

Their moments of mourning were interrupted by Lucy's tearful little voice, "Mummy, are you all right, what can we do?" Maisie looked down to see her two bewildered children looking frightened.

"Of course my darlings, I'm all right. Although we won't have Daddy any more, you've got me and I'll make sure that we'll all be fine. Will you take Jet for a run across the fields, make sure Joey's safe and sound in his stable, and please put your bikes in the garage and tidy up your toys that are scattered all around the garden. Don't forget to put on your macs and boots.

"I'll come and make sure you've done everything properly. Please just give me time to have a long chat with Uncle Mike in peace. We'll all have a nice tea later and perhaps play a game. Have fun."

With amazing resilience and probably still unaware of the finality of the situation Lucy and Tilly genially obliged.

"Are you feeling strong enough to tell me what happened Maisie? Have you any brandy in the house, as I think that might be a therapeutic medicine for you at this time, and I certainly wouldn't say 'no' to a glass."

"How very remiss of me Mike, of course, I couldn't agree with you more." With that she hurried to the drinks' cupboard and took out two large balloon glasses and a bottle of Cognac. As she was pouring them out the cuckoo clock struck six o'clock

"Very aptly timed," said Maisie. "You know Johnnie, on an impulse buy one day, came home with that wretched clock, and one lunch time when he had been out with the boys, he threw a bread roll at the cuckoo as it was 'cuckooing' and knocked it off its perch. Ever since then on every hour the door opens "Cuckoo, cuckoo" it goes, but no cuckoo."

She paused "Oh dear, I'll never be able to get rid of it now, I shall have to continue to put up with its incessant 'cuckooing'." They laughed, although perhaps a little superficially.

After the Cognac Maisie felt strong enough to continue. "Mike, I can hardly bear to tell you this awful story, but I'll try."

"As you know Johnnie has been yearning to be given the green light to resume testing Spitfires. Well, yesterday was the day. He passed his medical in Oxford with flying colours and was given the all clear to go ahead to start testing again. You should have heard him on the telephone last night. He was overjoyed and decided to spend the night in a pub nearby.

"I don't know the full story yet, but he evidently met some convivial Irish Guards Officers whose regiment was billeted in a nearby village. After a few drinks the conversation moved on to motorbikes as three of them were motorbike nuts. Johnnie obviously inveigled his way into driving one of these machines, in fact not just driving one but taking on two of the others in a race. All I know is that this race took place early this morning and due to the slippery conditions Johnnie's bike came off the road headlong into a tree. He was killed instantly."

After a long pause, trying to compose herself, Maisie continued, "I know he hasn't left a will because he always said it was like signing his death warrant. The likelihood of his being killed flying was so great that he didn't think it necessary to take out any additional life insurance – of course, like you, Vickers had insured him to the hilt if he had been killed flying. It wouldn't be so bad if I didn't have Lucy and Tilly who we were hoping to educate privately. I just don't know what I am going to do Mike."

Tears again were rolling down her cheeks.

Mike took her hand. "I know everything seems so awful tonight. Maisie, you don't yet know the facts so try not to panic, tomorrow . . .." She interrupted "Mike I knew something like this would happen, it wasn't so long ago, when he stupidly flew that Spitfire under the bridge, that I told him to realise that he had a wife and children who loved him and didn't want to lose him. Being a test pilot was stressful enough for us to have to contend with, without having to suffer his other hare-brained capers."

Mike continued, "Yes, of course it was a bloody stupid thing for him to have done. That was the man for you, that was the man you fell in love with and married. You knew he would always live life to the full. He was a wonderful man, courageous, a conscientious pilot, witty, considerate and adored by all who knew him. So now you must be courageous, I know that whatever life throws at you, you will grasp with both hands and take up the challenge. If it's any comfort Maisie I will be there for you, to help you through the difficult days ahead. That's the least I can do.

That heart to heart had raised Maisie's spirits. She decided there and then to tackle one hurdle at a time. Her future did look daunting.

Trying to dismiss negative thoughts, she realised the first hurdle was to make sure Johnnie had a befitting funeral. She could have done without the hindrance of her ageing mother-in-law, Alice, who was beside herself with grief and unable to come to terms with the fact that her only son had predeceased her.

"Darling, how could God be so cruel to take Johnnie away before me?" After hearing this for the umpteenth time Maisie eventually retorted somewhat impatiently. "Well Mrs. Kershaw, it is always the best that die young." That seemed to have the desired effect.

It was a moving and heart-wrenching funeral. Johnnie, who had so loved life, played a significant part in the production of the Spitfire. His light-hearted and cheerful manner had contributed to the high morale inherent throughout Supermarine. His needless death emphasised the sadness of his passing.

Johnnie would certainly have been aggrieved to have missed out on his wake, on what he would have described as a 'spanking good party'. The forecourt outside the Hampshire Aeroplane Club was heaving with not only his large circle of friends, but also, it seemed, most of the flying fraternity. The high esteem and affection held for that warm, but reckless man was evident as they bade - 'Cheerio Johnnie – God Bless.'

A subdued party of close family and friends met the next day to be taken by tender into the Solent. Lucy and Tilly, who did not attend the funeral, were there to say adieu to their father. The sound of the Merlin engine could first be heard, and then the charismatic little Spitfire came nearer and nearer. It flew so low over the boat that the expression on Mike's face was clearly visible. He released Johnnie's ashes, then did a victory roll, looped the loop before returning low over the boat. With a wave, Mike then did a final victory roll before fading into the distance. The silence was poignant. Maisie felt alone. She put her arms tightly round her children and tried to force a smile.

'Right', she thought, ' I've stumbled over the first hurdle, what next . . . ' The Grand National came to mind. Another twenty-nine fences to go. A formidable thought.

As Maisie had feared, Johnnie had died intestate with no life insurance. The laws of intestacy meant that half of Johnnie's estate, about ninety five percent of which was Rose Cottage, had to be put in trust for Lucy and Tilly. With no life insurance to fall back on Maisie was virtually left penniless. Because of contracting tuberculosis as a child she had lacked a sound education, so any job she was likely to find would, she realised, be pretty mundane.

A position as a matron at Tilly's school where they had a few boarders was in the offing, then followed a job running a residential club for officers and professional people in Southampton. It was where Johnnie used to stay during the week. Both prospects filled her with a sense of foreboding.

Mike's words "I know that whatever life throws at you, you will grasp with both hands and take up the challenge", came echoing back to her. In her heart Maisie knew she had little choice. She also questioned her own capability.

The Southampton job would mean uprooting Lucy and Tilly from their school, their friends, their animals and move them to a war stricken depressed town like Southampton. This proposition filled her with horror and made her feel it was too much to ask of her two little girls, especially when they had just lost their father.

It was while she was still weighing up the pros and cons of this nightmarish venture that Mike phoned her.

"One of the senior management team at Vickers would like to see you. He would be willing to come over to Rose Cottage and suggested the day after tomorrow – preferably in the morning."

"Oh what now Mike? Do you know what about?" she enquired. "Not really Maisie, but I think it could be to your advantage." An appointment was made and Maisie put the club proposition on hold until after this meeting.

To her amazement, Vickers confirmed that due to Johnnie's accident, they had no legal obligation towards any of his dependants, but because of the important part he had played in the production of seaplanes and the Spitfire they would be prepared to give Maisie some financial support and would pay for Lucy and Tilly to have a private education.

This put a different complexion on everything and gave Maisie the impetus to chisel out a new life for herself and her children.

In September Lucy and Tilly were sent off to their existing schools as boarders. It was no hardship to Lucy as she had been looking forward to this venture throughout the holidays and was enthused with excitement. As soon as her trunk had been lugged into the hall, she merely gave her mother a peck on the cheek and with "Bye bye, Mummy, see you soon" she was off to join a throng of chattering girls assembled in the common room.

Not so with little Tilly; she felt sick, had stomach pains and begged Maisie not to leave her. By any standard, the boarding house was a dark and austere environment. Maisie felt terrible. After all Tilly was still only six.

A sense of guilt swept through Maisie's conscience as she kissed Tilly goodbye. She returned to her little Austin 7 and glanced back at the house. Tilly's tearful and desperate little face pressed hard up against the window magnified her doubt – 'how can I be so callous?' she wondered.

She spent her journey home trying to convince herself that she was doing the right thing. Her children would be safer away from Southampton, and it was now up to her to grasp the challenges and pave the way to a better future for them all.

# CHAPTER 13

Mike was suffering from an acute sense of loss at Johnnie's death. He missed the close working partnership, the sense of fun and often-outrageous behaviour that had lifted their spirits in these wartime years. Life, he feared, would never be the same.

Another problem was now presenting itself. Mrs. Honeywell's duties had been extended considerably and she appeared to be under some strain.

"Mrs. Honeywell, you don't seem to be your usual self. Is there something worrying you." Mike enquired.

After some hesitation Mrs. Honeywell replied. "I don't like to say this Mr. Pinkerton, and I don't want to tell tales, but I think Mrs. Pinkerton is spending too much time with those Americans. She is hardly ever here and I now seem to be working all day and nearly every evening. I know it's nothing to do with me, but if you don't want to lose her I think you should look into it. Dear Mary has been helping me out with some baby sitting, and Kate and Phoebe spend a lot of their time down at the Boathouse."

At the back of his mind Mike had wondered whether Virginia's flirtatious manner towards the GIs had gone too far, but it had been such a relief to him that she had ceased moaning about how badly done by she was.

He knew very well that he had shown complete intolerance to her selfish attitude towards the O'Reillys and was probably to blame for her succumbing to American flattery. He had lost so much respect for her and galled by the fact that she was not prepared to help in the war effort. He knew though, that for the sake of Kate and Phoebe he must make a conscientious effort to repair the deep cracks that had occurred in their relationship.

Virginia had certainly taken advantage of those attractive and attentive guys who not only relieved the boredom of her mundane life, but also had compensated for the feeling of rejection she felt from Mike's dismissive attitude towards her.

On the pretence of going to stay with an old school friend, Camilla Bowyer, she had now launched into a whirlwind, clandestine affair with an American army officer.

Camilla had been Virginia's chief bridesmaid, and lived in a studio flat in the Old King's Road, Chelsea. She had enjoyed finishing school at the Chateau D'Oex in Switzerland.

Her French, Italian and German had landed her a top job at The Dorchester, Park Lane.

She was a magnet for Eisenhower's staff officers who had acquisitioned the nearby Grovesnor Hotel as their London Headquarters. Nobody needed to tell her she was beautiful and she made the most of her perfect skin, chestnut hair and Bambi eyes. Camilla's fiancé was serving in Italy as a field surgeon with the Eighth Army, well out of sight if not totally out of mind.

Camilla was responsible for introducing Virginia to Joe Hanson Jr, the most gorgeous man imaginable in their eyes and too great a temptation for the sexy Virginia.

With accommodation laid on at the Grosvenor at Joe's expense, their frivolous flirtation soon grew into an uncontrollable love affair.

On Virginia's second visit to stay with Camilla Joe's infectious personality first attracted her. She felt rejected by Mike, and then to be confronted by an exceedingly handsome American, oozing wit and charm completely bowled her over. She first noticed him, leaning against a bar at the Dorchester, looking dashing in his uniform, laughing and joking with his friends, Once or twice he had caught her gaze, and it was only when Camilla, probably noticing her starry eyes said "Come Virginia, let me introduce you." Interrupting Joe in full flow, Camilla edged her way in. "Come on you chaps I want you to meet an old school friend of mine Virginia." She looked stunning, wearing a midnight blue décolleté silk dress and sparkling diamond earrings. With her dark hair in a soft pageboy cut, and her smiling face and alluring brown eyes, the American Officers were soon chatting her up, plying her with compliments and drinks. With the romantic music of Glenn Miller playing in the background it was an evening to remember ending up at Eve's, Nightclub in Piccadilly. Joe and Virginia danced all night eventually rolling into their respective beds about 4am.

The following night, Joe took Virginia to an exclusive restaurant which had mysteriously survived rationing. There was now no going back.

She told him how she was trapped in an unhappy marriage, and how her husband had virtually abandoned her. He took her hand and kissed it. "My dear girl, my heart goes out to you. I cannot understand how any man could ignore someone as beautiful as you. What is the matter with the man?"

"Are you married Joe?" she enquired after nearly an hour of Joe's flattery.

"No Virginia, I had a lovely gal in Boston and it was our intention to get married if and when I returned from this God-damn war. I have only heard this week that she has fallen in love with one of my best pals and they are soon to be married. It has shaken me to the core. Maybe we were not right for each other."

"So here we are Virginia, two abandoned people together in this war=shattered, vibrant and throbbing town. I'll get the check and then how about coming back to my place? I'm fortunate enough to be staying at the Dorchester – I'm told it's the safest building in London, because it's built of solid concrete." The safety of the Dorchester was not foremost in Virginia's mind – the thought of going to bed with this warm and empathetic American officer filled her with intense excitement. She had no sense of guilt. Mike did not enter her mind except the realisation that her night of passion in the Dorchester had been so much more favourable than in the back of Mike's Talbot.

An evening or two after he had received Mrs Honeywell's warning Mike arrived home an hour or two before Virginia.

She seemed surprised to see him sitting at the kitchen table. "My word you're home early, what do I owe you for this privilege?" she launched out. That really got the proceedings off on the wrong note.

"You're looking stunning. Where have you been?" She was wearing a short grey tailored suit, with prominent shoulder pads and a nifty little hat. Mike had certainly never seen the outfit before, and was sure Virginia could not have had enough clothing coupons to buy it.

"If you want to know, I have been to the pictures with some friends," she replied, stalking out of the room.

Mike followed her and called out, "We need to talk, let's sit in the breakfast room. Would you like a drink?" She shook her head.

Mike came straight to the point, "Are you having an affair?" The silence said it all. She blushed profusely, and eventually asked,

"What do you mean by 'affair'?"

"I mean, are you having sex with any bloody American?" She remained silent, completely lost for words.

"Well are you? I want you to tell me the truth. I repeat. Are you having sex with any of those bloody Americans? If so, what's his name, or maybe I should say what are their names?" Again there was a long silence.

Then, "Yes Mike, if you are that interested, I am having an affair. His name is Joe Hanson He's thirty-one, good-looking, kind, generous, and treats me as if I were someone special. And what's more Mike I'm in love him."

Silence prevailed once again. Mike was the one who this time was taken aback. He was not expecting such an abrupt and honest answer.

"Does this mean, you want a divorce? Is this Yank more important than your children? Is he married?"

Virginia continued "You are entirely to blame for this. For over two years now you've hardly given me the time of day. You come and go as you please; you bring a family of five off the street and expect me to welcome them with open arms. All you can talk about is the war and aeroplanes, and I don't mind telling you Mike I've had enough."

"Do you mean there's no going back? I admit that I have been pre-occupied with this terrible war. Of course I have; and so should you be. If we lose, the consequences will be too terrible to contemplate. I believe, and I sincerely hope, that the worst is now over and it will not be too long before we are able to put these terrible years behind us and once again live a normal life. Until that time, even if I lose you, I will continue to play, what I consider a significant part in the war effort and in its aftermath.

"In some way, I also feel responsible for the O'Reilly family and would very much like to give them a helping hand if they need it. Little Annie is so isolated in her own silence – you just try to imagine what it must be like. If it is within my power and financial means to help her I will.

"Virginia, I want our marriage to work. I will try to be more atten-tive towards you. I will take some of the blame for your unfortunate affair. I will completely forgive you, and not mention it again, if you are willing to end it now and put everything into our marriage. The cards are on the table. Our two wonderful children need us. Virginia, you must now make up your mind."

"I will make up my mind in my own time, Mike. I have made it so clear to you over the last few years that I was not prepared to put up with your attitude of virtually ignoring my existence.

"Of course, the children matter. But it would be equally damaging for them to be brought up in an unhappy environment. I have now been given a tempting opportunity to move on, which I am seriously thinking of doing."

Before giving Mike time to reply she walked out not wishing to prolong the conversation any further." Mike had no one to console him. Even Johnnie was no longer around to consult.

The next day he kept asking himself where had he gone wrong? He knew he had become too obsessed with his work, and the war. He knew his over zealous help he had given to the O'Reillys had antagonized Virginia, but above all he knew that his love and respect for Virginia had gone.

On his arrival home that evening he was alarmed to see an American Willys Jeep standing in the drive. He got out of the car, slammed the door and stormed into the house. He was ready to confront the Yankee bastard face to face, or even fist to fist. How dare he? Pouring himself a stiff gin en route he pushed open the drawing room door.

Joe Hanson anticipating Mike's mood sprung to his feet, and half smiling, walked towards Mike to introduce himself. Putting his hand out he said, "Mike, I'm Joe Hanson, I'm here in the hope that we can sit down and discuss in an adult manner the relationship that your wife and I have recently formed."

Mike had no other choice than to shake his hand and say "How do you do." To lay him flat would, he felt, not be appropriate. Instead, Mike in a subdued manner offered Joe a drink. "I would love an iced beer Mike if that's OK."

"How about you Virginia," Mike added sourly "What would you like?"

"Just a small gin and tonic thanks Mike."

Joe certainly wasn't going give Mike an opportunity to let rip on any verbal abuse, so wasted no time in asking Mike to bear with him while he explained the reason why the two of them were having an affair. He told Mike how he had been swept off his feet by her beauty, and that although she told him she was married, she had also emphasised that her marriage was near breaking point and she was unhappy."

He continued, "I sure know Mike that's no excuse. As I shortly have to embark on some dangerous missions, I took the attitude of 'live for today', and by doing this I have fallen head over heels in love with Virginia, and I think she feels the same for me. We are both guilty and make no excuses. I am waiting to be called away any moment, so I'll be out of the way for sometime. I do hope you'll now both try to do everything to make your marriage work. You never know, perhaps our affair may even strengthen your marriage. I hope so anyway. I'm very sorry pal."

Mike sat there completely dumbfounded. "Let's have another drink" was his only contribution to the conversation so far. As he prepared the round of drinks he could not believe how ten minutes previously he had simply hated Joe Hanson's guts, and now he was almost admiring the guy.

"Thank you Joe for being straight with me. For the sake of our two lovely kids, it is certainly worth giving our marriage another go, don't you agree Virginia?" Half-heartedly and with tears in her eyes, she nodded.

"Tell me a bit about yourself Joe, what's your role in the army?" "Well I am what is called a ranger, it's the equivalent of your commandos, and in fact the whole concept was founded on your British commandos. We are at present being given extensive training on cliff assaults on the Isle of Wight under the direction of British Commandos. And are waiting for the OK to be given for, let's hope, the final invasion of this bloody war."

"Were you in the regular army before the war?"

"No Mike, I'm an attorney by profession, I had recently graduated from Princeton University, and had just gone into my father's law firm in Boston when I was called up. My father is a Senator, and before this war started I thought, I too might go into politics. Ambitions now are put to one side, first priority is to beat those vile Huns . . .. Well, I must be on my way."

He stood up and shook hands with Mike. "I'm sorry we had to meet under such a black cloud. I would love to have heard about your life as a test pilot. I'm sure we could have become friends. Good luck to you both, I so hope you can patch up your marriage." He tenderly kissed Virginia on the forehead "Goodbye, you lovely, beautiful girl, try to make a go of it" and then left without waiting for a reaction from Virginia.

Mike watched the Jeep drive away and went back to the house. Virginia had already gone to bed in the spare room.

# CHAPTER 14

The damage had been done. Virginia literally pined for Joe. She moped around day after day, and through not eating lost a good deal of weight. This was the first time that the fatality of war had made any impression on her.

The national and personal tension seemed at bursting point when just after dawn on June 1944 Eisenhower unleashed the invasion of "Fortress Europe." The stormy weather eased and airborne troops dropped behind the beaches, as British, Canadian and US troops began to move ashore on four different beaches.

Although resistance was fierce British and American beachheads linked up within days, and with support from Allied aircraft and the French Resistance Movement, German reinforcements were blocked.

Virginia was desperate for news of Joe. She now listened intently to every news bulletin, and asked Mike if he could find out if Joe had survived the carnage.

"Evidently, the Americans will only release details to relatives. I even told them I was a friend, but it didn't help."

Their marriage limped along with studied politeness, but no dialogue on the decision which lay between them. Without any formal discussion the rift in the marriage grew wider. Mike's love he once had for her was gone, and all he could see was a vain, cold and shallow woman. Virginia's heart was elsewhere, and her resentment towards Mike could not be camouflaged.

Following the departure of Joe from Virginia's life, she kept in constant contact with Camilla over the telephone pouring out her woes. She was her soulmate, the only one in whom she could confide. Camilla was still enjoying her Anglo American romances without the angst tearing her friend apart.

From an American colonel she got the news that Virginia needed and picked up the phone. "Joe's OK Virginia. He's wounded, in hospital here in London, but expects to be out within a week."

"Oh, thank God, Camilla, can I come and stay with you for a few days and find him? I'll leave a note for Mike. Our marriage is as dead as a dodo, I'm sure Mike realises it too."

Later that day, Mike read the note which was almost exactly what he expected:-

*"Dear Mike,*

*I have today discovered that Joe is alive and in London. I'm sorry but I cannot live without him and have gone to stay with Camilla for a few days to try and track him down. You and I both realise we have no future together and the sooner we can settle matters to the benefit of the children and go our separate ways the better. Try to understand.*

*Virginia.*

Just after the ecstatic celebrations of VE Day Virginia told Mike that she had decided to go back to America with Joe. To Mike, the feeling of euphoria that abounded after five torrid years of war was marred by the final admission that his marriage had failed.

"Our first priority must be the welfare of Kate and Phoebe. What are your views?" Mike asked.

To his surprise and without any hesitation, she replied, "Mike, I would like them to stay and be educated in England and for you to have custody. I would, however, like them to come and spend many holidays with Joe and me in Florida.

"I've enough money to look after myself and I hope you'll take care of the children."

This was music to Mike's ears.

At least he had retained the children and hopefully in this way too much disruption in their lives would be kept to a minimum. Ever the pragmatist, he thought it might even be better for them.

"This sounds like a reasonable formula – I am sure we can avoid too much aggravation.

We must both be together when we tell the children."

Virginia sighed with relief.

\* \* \* \* \*

Brendan and Mary had sensed, mainly through Mrs. Honeywell, that all was not well at Creek House. Fortunately, up to now Kate and Phoebe seemed oblivious to it all, apart from their mother's mood swings and spent more and more time in the company of Biddy, Annie and Paddy. The latter had now become a little terror and Mary was reluctant to let him out of her sight. He had an amazing knack of disappearing without trace – often he would be found with his bucket and spade making mud pies, the river had a magnetic attraction.

"Where's that dirty little urchin gone now?" was Mary's familiar cry.

Mary's religious fanaticism had become less extreme, although the 'Faith' had instilled a fear which had become permanently ingrained.

Grace was still said before every meal and the family would go to church every Sunday, but Mary refrained from using religious threats to her children in the way she had become accustomed to in her childhood. It was Brendan's strong influence that had prevented Biddy, Annie and Paddy from undergoing the same mental torture that Mary had endured. Mary's strong friendship with the laid back Mrs. Honeywell had also helped her to relax her beliefs a little.

With victory over Europe won and the hope that a victory over Japan would not be long in forthcoming, the Spitfire assembly line was not working at such a frenetic pace. There were even rumours of redundancies in the near future which Brendan found alarming. He knew that there was much expectation about a new jet fighter that was to replace the Spitfire but that did not seem to be imminent. He could not afford to be out of work, so maybe it was time he quietly started to look around for alternative work.

Churchill had led Britain through the war heroically and was probably the most popular prime minister of all times. His opinion poll rating was 83% in May and then in the General Election two months later, in July 1945, incredulously, the electorate turned against him and he was defeated by the Labour Party with Clement Attlee installed as the new prime minister.

Mike thought the ungrateful British people had been disloyal.

"I cannot for the life of me imagine anyone who could have lead this country to greater success, and who could now lead us forward in the days of austerity that we will now be facing," he told Mrs. Honeywell one morning.

Although he had enough of his own problems to contend with, he was visibly upset by the snub to such a great man.

The war in Asia came to a climax when Japan refused to surrender and America dropped an atomic bomb on Hiroshima killing thousands of civilians. As they still refused, three days later a second atomic bomb was dropped, this time on Nagasaki with the same further dire consequences. These lethal nuclear bombs sent shock waves throughout the world. Some 200,000 were killed, mainly civilians, leaving an aftermath of radiation and other associated illnesses for years after. Japan surrendered.

On August 15th 1945. World War II was finally at an end. It just happened to coincide with a holiday Maisie had decided to take by the sea. She had learned all the ropes at running her residential club and after working seven days a week for two years she thought it time for a little rest to spend some quality time with Lucy and Tilly. She took an apartment at Sandbanks with direct access on to the beach.

She had heard of Mike and Virginia's marriage break-up and invited Kate and Phoebe to join them all. It was the first holiday that any of the children had ever had so their excitement was almost uncontrollable. The 'oohs and aahs' that took place as they first set eyes on the sea gave Maisie an instant thrill, not to mention the look of wonderment as she bought them each a bucket, spade and a fishing net. They walked back splashing through the sea as it lapped up on the beautiful sandy beach. They couldn't wait to make their first sand castle.

Kate and Phoebe had been staying at Sandbanks for a week when the celebrations of the victory over Japan, or VJ Day as it became known, took place. Mike had arranged to come down and spend the day with them and then take his children back with him. Flags were flying, bonfires being built along the beach. There was rejoicing everywhere, and to Kate it was even more special as it was her ninth birthday. Her birthday present from Mike was a rubber ring. It was actually a big inner tyre from a lorry, but to Kate it was magical. Mike joined by Maisie spent most of the day sitting each one in the tyre and pushing them along by swimming behind. As the tide went out and with a glorious sunset they went paddling in Poole Harbour collecting winkles and crabs, but Maisie was not too keen to cook them. She insisted that they were put back into the water.

"What do you kids think about a barbecue on the beach?" There were screams of excitement from all four of them. "Right, what I suggest is that you play on the beach and see how big a sand castle you can make while we get everything ready. We can see you from the window and balcony, but you must promise you will not wander off. Do you promise?" In excited unison they shouted, "Yes, we promise."

Mike had saved up his rations and brought sausages and chops as well as plenty of twigs and wood for the fire. Maisie had some exciting goodies in the fridge and she had also made a surprise birthday cake. It didn't take them many minutes to gather together all the necessary equipment including some beer, and after a few trips to and from the beach, their party was ready to roll. Mike soon had a lively fire going, and it wasn't long before the sausages and chops were sizzling away and Maisie was dealing out the plates and cutlery.

To add to this great feast Maisie had pre-cooked some baked potatoes in the oven and a big pan of baked beans which they all happily tucked in to.

The ambience was enhanced by the strains of music in the distance and the sounds of rejoicing and laughter as everyone that night was celebrating the end to what had been six years of hell. By the time Maisie had produced the cake and they all sang the customary "Happy Birthday" darkness had fallen, and suddenly could be seen towards The Old Harry Rocks a bonfire, and then another, and another, until the entire coastline, including the Isle of Wight seemed alight.

With the children all safely in bed Mike and Maisie sat on the balcony contentedly sipping a brandy overlooking the beach and listening to the sea breaking on the shore. The nearby rejoicing had mellowed and through the night air now could be heard the poignant songs of Vera Lynn singing 'We'll meet again,' and 'The White Cliffs of Dover,' accompanied by inebriated and weary revellers.

Mike slipped his arm through Maisie's and held her hand squeezing it affectionately. "Dear, dear Maisie, so much has happened over the last few years, and now here we are, the two of us left alone. I love and admire you so much. Do you think that perhaps when I've got this wretched divorce out of the way, that you and I could get together? There is no one in this world I would rather spend the rest of my life with."

There was a lull in the music and for a minute or two there was silence except the sea gently lapping on the beach while Maisie hesitated in her reply.

"Darling Mike, I love you too, but the stress that Johnnie put me through during our years together has made me realise that the wife of a test pilot is not for me. I know you are not nearly as reckless as he was, but nevertheless I know I would spend my life worrying about your safety, and that would drive us both crazy. You have an exciting life ahead Mike with the new jet fighter not too far off. Flying is in your blood, it is your future, and you are such a wonderful guy that you will have women fighting over you. I know you won't be on your own for long."

She leaned towards him and holding his other hand gave him a kiss. "Please Mike, I do hope we can always be friends, I feel you are part of my beloved Johnnie and I love you as much, but it is not to be. You are emotionally unstable at the moment, and it was at your instigation I took on running the Club. I am enjoying the challenge and am determined to make a success of it."

"Maisie, I am heartbroken you feel that way, but I do understand." He put his arm around her and they snuggled up together in silence listening to the familiar wartime songs still wafting through the late night air.

Sadness lingered in both their hearts.

# CHAPTER 15

There was a message waiting for Brendan when he arrived at the factory one morning in September. A Rory Kennedy would like to meet him in his lunch hour and would return at 12.30pm.

'Rory Kennedy, Rory Kennedy', who on earth is Rory Kennedy?' he wondered. He could not recollect ever meeting a Rory Kennedy. This name filtered through his mind on and off all the morning. Still none the wiser he walked through to the office and there stood a tall, reddish haired young man looking extremely agitated.

"Hello, I'm Brendan O'Reilly, I believe you want to see me." With a nervous shake of the hand he answered

"Oh yes, I'm Rory Kennedy, we haven't met but I am your brother-in-law." Brendan was still trying to place him, when he continued, "I'm married to Bryony, your wife's sister."

Alarm bells began to ring in Brendan's mind. "I wonder if there is a bar we can go to where we can have a chat?" Rory continued.

"Of course. I'm sorry, I now know exactly who you are. There's a nice pub a few minutes away. I'll buy you a beer."

Even Brendan was taken aback with the story Rory revealed. His voice quivering he meekly began.

"Although I was unaware of her age, I met Bryony when she was still only fifteen and I was a priest. She sought help from me as she was suffering from a lot of abuse from her father. She was desperate, and I felt very sorry for her. I'm sure Brendan you can guess what happened. I realised what I had done was one of the worst sins I could commit, especially being a priest, but instead of leaving the church there and then, I told no one and got myself moved to Dublin.

"I was too frightened to confess my terrible sin to God, and knew deep down I was a fake priest living a lie.

"I had no idea that Bryony had become pregnant and it was only much later when I returned to Limerick that I met her again. She told me she had had a little boy and that Mary, her sister, had taken him on as her own baby. I immediately confessed everything, gave up my priesthood, and asked Bryony to marry me. We had a quiet wedding and have now moved out of the area."

"My word Rory, that is certainly some story, I'm still trying to get to grips with it. I think another beer would be a good idea," said Brendan getting out of his chair.

"No, no Brendan, stay there, it's my turn, will you have the same again?" "

While Rory was at the bar, Brendan tried to digest the saga that had just been divulged. 'How would Mary take it all?' he wondered. He also recalled Bryony's last letter to Mary, and was now even more fearful of what was to follow.

After Rory had sat down with the drinks, Brendan lifted his glass. "Well here's to you and Bryony. I hope you can forget the past and will both be very happy. Now that the war is over perhaps we'll be able to come over and see you."

Rory was ready to continue. "I will, of course, always have that guilt on my mind Brendan but I do feel so relieved that I have now done the right thing and we can move on. The reason I'm here is to tell you that Bryony is pining for her little son. Do you think Mary would be upset if Paddy was reunited with his mother?"

Brendan, having read between the lines of Bryony's letter, knew at the back of his mind that this was on the cards.

"Yes Rory, I think she would be completely devastated. I, too, would be upset. I really love the little fellow. Since Mary and I have been together life has been very tough. As you probably know, her life at home in Limerick was a nightmare, and you have no idea the effect that the war has had on her. Being bombed; with Annie being left deaf and not really being able to speak, and now if she were to lose Paddy, I just fear for her sanity.

"I suppose legally he is yours, but I think after everything Mary did to help Bryony out of a difficult situation I'm not sure where we all stand morally. I can completely understand you both wanting your lovely son back. All I can say Rory, is perhaps I can gently ease Mary into believing that if at any time you wanted to have Paddy back that she may have to agree.

"If you don't mind I would rather not tell her you have been here. Perhaps we can talk again in a few months time. Is that OK with you? I must now rush back to work."

"It has been a good conversation Brendan. I am so pleased to have met you. I will go back and tell Bryony and let's hope we can sort this out in a friendly manner." They shook hands and Brendan hurried away.

Brendan arrived home that evening to find Mary at her wits' end with Paddy. "Oh Brendan, I'm so glad you're home, Paddy has been a right little devil all day, I don't know what to do with him. I even smacked him and sent him to bed for an hour – just look at him now."

Brendan could see Paddy picking up clods of soil and throwing them at Mary's clean washing hanging on the line."

"Hi Paddy! Stop that immediately – what DO you think you're doing? That's Mammy's clean washing that she has taken a long time to wash. You are a very naughty boy. I've heard that you have been naughty all day Paddy, what's got into you? Go and say sorry to Mammy straight away. If I hear from Mammy again that you've been naughty again I will give you a good walloping," Brendan threatened.

That evening Brendan approached the subject of Paddy's rightful parentage. "Mary, have you ever thought, now that Bryony's married she and her husband might want Paddy back."

"The way I feel now they would be welcome to have him," chuckling she instantly replied. Then continued "No, I don't really mean that Brendan, I really love the wee lad, but he can be a little sod."

"Seriously", Brendan continued, "I think this could easily happen, and legally I don't think we would have a leg to stand on. I think Mary, you must, perhaps, prepare yourself for this. At least he would still remain within the family and we could keep in touch."

"It's an awful thought, I don't really want to think about something that will probably never happen," Mary replied, trying to dismiss the subject.

"Prepare yourself Mary. I think it might."

Biddy's attitude towards Annie had certainly improved, but the gap between them was widening at an alarming rate, and Annie was becoming more and more isolated in her own world, realising how much she was lagging behind her twin sister. When Kate was around she would always take Annie under her wing and there was a genuine companionship between the two of them. Kate was able to talk with Annie better than anyone else and it was only while Annie was in Kate's company that she became notably animated.

Kate had now been at her prep school for two years and Annie and Biddy had moved on to the local primary school, where it appeared Annie was making no progress. The time had come for Annie to go to a special school where she would meet children with similar disabilities and with whom she could relate. She was lost and lonely in a world of silence and nowhere to go.

Brendan's could no afford school fees so it was presenting quite a problem.

Brendan had been brought up with the belief that life was all about solving problems. He certainly had more than his lion's share.

Winter was setting in, and one damp and foggy evening he arrived home to find Mrs. Honeywell at the door to meet him.

"Brendan, I am a little concerned about Mary, she has severe tummy pains and has been sick. I think she has quite a fever, but I could not find a thermometer. I think we should call the doctor."

Brendan found Mary vomiting into a bucket. She looked awful.

"My darling Mary, when did this all start? What have you eaten?" Mrs. Honeywell came in with a cool flannel and sponged her head.

"It started about three hours' ago" Mary began. "Oh! I do feel really awful, but please don't get the doctor, I'll feel better in the morning."

"Sorry Mary, I am going to call a doctor before he goes off duty" answered Brendan walking towards the door.

Doctor Robinson arrived about an hour later and diagnosed what he was pretty certain was an acute appendicitis and asked Mrs. Honeywell to call an ambulance. He explained to Mary that she must go to hospital as soon as possible where subject to a definite diagnosis she would have her appendix removed.

"Sorry doctor, I'm not prepared to have an operation."

Politely, Doctor Robinson assured her that it was a straightforward minor operation and there should be nothing to worry about. She would only have to stay in hospital for a few days. Mary was adamant nothing would induce her to agree to an operation. She was still protesting as she was stretchered into the ambulance.

"Mary, come on, come on, you must have this operation. It will be over so quickly and you will soon feel better." "I must now tell you everything Brendan. The reason I won't have the operation is because I have committed a mortal sin and the priest will not give me absolution."

Brendan looked askance. Mary heaved with pain before continuing.

"Just after the bombing I found out I was pregnant, and it was all too much." Tears were now streaming down her face. "I couldn't cope Brendan, and Mrs. Honeywell took me to someone she knew and I had an abortion. I had our little baby killed because I couldn't cope and I knew that it would have finished you. I was too frightened to tell you. Over the years I have asked for absolution, but I know I have committed an unforgivable sin. I feel better now that I have told you my darling Brendan. I wish I had done it years ago. It has been haunting me all these years."

"Darling, darling Mary, I would have understood and even admired you for what you did. Please don't give up now. God understands why you did it. He is the one who really matters, not a priest. A priest is just a man who so often has failings just like you and me. Let me tell you now Mary, Paddy's father was a priest. They're not all perfect you know."

Before any more could be said, the ambulance drew to a halt and the doors opened and Mary was carried through into the Emergency Department.

"Brendan I will agree to the operation, but I would like to see a priest first." It was a further three hours later that Mary finally went into theatre for her operation.

Brendan sat in a cheerless waiting room listening to the monotonous tick-tock of the clock. It wasn't long before a sombre-looking surgeon opened the door.

"I am so sorry to have to tell you Mr. O'Reilly that your wife passed away under the operation. The appendix had burst, causing peritonitis, and there was nothing we could do. I am so sorry. This is normally such a straightforward operation, but regrettably the damage had already been done.

Brendan had been so relieved that she had agreed to have the operation and somehow never dreamed she wouldn't come out of it. His loyal and devoted Mary now no more. This was more than he felt he could cope with.

Death over the last few years had become a common occurrence at the hospital, and the nurses were well experienced in dealing with such situations. They encouraged him to stay in the hospital until he had come to terms with Mary's death and plied him with sweet cups of tea to stave off the shock.

One of the kindly little staff nurses volunteered to take him home as she was about to go off duty.

He felt unable to face the children so soon, he knew Mike would be at work, so Mrs. Honeywell he knew would understand the complete hell he was going through and give him a little solace.

The expression on Brendan's face was enough to alert Mrs. Honeywell that something was wrong. "What is it, can I help?" Brendan was too choked up to reply, and then eventually he managed,

"It's Mary – she's dead."

Even Mrs. Honeywell, who could normally give a positive reply to any problem, was shocked. "Oh my dear dear boy, I just can't believe it." She put both her portly arms round him and gave him a hug. "I'm just making a pot of tea, come and sit down and then try to tell me all about it."

As she poured out the tea Brendan sat shivering in the chair with his eyes closed looking almost comatose. "Here you are Brendan, you'll feel better when you've got this inside you. Are you feeling cold? I can light the fire."

He slowly shook his head. "I don't know how I am feeling."

Mrs. Honeywell took his hand. "Come on now. Just try to tell me what happened." While he was trying to relate the tragic story, Mrs. Honeywell saw Mike's car flash by.

"Just stop there Brendan, I've just seen Mr. Pinkerton go by, I will just nip over and fetch him. He will be a good one to talk to and it will save you having to tell him the whole sad story over again."

"Please come quickly Mr. Pinkerton, Brendan needs you, something terrible has happened." As the two of them hurried along the road Mrs. Honeywell put Mike in the picture.

"Brendan, what on earth has happened?" Brendan went to get up.

"Please don't get up." Bending over and affectionately squeezing both his arms together he said, "I'm devastated to hear from Mrs. Honeywell that Mary has died. This is awful, and so sudden, I am so sorry, what an awful catastrophe. Are you able to tell us what happened?" Mike slumped down in the chair next to Brendan.

Next followed the story from beginning to tragic end. "Well, we can't really blame this one on the war can we Brendan?" said Mike. Mrs. Honeywell intervened.

"From what I have just heard Brendan, I feel that perhaps it is me who is to blame for this whole horrible episode. When Mary found she was pregnant, she virtually had a breakdown, and for your sake Brendan, and for the sake of Annie, Biddy and Paddy, I persuaded, and might even say pushed her into ending her pregnancy. I did not understand her strict religious leanings although she did tell me she would be committing a terrible sin. I am afraid I poo pooed her beliefs and told her that her husband and children should come first and they were the most important ones to protect."

Mrs. Honeywell's voice was beginning to break as she continued. "I can't bear it. To think if I hadn't persuaded Mary to have that abortion, she might be here today. What have I done?" Tears now were very evident.

"Please, please, don't say that Mrs Honeywell, you are certainly not to blame," said Brendan trying to reassure her.

"You, and of course, you Mike, have helped Mary, me and our children through such terrible times that it would take us a lifetime to repay you. I know I shouldn't say so, being a Catholic, but I am afraid I blame the 'Faith' as she always referred to her religion.

"Her childhood in Limerick was spent in constant fear of the Faith which seemed to rule Ireland at that time. The poor girl was fanatical and lived permanently in a state of fear that if she did not comply rigidly she would be doomed or burned in hell. I feel angry, because regrettably it ruined her whole life. And now she has gone for ever."

Mike quickly came to the rescue. "It's no good trying to apportion the blame for poor Mary's death. It is really nobody's fault and it is not going to help any of us to keep harping back on it. Brendan you must put it right out of your mind, you must not become bitter, and you Mrs. Honeywell you too will become bitter and twisted if you think in any way you are to blame. Of course you're not.

"You have brought such help and stability to both our families for which we will always be eternally grateful. You must both put these negative thoughts right out of your minds, and let's now think how you, Brendan, or all of us are going to break the news to first of all Annie, Biddy and Paddy, and then to Kate and Phoebe."

## CHAPTER 16

Mike Pinkerton's life was now subject to a radical reassessment. The arrangements of his divorce with Virginia seemed to be going through amicably, and they had agreed that Kate and Phoebe would spend six weeks each year in Florida. After much deliberation he decided to let Kate finish her last year at her present school, Rookesbury, and then join Lucy at the Godolphin School, Salisbury, as a boarder. Mike felt that Phoebe was too young to be sent away, so she could stay on at Rookesbury until she was twelve and then join Kate at the Godolphin.

As Mrs. Honeywell was in her late sixties he had to reduce her workload, so he decided to employ a 'mother's help.'

Brendan O'Reilly also had to reappraise his life. Having come to terms with the death of Mary, he had to break the news to his frail mother-in-law, Molly O'Shea, in Limerick.

It was more than six years since he left Southern Ireland, and due to the war, and the traumas that had beset the family little contact had been made. This was yet another formidable challenge for the kindly Brendan. Now fifty-two years old, three children in his care and his future uncertain, he decided to take a boat back to Ireland accompanied by Annie, Biddy and Paddy. This trip, put a strain on his pocket, and he was determined to return as soon as was possible to avoid extreme religious pressures on his children. Vickers gave him three weeks' compassionate leave at the beginning of December, the idea being to return to Hamble before Christmas.

Fortunately, he would still have a well-paid job to come back to, but for how long he was not sure.

A mixed reception greeted Brendan in Ireland Nothing much had changed in the O'Shea household. 36d St. Thomas Street looked exactly the same as it had done six years previously - same carpets, same curtains, same furniture arranged in exactly the same way. What was strikingly evident was how Molly had aged in that period. She was still in her fifties, about the same age as Brendan, but looked over 70. She was sitting hunched up in a chair fiddling with her Rosary. Her hair was white, she was painfully thin, shrivelled and wrinkled. 'At least Mary was saved from seeing her darling Mammy in such a state of deterioration,' Brendan surmised. Mary, he knew, would have blamed herself for it all.'

Brendan approached her gently.

"Hello, Mrs. O'Shea, it's Brendan, your daughter Mary's husband."

At first she looked startled, then nodded in recognition, "Hello my dear, well I'm surprised to see you - where's Mary?"

He had hoped to break the news slowly, but Molly had put him on the spot.

"I'm afraid I am here to tell you some sad news. Our darling Mary passed away two weeks' ago. Brendan's voice was breaking.

"She died of peritonitis, a burst appendix, and this is why I have come here to tell you."

He put his arm round her. "I am so sorry Mrs. O'Shea to have to bring you such terrible news. Mary meant everything to me, I loved her so much. She was a wonderful mother, and it was my fault that she had to undergo six difficult years. She was so brave – you would have been really proud of her."

Mopping away her tears with the back of her hand, it took Molly a few moments to compose herself. "Oh dear God, it is indeed awful news Brendan that Mary has been taken away so soon. She was a good girl, so I know she'll be in the safe hands of God and will now be with her brothers, Tommy and Sean, and my two other babes who died in birth."

"Five of my children have now died Brendan - I wish I could join them. Bryony and Seamus have both left home and I'm now only left with Jimmy, that drunken, lying scoundrel. I have nothing more to live for."

Brendan had hoped to talk to Molly without the presence of the three children, but it had all happened so quickly that they had to undergo this further torment. "Biddy, Annie and Paddy, come and meet Granny O'Shea, she hasn't met you since you were all very tiny."

"Which twin's which?" enquired Molly. Brendan then had to go into further detail about the night during the Southampton Blitz when their house was bombed, as a result of which Annie had been left deaf and virtually dumb.

He decided it would not be wise to wait for Jimmy's return. Biddy, Annie and Paddy had suffered enough without having to see Jimmy come staggering home, and watch his reaction to the news of Mary's death.

Brendan excused them all and told Molly that they were going to stay with Fred, his brother, but would be back the next day to see her.

Brendan had already had enough. He looked forward to seeing Fred again, and knew they must spend a few days with Bryony and Rory. After that he could hardly wait to be back on the ferry to England, which in spite of everything, he had grown to love.

After another brief visit to Molly, Brendan and the children caught the Tipperary bus to Pallas Grean where Rory worked on a large estate. He met them off the bus just outside a thatched inn, Chaser O'Brian's Pub as it was called.

Rory was pleased to see them, and no sooner had he been introduced to Annie and Biddy and then to meet Paddy, his son for the first time was an emotional experience.

"I should think you could be doing with a glass of Guinness, Brendan before we go home."

"That, I think Rory would be a good idea."

Putting their luggage in the back of the truck, and installing the three children they disappeared into the pub.

"My word Rory, this is quite some pub," Brendan exclaimed, as his eyes focused on a huge fireplace in which roared a welcoming log fire.

Brendan then noticed a shelf full of Irish malt whiskeys. Almost drooling, he remarked, "just look at those, this is the Ireland of my dreams, this is how I want to remember it."

With no time to enjoy the 'other half' they were soon being thrown around on a rough potholed gravel road driving through spectacular countryside. About twenty minutes later, through the gates of the estate, they drew up to the cottage which came with Rory's new job.

Bryony came rushing out of the door. "It's just wonderful to see you all my darlings," she began "I thought you were never coming."

"It's been a long time Bryony, I would hardly have recognised you. Now, this is Biddy, Annie, and of course, Paddy – this is Auntie Bryony, Mammy's sister." Brendan then repeated very slowly for Annie's sake and asked her if she had understood.  She half smiled and nodded.

Bryony gave them a hug. She was awestruck by the sight of Paddy. "I can't believe Paddy this can be you, you are so much bigger than I'd imagined, and so good looking." She could not resist in giving him an extra big hug. "Come in, come in, and make yourselves feel at home."

So much had happened in such a short time. The realisation that Mary had disappeared from their lives for ever, and then to be suddenly taken to Ireland, had, Brendan thought, greatly impacted on the children.

"Who's going to come and help me feed the pigs?" asked Rory. That galvanised them into action. Even Annie could detect that something had aroused Paddy and Biddy's enthusiasm.

"Annie,would-you-like-to-go-and-feed-the-pigs-with-uncle   Rory," repeated Brendan. She nodded and chased after them.

Brendan now faced another problem, one that he had not been looking forward to - Paddy's future. Bryony sat down close to him, and after a few stilted moments, asked him whether there was any possibility of Paddy coming back to live with his rightful parents.

"Well Bryony, I knew you were going to ask me this question, and it has been worrying me for a long time. It is difficult to know the rights and wrongs of it all, so I think we ignore that, and ask ourselves what is best for Paddy, and secondly, what Mary would have wished. I now look upon Paddy as my own son and love him as much as Annie and Biddy. He can, you know, be a right wee bugger at times." They both smiled.

"I know Rory and I can give him a very loving home. We realise we've made a disastrous start, but that is now all behind us. Rory has a steady job, and is also going to evening classes in Tipperary. You know he never wanted to be a priest"

"Like me he had religion thrust down his throat as a child. He was frightened, and his papa really forced him to go into the church. That, he believed, was the only way forward.  He did not like a lot of what he saw, especially the fear that priests instilled into people. I know Rory has committed a cardinal sin and has now fully repented, but, of course, he will never be forgiven by God. I, too, have sinned Brendan, but we now both know the way forward."

Brendan was impressed. "What we have to consider, Bryony, is whether Paddy would be happier with you here in Ireland, or with me in England. I think it all comes down to that, and I believe, that given time, Paddy himself will show us the way."

It was amazing how quickly the children had lifted themselves from the doldrums. Rory had not only helped them feed the pigs, but had taken them all around the farm. They had seen sheep and cows and met Kep, the sheepdog, numerous farm cats, and Rory had promised they could help him to get the cows in for milking the next day if they got up early enough. The entire atmosphere had lightened within an hour.

When the children were tucked head to toe in one big bed, the subject of Paddy's welfare returned.

Rory had an idea. "Bryony, why don't you go back to England with Brendan for a few weeks to help him get back to normal? This will give you a perfect opportunity to get to know Paddy." Bryony and Brendan thought this, in principle, a good idea, but Bryony was reluctant to leave Rory for so long on his own.

"I shall be fine Bryony, I shall be so busy and I'm quite capable of looking after myself. There is so much at stake here, and whatever decision is made it will not be easy. For Paddy's sake I feel this is what you should do. Any transition should evolve." They soon agreed.

This took another four days by which time Paddy had become acclimatised to farm life, and he could not stop talking about the pigs, cows, Kep, tractors, and 'Uncle Rory said this.., or Uncle Rory said that...'

It almost seemed that cowpats had replaced his craze for mud pies, because after every outing with Rory he came back caked in the stuff.

Brendan and Bryony paid a last brief visit to Molly taking with them some vegetables Rory had gathered from the farm. It hardly seemed she had moved since their last visit, still huddled up in a chair, clasping her rosary.

She was a pitiful sight. She had not recovered from the news that 'Father' Rory was the father of her grandson, and it was completely beyond her comprehension that Bryony was now to accompany

Brendan and the three children to England.

They refrained from going into too much explanation thus confirming Molly's belief that Bryony was a thoroughly immoral girl, and would surely burn in hell.

"Mammy, I'm going away for only a few weeks to look after Mary's children and help Brendan get back on his feet. I'll call in and see you on my way home and tell you all about it. Please look after yourself. I love you Mammy." Molly looked up at them all, and one by one they gave her a peck on the cheek as they said goodbye. There was a look of utter amazement on her face as they left.

'What ever next?' she wondered.

# CHAPTER 17

With Bryony by his side, Brendan looked at life in a more positive light.

Christmas was less than a week ahead. This filled the children's minds with excitement. Kate and Phoebe were spending the holidays with their father; the new mother's help was in residence, and Mrs Honeywell, like a conductor of an orchestra, coordinated operations in all directions. A wind of change was already blowing through the Pinkerton household.

Mike seemed pleased that the O'Reilly family had returned and was delighted that Brendan brought Bryony, his sister-in-law, back with him. He invited them all to spend Christmas day at Creek House, which came as a great relief to Brendan. All he had to do was rustle up some stocking fillers and presents. Even that would not be easy.

Kate and Annie were soon back on the table tennis table – backwards and forwards, backwards and forwards. This was their way of bonding, and although Kate went out of her way to try to help Annie to lip-read and speak, it was mentally exhausting for both of them. Their game was getting faster and faster and they were becoming quite proficient little players. Of prime importance, it was the one pursuit that Annie could compete with Kate on level terms This gave her a great deal of self confidence – at times she was even able to beat Kate, which brought wide smiles to her face.

That Christmas Brendan felt just was not Christmas without Mary. His anger towards religion still ran deep. Bryony, and the children including Kate and Phoebe went to morning service at the Hamble village church, while Mike, Mrs. Honeywell, and Inga, the Icelandic mother's help, prepared Christmas lunch. Neither Brendan nor Bryony could bring themselves to attend the Catholic Church, although deep down they felt they should go to pray for Mary.

Even Mike, who did everything to make it a happy time for everyone had to admit to Brendan, "It's a funny thing Brendan, although Virginia and I could not see eye to eye on almost everything, I do miss her. I am almost missing her whingeing and dissatisfaction with everything and everyone."

Even Mrs. Honeywell was not her usual jovial self and Inga was a little homesick as it was the first time she had been away from her parents. Bryony admitted she was concerned about Rory being all alone. It was a low key Christmas, but the children seemed happy with it all, and played boisterous games until exhausted they fell into their beds.

On Boxing Day, Mike took Kate and Phoebe to visit Maisie, Lucy and Tilly at the Club in Southampton. It was not quite the same as their visits to Rose Cottage, but nevertheless Maisie put on a special lunch, and afterwards the children met the cats, rabbits and guinea pigs that the family seemed to have accumulated. They then disappeared to the large playroom on the third floor of the house.

Mike regularly called into the Club to see whether Maisie was all right, but either he had friends with him or otherwise Maisie was too busy to sit down and talk. This was the first time they had been together, alone, for some time.

"It's so good to see you Maisie, and wonderful to have you on your own for a change" he said, taking her hand.

"How's life treating you?"

"I can't grumble, Mike, I don't really have time to think, I'm tied here seven days a week, it's such hard work, but I find it gratifying. I'm earning a good living, meet lots of lovely people and feel at long last that life's worth living again. How about you Mike?"

"My working life is going just fine. As you know I have a job in a million, that's always exciting and keeps the adrenalin pumping and shortly I will be testing jets, which will be even more challenging. But I realise that there's more to life than flying, and I need someone to love and cherish. Family life is very important to me. You may not believe this, but yesterday I really missed Virginia not being there. Christmas didn't seem the same without her. I do blame myself in many ways, but I'm equally certain that our marriage could never have worked."

"If you want my opinion, you were completely incompatible Mike. It was her beauty that swept you off your feet. You were immature, and I expect you thought it was good for your image to have such a beautiful woman on your arm. You married her on impulse and discovered that her character did not match up to her looks."

"You both produced two wonderful children – be thankful for that Mike, and now move on."

He took her in his arms. "You've no idea, Maisie, how much I love you, please say you will give me a chance. I will do everything possible to make you happy. I am sure our children would want us to be together.

Extricating herself gently from his embrace, Maisie replied, "Mike, I've already given you my answer and the reason why. Please understand. You know I love you, but, I feel we must go our separate ways. I'm not ready to enter into another relationship" . . . and then added, jokingly "You wouldn't really wish another test pilot on to me, would you?"

"No, I suppose not, you stubborn mule, but it makes me sad. You know Maisie, not only do I love you, but I'm in love with you. I ache for you, I'm certain I could not have the same feelings for anyone else. You . ."

Maisie interrupted "That's just lust. Don't spoil the relationship we have already. It would break my heart if our deep friendship suffered."

"There's someone out there Mike who would make a far better lover, wife and mother than ever I would. But please don't be stupid enough to only judge her by her physical attributes. At the end of the day internal beauty is more important."

"To me Maisie, you just happen to have it all, I will not dwell . . . . ." The door burst open and in rushed four rowdy children.

Maisie wondered why she was inflicting so much emotional pain on herself. Deep down she knew she would never find a lovelier guy than Mike, but her own mission was not yet accomplished, and she was convinced that he was acting impulsively, looking upon her as a safe port in a storm.

# CHAPTER 18

By 1947, there was a growing impatience, and people began to ask themselves 'who won this war anyway?' To the man in the street, Western Germany seemed to have become more affluent than Britain. Stringent food, petrol, clothes and even coal rationing remained. Even with Mike's assistance, Brendan was finding it hard to make ends meet. It appeared that austerity was here to stay.

To add to the doom and gloom, the January weather had come in with a vengeance. Deep snow covered the country. Large drifts caused roads and railways to be blocked. The bizarre weather had a worsening effect on Britain's economy, and was to continue for the next two months.

Bryony stepped in admirably to shore up the breach of Mary's absence, so much so that within a week she had been nicknamed Bryma by Biddy, Annie and Paddy. This name was soon affectionately adopted by Brendan and all at Creek House. She was at everyone's beck and call.

"Bryma, will you come and play football with me?" was Paddy's constant plea.

"Yes, Paddy, when I've finished the ironing." Realising she mustn't outwardly favour Paddy, she had to succumb to the requests of the rest.

"Bryma will you come and play a game of doubles at ping pong with Annie, Kate and me?"

"Yes Biddy, when I've played football with Paddy." So it went on, and then . . .

"I have an idea, why don't you set up make-shift goal posts each end of the lawn, and then go and find Phoebe, and we can play three a side football, a game we can all join in?" That was met with great enthusiasm. So much so that Bryony thought it should keep them all happy, and would kill two birds with one stone. Before she knew where she was she was playing football, followed by progressive ping pong, and then the monkeys had even lined up yet another game for her. She never stopped.

It did not take Annie long to relate to Bryony's warm personality. In the past she would hold Mary's throat to feel the vibrations of her speech, which somehow helped her to understand. She soon adopted this remedy with Bryma much to Brendan's delight.

All too soon Bryony's visit was drawing to a close. The evening before her departure, she and Brendan decided to break the news to Paddy about his real parentage. Brendan approached the subject first.

"Paddy what would you say if I told you that your real Mammy was still alive?" Paddy looked puzzled. "What do you mean?"

"Well, let me tell you a little story. You, like Annie and Biddy, were all born in Ireland. Mammy and I had Annie and Biddy, and 'Bryma' and Uncle Rory gave birth to you, a lovely baby. Due to some big problems in Ireland it wasn't possible for Bryma and Uncle Rory to take care of you properly so Mammy and I brought you with us to England, until Bryma and Uncle Rory could give you a proper home."

"Then of course Paddy, the horrible war happened, so you stayed with us. You are so lucky Paddy, because now you still have a real Mammy and Daddy, and you have me who will always love you. Bryma says she will come again next holidays to stay with us. Then perhaps in the summer you might like to go back with her and see what life is like on the farm."

Paddy looked at Brendan and then at Bryony.

"Are you going back already Bryma?"

"Come here Paddy." She opened her arms, and he went straight to her cuddling up close. "Yes, I'm going back to Ireland to look after

Uncle Rory, and when you've finished school at the end of this term I will come back and look after you all during the holidays."

"I don't want you to go Bryma, please stay here." Paddy urged.

"No, I really must go. Uncle Rory will wonder what has happened to me. I love you Paddy, I'll write to you and hope you will write back. I'll see you very soon."

After giving him one last big hug, Brendan then took him briskly by the hand. "Come on boy, Biddy and Annie are waiting for you. Inga's taking you all out tobogganing."

Brendan returned looking strained. "I hope that was OK Bryony. I kept as near the truth as I thought possible. I have come to the conclusion that the little boy will be much happier with you - he so needs a mother, and I know with my work, I could not cope being a mother and father to all three of them. As it is, I don't know how I am going to manage. It breaks my heart, but I know it is the answer for us all, and it is not as if he will be completely disappearing from my life."

With Bryony gone, Brendan now felt isolated. He certainly did not want to lose Biddy and Annie.

\*　\*　\*　\*　\*

"What are you doing Brendan, are you busy?" asked Mike as he walked into the Boathouse.

"Oh, don't talk to me Mike, those kids seem to run rings round me. I know I'm a bit cack-handed at doing everything in the house and I'm sure I will improve, but at present I'm finding it hard work. Paddy seems to go out of his way to make twice as much work as is necessary."

"Look Brendan, I have asked Mrs. Honeywell if she is able take care of your kids this evening while you and I go down to the Bugle for a few jars. Does that appeal to you?"

"Appeal? I should say so Mike, it's the best thing I've heard for many weeks." Brendan unhesitatingly replied.

"OK, that's great, I'll ask Mrs. Honeywell to come down to you about six thirty, and she can help you get the kids sorted before we go out. I've got one or two ideas I would like to put to you. Shall we walk down to the pub? It's going to be frosty but I don't think too slippery."

The Bugle was heaving. The smell of beer, cigarette smoke, fish and chips, and a throng of noisy men, greeted them.

"There's nothing better than an English pub Mike, except, of course, maybe an Irish pub – they take a lot of beating." Mike nodded in agreement.

"Cheers, down the hatch." Brendan lifted his glass.

"Cheers Mike."

"Brendan, I think I have problems, but when I see what you are up against, they pale into insignificance. But I have one or two suggestions. Now that I have Inga working for me as a mother's help, I do not really need Mrs. Honeywell except when my children are here, and not when they are with Virginia, during the holidays. She is an absolute treasure, and I want her to stay but not to do too much. If you are prepared to keep my lawns mowed, and help with odd jobs, I would like to suggest that at my expense, Mrs. Honeywell comes down to you for an hour and half every weekday morning, and for the same amount of time every evening during term time. Then perhaps during the holidays she can come for a longer period during the day while we are both at work. This could help us both. What do you think?"

"You have done so much to help us over the last few years Mike, I feel that would take me a lifetime to repay. I do not like feeling so indebted; my father's motto in life was always give more than you take. This I have always tried to live up to, but recent circumstances have made that impossible."

"Steady on, Brendan, you would indirectly be paying for Mrs. Honeywell, so the 'give and take' issue does not come into this. Now I have another proposition to suggest."

"My father died a few months ago and left me a healthy sum. Rather than give some of this to charity, I would rather the money go somewhere to help someone who would really benefit, and a cause that I could closely follow"

"Brendan, I want to help Annie. I know you're doing everything you can for her but she needs specialised help if she's to live a near normal life. Having helped in her rescue, I have felt a sense of responsibility towards her."

He paused and looked at Brendan who had gone a bright puce colour and wondered whether he had upset him. "Oh God Brendan, I hope I haven't upset you."

"No, Mike, you haven't upset me, I am just overwhelmed. It's another shock to my system that I hadn't bargained for. In what way do you feel you could help her?"

Mike then told him that he had recently met speech therapist, James Morrison, in London, and although not mentioning Annie, had asked him what he considered the best way forward for a nine year old who due to an accident had been left deaf and virtually unable to speak.

"He told me Brendan that great strides were now being made in that field, now that speech therapists were being medically trained. Ideally Annie should already have been having regular therapeutic tuition. He told me that no more time should be wasted before she had a thorough assessment and be sent to a school that specialised in deaf children."

"He is a consultant at a very good school for the deaf on the Isle of Wight and pays regular visits there. He has given me a telephone number, and would be happy to meet Annie, if you agree, when he comes down to the Island."

"Talk about everything all happening at once. It's too much for me to take in. I would obviously do anything possible to help Annie come out of that isolated world that she is trapped in. Mike are you suggesting sending her to this school on the Isle of Wight?"

"One step at a time Brendan, let's first take her to see James and see what he has to say. He did say that children make far more progress if they are in a residential school, so you might have to prepare yourself for this. It's your decision, and whatever you agree to Brendan, I don't want you in any way to feel beholden to me. It is not me helping Annie, but my father. He was such a great guy, and would have been so proud to know that some of his hard earned money was going to help a girl like Annie."

"He would have been relieved to know that I was not going to blue it on wild women and fast cars. He may even have thought that perhaps I was maturing at long last!"

They sat in silence for a few moments with just a background of chatter and laughter from the bar interrupting their thoughts. Brendan was the first to break this pause.

"This, Mike, is really beyond my wildest dreams that Annie might be given the chance to live a near normal life. With this unbelievable offer come negative thoughts. For instance, my job with Supermarine is insecure. So much so that I have been expecting to be made redundant."

"I have applied for a job with Shorts in Belfast. My other worry Mike is if your friend James recommends Annie goes into a residential school, she might think that I don't want her any more, especially as Paddy will probably go back to live with Bryony and Rory in Ireland. What a dilemma, to be sure!"

Mike cut in: "I quite understand, it all has to be thought through carefully, and I certainly do not want to put pressure on you. If you lose your job, I'm sure you will not find it too difficult to find another locally. Also with Kate and Phoebe, and for that matter Tilly and Lucy, all going off to boarding school, should make it easier for Annie to understand. Kate will help Annie with that issue.

"Let's not discuss it any more this evening, we must get back anyway. Oh, I'll just add Brendan, don't you think it may be a good idea if Biddy and Annie went to separate schools?"

"Annie finds it impossible to compete with Biddy. Think it over, and perhaps we can discuss it again in a day or two. Whatever decision you make Brendan I'm right behind you."

With that Mike paid the bill and they walked briskly home, hoping their late arrival had not upset Mrs. Honeywell.

Brendan went to bed that night unsure whether to be excited or saddened by Mike's generous offer. His mind was in turmoil.

# CHAPTER 19

The only bright prospect to lift the gloom of 1947 was the engagement of Princess Elizabeth, the King and Queen's elder daughter to Lt. Philip Mountbatten RN, the only son of Prince and Princess Andrew of Greece.

The hard winter continued until mid March, when milder air eventually thawed the snow. This caused widespread flooding affecting 100,000 properties. The army and foreign aid agencies were called in to provide humanitarian aid.

The pound having to be devalued and the aftermath of the war reduced Britain from super power status.

In August Annie went to see James Morrison at Seaview School on the Isle of Wight. Brendan had asked Mike along, so they took the ferry from Southampton to Cowes. Kate and Phoebe were spending a few weeks with their mother in Florida, and Inga had gone home to Iceland to see her family, so it was decided as a treat to take Biddy and Paddy as well as Mrs. Honeywell.

After a picnic lunch, Brendan, Mike and Annie drove off to meet the speech therapist, leaving the others on the beach. They had tried to explain to Annie where they were taking her and she seemed to understand.

Mr. Morrison chatted to them for some time and then he said he would like to see Annie alone. Although the school was closed for the holidays, there was much to see, and Mike and Brendan were impressed It even had steps going down to a small sandy beach – quite a children's paradise.

Mr. Morrison stood up as Mike and Brendan returned. "Well, Annie and I have had a very interesting time. I hope you were able to see some of the school. It's a shame that it's not term time. I believe the children love it here, and I'm told some often don't want to go home for the holidays."

"I know there's a lot we can do to help Annie. I'm sure she is not totally deaf, and I wonder whether you could bring her up to London as there are one or two further tests I would like to carry out?"

"Is there any chance of her attending this school?

"I'm sure she would enjoy it. She would then have continuity with her therapy as most of the staff has been trained to deal with deaf children, so unconsciously Annie would be learning all the time. You would notice an overwhelming improvement in no time at all. Equally important, it would give her an opportunity to make friends with children with the same disability, and this alone would help her and give her self confidence."

Brendan looked embarrassed, and briefly related the story of how he had just lost his wife and was afraid that if Annie went to boarding school, it might deeply disturb her, believing, perhaps, she was no longer wanted.

"This depends on how it is handled Mr. O'Reilly. How about if to begin with she just came for a week or two to see how she liked it, and then we could go from there?"

"That sounds like a good idea. Would you mind if I think about it for a few days and then get back to you?"

"I will inform the Head of the suggestions I have put to you, make sure they have a vacancy for next term, and then, perhaps, when you have made up your mind you could contact the school direct?" After making an appointment for Annie to go to London for a further consultation with Mr. Morrison, and being given a school prospectus, they left. Taking Annie by the hand, Brendan felt more relaxed as they returned to the car. He still had mixed emotions over the emotive decision he must shortly make.

A day or two later Kate and Phoebe, accompanied by Virginia, returned from their American holiday. Mike seemed pleased to see his ex-wife, but this pleasure was not reciprocated. Mike politely asked after Joe and how she liked living in the States. She had already developed a slight American accent, accentuating her usual affectation.

"Joe's fine. I expect you know he received a Bronze Star Medal, a Presidential Unit Citation, and a French Croix de Guerre with Silver Gilt Star after the war."

"That is quite something, and from what I hear well deserved," replied Mike. "Please send him my congratulations." She could not bring herself to ask Mike how he was coping, and after a few minutes of pleasantries she had to rush off to stay with her mother. Mike felt snubbed. Although the girls, both looking happy and suntanned, seemed excited to be home again.

Mrs. Honeywell had been busy sewing name tapes on Kate's new school uniform which she had laid out meticulously on the spare room bed. On the floor lay the large school trunk. To Kate it was an awesome sight.

"Wow, just look at all that!" she then added excitedly drawing a deep breath "it won't be long now." She picked up a pair of navy blue knickers and held them up. "Oh no! don't say I have to wear these? They're horrible and look enormous."

She gave Mrs. Honeywell a kiss.

"Thank you for doing all this Mrs. Honeywell." "That's a pleasure dear girl, I have got the clothes list, and when we've got time I would like you to help me check everything off as we put them into your trunk."

"Yes, of course I will, it makes me feel quite nervous looking at all that!"

Brendan knew it would not be fair to ask Annie if she would like to go to Seaview School. When it came down to it, the decision was his alone. After hours of deliberations he made up his mind – he would definitely take up the offer for Annie to go for a trial period, and if he thought it was having an adverse effect on her he would bring her back home.

Mike assured him he was doing the right thing. "Brendan, Annie has her whole life ahead of her, in my mind it's vital that she goes to a special school, her whole quality of life depends on it. Well done old boy! I knew common sense would prevail. It's going to help her to know that Kate is going away at the same time, so I will ask her to encourage Annie as much as possible. You must make sure now that Biddy doesn't feel left out! It's not much fun being a parent is it, especially having to play the role of mother and father? We'll get there Brendan."

Brendan must have wondered why he had put himself through so much agony, for once he had told Mike of his decision, he broke the news to Annie. To his utter amazement, her whole face lit up and she enthusiastically nodded her head.

"Yes, I want to go" she mouthed. Brendan then elaborated "Annie, you know..you..will..have..to..stay..there..during..the..week?"

"Yes" she said nodding and still smiling. 'All that soul searching for nothing.' Brendan thought.

"Why can't I go to boarding school Dada?" Biddy asked as soon as she heard that both Annie and Kate were going. "It's not fair, I don't want to stay at home." Brendan, slightly losing his patience replied, "Look Biddy, you're doing very well at your school, and I want you to stay there. Besides, I want you to stay and help look after me." With that remark she made a terrible face as if about to be sick and walked away. "Oh well I can't win them all" he muttered under his breath.

* * * * *

All packed up and ready to go, Kate came down to the Boathouse to say her goodbyes. She was wearing a boater with a bright red band around it supporting the school crest, a smart navy blue suit with a white shirt and a red tie. Suddenly, within an hour she had changed from almost a scruffy urchin into a sophisticated young lady. Her eyes were sparkling with excitement as she went up to Annie and gave her a big hug, wished her good luck and told her she would write to her.

"Bye, bye everyone, see you next holidays" she said cheerily as she disappeared up the path to the waiting car. Annie looked bemused.

Three days later, the day that Brendan had been dreading arrived – Annie's initiation into a new life. It had been difficult for him to ascertain Annie's feelings in the run up to this new venture. In the last week she and Kate had been inseparable, and certainly Annie had looked more animated than usual. Mike had also been administering plenty of Dutch courage to Brendan, so it was with a certain amount of confidence that the three of them set forth for the ferry.

Mrs. Lovelock, the Head, or housemother as she was known by, warmly welcomed them. She was about forty, brown hair and blue, blue eyes. She had a partially deaf daughter Sophie, a little older than Annie, who attended the school. Mrs. Lovelock was a war widow. She was already working at Seaview when she heard that her husband had been killed at Dunkirk. She then dedicated her life to Sophie and the school. On the retirement of the principal in 1945 she took over the running of the school.

The preliminaries were soon over when it was decided that Annie would stay there on a two-week trial. If by then she was really unhappy Brendan would collect her.

"Annie,..my..daughter..Sophie..is..going..to..show..you..   around.. and..help..you..unpack..She..will..also..look..after..you..so..you..have.. nothing..to..worry..about.

Say..goodbye..to..your..daddy..and..uncle..and..I..will..take..you.. to..meet..Sophie..and..the..others..Do..you..understand..my..dear?"

Annie nodded. Mike gave her a tight hug. "Keep smiling Annie. See you very soon."

Brendan holding back the tears said, "Bye bye darling, I..think.. you ..will..love..it..here. I..love..you.." He could say no more. A new life lay ahead for Annie.

# CHAPTER 20

How strange the Boathouse seemed without Annie. In spite of her life of silence and isolation, she always had a great presence, and now it seemed uncannily quiet without her.

Even Biddy, whose natural instinct was to outshine her twin sister, mooched around complaining how much she missed her. However, Paddy could be relied on to compensate for this noticeable lull.

A letter dropped through the letterbox addressed to Master Paddy O'Reilly. It was from Bryony.

"Look, look, I have had a letter from Bryma," he said excitedly, running round the housing waving the letter. He read it carefully, thrilled by its contents, then neatly putting it back in its envelope, put it in his satchel to take to school.

"Can't I see it Paddy?" Biddy asked.

"No not yet, I may show you when we come back from school." It was a cheerful Paddy that went off to school that day, accompanied by a pretty grumpy Biddy.

Paddy's schoolmates had been sympathetic when they had heard of the death of his mother, but now to be told that the one who died wasn't his real mother, and that he now had a new real mother and a real father must have baffled his friends.

Paddy was an enigma, but with his Irish drawl, devilish sense of fun and happy-go-lucky nature he was a loveable boy, always getting away with the most mischievous pranks.

He couldn't wait to get home from school to answer Bryma's letter. He opened it up  and put it proudly on the kitchen table.

"Can I read it now Paddy . .please?" pleaded Biddy.

"Oh, all right then", he said passing it to her, "but give it back."

As Biddy was reading it Brendan walked in "Paddy's had a letter from Bryma, Dada, can I read it to you?"

"Only if Paddy agrees." replied Brendan. Paddy nodded a little reluctantly.

"Right, here goes . . .

*My darling Paddy*

*I am so happy that you now know that Uncle Rory and I are your real Mammy and Daddy and that you have another special father in Dad O'Reilly. Without him and my lovely sister, Mary, life for you would have been very different. We will never forget how very kind they have been to us, and dear Paddy it is important for you to remember this.*

*I loved my visit to England, and being able to look after you all. How are Biddy and Annie? They are such lovely girls and made me feel so much at home – I hope they will soon come back to Ireland to stay with us.*

*I can't wait for the holidays. You must let me know what you would like to do. I would also like to know Paddy how you are getting on at school. What lessons do you like best? Do you play football?*

*Please write to me soon.*

*With lots and lots of love to you all. See you in a few weeks.*

*Bryma xxx*

Biddy looked up "Why is it I have only one daddy and no mammy, and Paddy has one mammy and two daddies? It's not fair. It's not fair that Annie can go to that lovely school and I can't?

"Look here my Biddy, "life isn't fair. It isn't fair that Annie is deaf. It isn't fair that Mammy has died. It's good for you to realise that life isn't fair, and it never will be. You're a very lucky girl – you're clever, healthy and beautiful – remember that. I was thinking of getting you a little kitten for a surprise, but I certainly won't if you keep moaning 'it's not fair', 'it's not fair'. Away with you Biddy, I don't want to hear you say 'it's not fair' again."

Putting the letter back on the table, she skulked off.

Annie's progress report was most encouraging. Mrs. Lovelock phoned Brendan regularly to keep him in the picture. She did not seem homesick and was mixing well with the others, and had bonded well with her daughter Sophie. They were carrying out numerous tests to discover whether or not she had some degree of hearing. It was suggested that Brendan left her alone for at least three weeks, and then took her out for the day either on the third or fourth Sunday of the term. "I am aware Mr. O'Reilly that Annie is only here on trial. I can only say that she has settled in exceptionally well and her response to both the children and staff is excellent. I'm certain she will now go from strength to strength, and I implore you not to think of taking her away. I told her that I was phoning you to say how well she was doing, and she asked me to send you her love."

Brendan was quick to respond. "I am so relieved that she has settled in so well, and I am now feeling much happier about sending her away. Please Mrs. Lovelock will you send her lots of love and tell her we are longing to see her." He felt a shudder of excitement as he replaced the phone. 'Thanks Mike for making me do this' he muttered under his breath.

Later that evening Brendan strolled up to Creek House to tell Mike the good news about Annie. Mike opened the door and welcomed him in.

"Brendan, I want you to meet Gina Galbraith, Gina, this is Brendan O'Reilly who lives next door."

Brendan was taken aback. The resemblance to Virginia was amazing. His immediate reaction was that she must be a niece or close relative.

The body language between them soon dispelled that assumption. This was Mike's new girl friend. She was tall, dark, and statuesque with the same rather disdainful look and appeared no more than twenty. Gina and Brendan politely shook hands, and then Brendan, feeling a little embarrassed, immediately apologised.

"So sorry Mike, I had no idea you had a visitor, I thought I would just pop in to tell you how Annie's getting on at school. It can easily wait."

"No, no, I wouldn't hear of it dear boy, I have been thinking of her so much wondering how she was settling in. Please come and join us. I'm just getting us both a drink. A beer Brendan?"

"Thanks, just a half though Mike, I must get back to Biddy and Paddy." While Mike was getting the drinks, Brendan explained to Gina about Annie's disability and that she had just started at a boarding school for the deaf." Putting the drinks down on the table Mike asked "well how's it all going with lovely Annie?"

"I am delighted to tell you that according to Mrs. Lovelock, she's doing really well. She seems to have made friends, is already making progress, and I'm assured is happy. If only you knew what a burden has been taken off my shoulders. All thanks to you Mike I might say. Mrs. Lovelock asked me not to go and see her until she had been there between three and four weeks; so it looks as if she may well be there to stay."

"It's about time things began to go your way. I'm sure you have now rounded the corner, and everything will now start going right for you. You certainly deserve it." Mike replied. Feeling a bit of a gooseberry, Brendan gulped down his beer and hurriedly left.

Mrs. Honeywell had fed the children and was doing the washing up when Brendan got back. "You will have met Mr. Pinkerton's young lady

I expect," were her remarks as he walked through the door.

"That I did Mrs. Honeywell."

"Will the man ever grow up." Mrs. Honeywell continued. "He's old enough to be her father, and from what I can see she is too like Mrs. Pinkerton – even her name is almost the same – Ginny and Gina. They talk the same way – I'm really worried he may end up going from the frying pan into the fire."

Brendan put his arm round her "Please don't fret, Mrs. Honeywell, It's probably just a little dalliance he's having. I think he is pretty lonely."

"That's what's worrying me Brendan, he hates living alone – I can't see her playing the role of a stepmother to Kate and Phoebe."

This 'dalliance' as Brendan called it was no flash in the pan as over the next few months Gina's presence became more and more to the fore. Phoebe found it difficult to accept this young woman taking up so much of her father's time, especially as she took no interest in her at all, and even worse she disliked Timo the cat. Phoebe soon built up a noticeable resentment.

Mike, seemingly oblivious to any disapproval of his young amour, was anxious to introduce her to all his friends. Gina had heard so much about Maisie from Mike – from the outset of their courtship she had come into many a conversation; so often in fact that Gina had realised Mike's strong affection for her. Somewhat naively, Mike had assumed that Maisie would be happy for him to have found someone to fill the gaping hole in his life.

One day he proudly walked into the club with her on his arm, and having introduced her around to a few of his chums in the bar. He inquired after Maisie.

"I think she's in the kitchen overseeing the lunches," said Rob Forfar, one of the regulars.

"Thanks Bob, I'll go and drag her out." Maisie, as always, was thrilled to see him.

"Hello Mike, it's great to see you" she said giving him a big kiss. "I haven't seen you for such a long time. I've been so busy, I haven't had time to phone you, and what's more you haven't phoned me."

Mike took her by the hand "Can you spare a few minutes, I want to introduce you to someone special."

"Mike, I can't come into the bar looking like this, I must go and tidy up a bit." Mike insisted. "You look lovely as ever Maisie, come on." She reluctantly followed him into the bar.

"Maisie, this is Gina, the lovely young lady who has recently come into my life. Gina, this is Maisie a close friend, and the widow of my greatest mate Johnnie." The two women politely shook hands without the semblance of a smile on either of their faces. After a short stilted conversation, Maisie excused herself saying she must get back to the kitchen as they were short staffed.

A wave of jealousy rushed through her veins. This young 'imposter' had aroused her emotions. She now realised her love for Mike was over-whelming. She had shunned his love for three years and now she feared she had lost him. In their brief encounter Maisie, too, had noticed the striking resemblance between Gina and Virginia.

'She's far too young for him, he's going to make the same mistake again, the silly immature man, will he ever learn.'

All these thoughts were going through her mind, and then when Mike finally came into the kitchen to say goodbye, she had whipped herself up into an anger, jealousy dominating her emotions.

"We're off now Maisie, I would like you to come over to Creek House soon, because I want you to get to know Gina, I know you'll like her."

Trying to quell her anger Maisie replied, "Thanks Mike, I'll see what I can do. I hope you know what you 're doing. Don't you think she is a bit young for you Peter Pan?"

"Jealousy will get you nowhere, Maisie my darling." Maisie's automatic retort did her no favours.

"You kid yourself." With a peck on her cheek he was gone. Mike's abrupt departure and her cack-handed way of handling the situation sickened her. She was ashamed of herself. 'Why did Mike have to meet someone else, to make her realise how deeply she was in love with him?

Why should he have hung around in the hope she might change her mind?' These thoughts rankled round and round in her mind, concluding with 'and now I've lost him – my own fault.'

# CHAPTER 21

With the leaves falling and winter beckoning, the allure of a day on the Isle of Wight did not have the same attraction to Biddy and Paddy as it had during the summer.   Mrs. Honeywell offered to take care of them while Brendan and Mike went over to take Annie out for Sunday lunch.

It was a happy and smiling Annie who came running out of the door to meet them. As she hugged them both another little girl came and stood by.

"Dada, this is my friend Sophie" she mouthed, "can she come out to lunch with us?"

"Hello Sophie, we-would-love-you-to-come-out-to-lunch-with-us. Is-it-all-right-with-your-Mammy?"

"I'll go and ask her." A smiling Mrs. Lovelock soon appeared and told them she would be happy for Sophie to join them. She then asked Brendan and Mike how they thought Annie was looking. "Quite radiant, Mrs. Lovelock" was Brendan's immediate reply, followed by Mike "I can notice an amazing difference already – she seems a different person."

As soon as they were in the car Mike told them he was taking them to an interesting hotel for lunch. Annie and Sophie were now learning to communicate in a sign language, which occupied them all the way to the Farringford Hotel. Their eyes opened wide as they tumbled out of the car.

"Very nice," mouthed Annie looking at the large house clad in virginia creeper. Sophie nodded enthusiastically.

A circular table made it easier for them all to enter into conversation. Mike explained that the Farringford Hotel had once been the home of Lord Tennyson who had written many of his poems there. Although neither Annie nor Sophie had heard of Tennyson, they understood what he told them.

Likewise, Mike and Brendan were able to understand Annie and Sophie when they told them all about school and the different methods being used to aid them in their hearing and speaking. In just a few weeks the improvement in communication with Annie was remarkable.

It was still difficult to understand her, but there was some detectable form of speech ruling out that she was dumb. Her world of silent isolation was gradually being lifted, and she was moving into the real world. Brendan was ecstatic, and Mike had a feeling of enormous satisfaction that he was donating some of his inheritance to such a worthy cause. Fortunately, Brendan just scraped enough money to pay the bill. He was adamant that lunch was on him.

On the return journey, the subject got on to Gina. Mike was obviously smitten by her, and he even told Brendan they were talking of getting married.

"Mike, you have given me such sound advice over the last few years, for which I will always be eternally grateful. Now it's my turn. Please think this one through very carefully. As you know, I've only met the young lady once, and so cannot give an opinion. To me she looks young enough to be your daughter, and as the years go by I feel this gap will widen.

"Although I loved dear Mary, I was nearly twenty years older than her, and believe me it was too much. She, I know thought I was much too old for her, and continuously reminded me of the fact. That's my opinion Mike for what it's worth. At the end of the day it is the two of you who have to decide, nobody else; although of course it would make your life much easier if your children approved."

Mike was quick to reply. "Kate, of course, being away from school has not yet met Gina, and I'm afraid Phoebe has taken an instant dislike to the girl. But, Brendan, I think both my children would resent anyone coming into their father's life, though, oddly enough, they seem to have accepted Joe. It's a funny old world that's for sure.

"Gina's parents are also horrified that their darling Gina is going out with a divorced man much older than herself. So much so they have taken her away on a holiday to try to get me out of her system."

They both chuckled, before Mike continued, "I suppose I would be equally protective if Kate or Phoebe were to bring home a divorced man with two children whatever his age. It's good to be able to have someone to confide in Brendan; Johnnie was always my soul mate with whom I knew I could discuss anything in the strictest confidence."

"My god how I miss that man. Maisie, also I love to pieces, but I received such a cold reception when I introduced her to Gina. She didn't say much, just insinuated that I was a bloody immature fool and should know better. I certainly won't go down that road again in a hurry."

"Come on, cheer up boy! It's quite a nice problem to have. Look at me - my age, no money, complicated responsibilities. I have little or no prospects of meeting anyone else. It is, to be sure, pretty lonely having no one, apart from your children, and, of course, dear Mrs. Honeywell to share your life."

Fortunately, the ferry arrived at Southampton Pier, which brought a halt to their conversation.

Mrs. Honeywell couldn't wait to hear how Mike and Brendan's day had gone. She too had had misgivings about Brendan's decision to send Annie away, and was delighted to hear their encouraging news. "Oh, that's a relief, I can't tell you how worried I was when you decided to send her away. You know inside that world of silence, there's a young girl with a  really strong character. I know she will win through and surprise us all."

Even Biddy and Paddy were interested to hear news of Annie, and seemed pleased she was making such good progress.

Biddy too had come to terms with the fact that perhaps she wasn't so hard done by. Now she was no longer encumbered by Annie at school, she seemed to be going from strength to strength and had been told that if she continued to work hard she could easily obtain a scholarship to a grammar school. Being competitive, this encouragement acted as a good stimulus, and she conscientiously swotted away, almost to the exclusion of everything else.

As for Paddy, he continued to be a law unto himself. The more Biddy ignored him the naughtier he seemed to become. Although he appeared to get by on the academic side of his life, somehow his surplus energies needed to be channelled into more constructive ways. He seemed to run amok not only at home but also at school. His latest escapade was being caught on top of the three-storey school roof to retrieve a ball. How he managed to do it remains a mystery, but he had to do three weeks detention for that little sortie. Although completely unpredictable he had such a lovely nature, always smiling, and seemed oblivious to his reckless behaviour. It was only when he kicked a football into Mike's greenhouse breaking numerous panes of glass that prompted Brendan to visit the Hamble Football Club where he had been told they had some junior teams.

This turned out to be a good move, as twice a week Paddy would cycle to the ground for training, and it wasn't long before he was playing for the Hamble Under 12's. This, at least, used up some of his surplus energy.

As his term was drawing to a close, Paddy heard the news that Rory was to accompany Bryony to England for Christmas. This news was met with approval from the entire O'Reilly family, particularly Brendan who had now completely come to terms that Paddy's destiny would shortly be in the hands of Bryony and Rory. Their arrival would reduce the pressure on Brendan to organise the family Christmas. He was anxious that it would be a special time for Annie on her return from school. He had already sorted out the twins' presents – a kitten for Biddy and a rabbit for Annie.

Annie had made it known that she was allowed to take pets, either a rabbit, guinea pig or hamster back to school with her, so a rabbit was a perfect present for her. The bonus was that both these pets were gifts from friends, so the only expense that Brendan would encounter was for the hutch and a run. Fortunately, Sherbert, who had helped with the refurbishing of the Boathouse agreed to make these two items, so Brendan felt he was financially let off the hook. He had also organised six riding lessons for Paddy, so by the time Bryony and Rory arrived, Brendan felt he had Christmas done and dusted.

The final plans for Paddy's 'adoption' took place during that holiday. As Mary and Brendan had never registered Paddy on his arrival in England, and nothing had been done in Ireland, it was decided that Rory and Bryony would try to sort out the legal formalities required on their return to Ireland. Paddy would finish his school year and then move to Pallas Grean for the summer holidays and then Bryony and Rory would find him a good school locally for the autumn term. Rory, having benefited from a good education, had already been doing some research and visiting various state schools. Paddy found this whole prospect an exciting challenge, and it looked as if this major transition in this young boy's life would evolve uneventfully. After all the anxiety that Brendan had suffered, he was stunned that Paddy appeared to be taking everything in his stride. To him it was one big adventure which, as it looked, he would continue to relish.

As 1949 drew to a close, there was an air of optimism in the O'Reilly household. Annie had returned from her first term at boarding school buoyant, and Biddy was outwardly pleased to see her twin sister again. She found that she too was able to communicate with her so much more easily.

Kate had noticeably grown up during her first term at the Godolphin, and her close relationship with Annie resumed where it had left off. What was so encouraging, Biddy no longer tried to upstage Annie and the three of them all enjoyed each other's company which previously had been thwarted with tension.

Rory's presence was an added bonus, as he took Paddy off on long bike rides, spent hours kicking a ball around Mike's orchard, and the ping pong table was in constant use throughout the holidays. Paddy's energy was kept in check, to everyone's relief.

There were, however, one or two black clouds. Although Mike's relationship with Gina seemed on an even keel, Kate like Phoebe, was unable to relate to their father's new love. Likewise, Gina found Mike's children an encumbrance, and made no effort to win them over. With her parents continued disapproval of Mike, and Mrs. Honeywell putting the odd spoke in the wheel, there was discord at Creek House.

A day or two after Bryony and Rory's return to Ireland, Brendan received his redundancy notice. He had for sometime thought this to be on the cards, but now to see it in black and white, filled him with despair. Where was he to go from here? It seemed that no sooner had he solved one problem that another would rear its ugly head.

# CHAPTER 22

Much to Mike's consternation, Gina's visits to Creek house became more contentious as the holidays proceeded, so much so, that finally Mike blew a fuse. "For God's sake shut up, I've had enough of you bickering females. What is the matter with you all? Every time Gina's here there is nothing but arguments and bitchiness. I don't expect this behaviour from either of you two children - you're not giving Gina a fair crack of the whip." He stormed off.

"How about coming down to the pub for a pint Brendan. I've had enough of women's company for a bit. I must get out." Brendan who never needed much persuading quickly replied,

"Sure Mike, I'm with you, one tick while I check up on the kids and make sure Mrs. Honeywell will be around for a bit."

Mike found it incomprehensible how Kate and Phoebe were not prepared to accept Gina, and the distress that it was causing him.

"Mike, I can quite understand it all. Forgive me when I say, Kate and Phoebe are looking for a surrogate mother, and with the most vivid imagination Gina is not that, and does not pretend to be. She makes it clear to both of them that she finds it difficult to even tolerate them, making your own children feel like outsiders in their own home. Gina wants your undivided attention Mike, a glamorous lover, and the lure of the older man, she finds irresistible.

Have you not been down this road once before? Gina is a younger version of Virginia. There is no one I respect more than you, but don't you think it's time you stopped thinking with your genitals?" Brendan was surprised by his own verbal foray, so much so that he felt himself blush with embarrassment.

"That's a bit below the belt Brendan," said Mike, quickly adding "literally!" They both chuckled.

"Mike no hard feelings, I probably should have kept my mouth shut."

Brendan continued changing the subject, "Guess what's happened to me? I've been made redundant. Just as everything seemed to be going right in my life, and now this. Mind you Mike, I half knew it, but kept putting it to the back of my mind hoping it would never happen."

"Oh I'm so sorry. That is a bugger, as if you haven't had enough setbacks. I don't know how much you enjoy the gardening work you do in my garden, but I can give you a few more hours and probably find you further work in the village if you're interested in that type of work."

"I'm happy to put my hand to anything Mike. I did wonder about asking Charlie, the landlord here whether he needed anyone. I know a couple of months ago they were looking for extra bar staff. It's my round, so I think I will go and sound him out." He picked up the two empty glasses and walked to where Charlie was standing behind the bar. Mike remained seated. It gave him time to reflect on Brendan's frank outburst.

"Same again, please Charlie. I suppose you're not looking for anyone to help in the pub, as I have just been made redundant and am looking for work." Charlie hesitated, "I might well be Brendan, it's no good discussing it here in a busy bar, when can you come and see me? If you could make it about ten o'clock one morning."

"I'm working all this week - my last week, so can I come and see you on Saturday morning?"

"Sure. That will be fine, we'll see whether we can come to some kind of arrangement. Cheers."

"Thanks Charlie, I'll be there," said Brendan as he squeezed his way through a throng of customers to a despondent looking Mike.

As he put the drinks down on the table he felt a pang of guilt. "Mike, I was completely out of order, I should never have spoken to you like that."

"Really, Brendan, I should thank you. You have really made me think. I can see that by pursuing this 'lustful' relationship I could jeopardise the happiness of so many near and dear to me. You're right, Gina could be far too young for me, and although I hate to admit it, outside the bedroom we don't have much in common. There is someone I love far more than Gina, and it's because of her rejection of me that prompted me to pursue the beautiful Gina."

"Gina too, deserves more, and I do understand why her parents are so opposed to me. You are right Brendan, I should have learned by my previous mistake."

Mike was now on a roll. "You know, we put everything into winning the war, dreaming of the days of Utopia. We have now encountered nearly five years of 'peace'. 'PEACE'? Some peace! If you ask me it has been one long struggle. Food and petrol still rationed, we can still only take £5 abroad – some bloody miserable holiday that would be."

"Sorry Brendan to rant on, but I feel completely disillusioned. At least we now have a General Election in the offing, so let's hope we can get rid of this bloody government, and it can be replaced by something more positive that gives us the incentive to dig ourselves out of this black hole. Your verbal punch has certainly brought me to my senses."

"Come on Mike, we must get back. I don't like to take advantage of Mrs. Honeywell, and you may have a little matter to sort out."

Patting Brendan on the back Mike nodded and with a broad grin said, "You can say that again."

In Mike's short absence things had come to a head. On his return from the pub he was met by Kate and Phoebe looking distraught.

"Where have you been Daddy?" Kate remonstrated, and not waiting for an answer continued, "Well, I'm sorry to say that your friend Gina has left in a terrible huff. She told us to say 'goodbye' to you and says she never wants to see or hear from any of us again."

Tears began to swell up as she walked into Mike's arms. "I'm so sorry Daddy, I know you'll blame it all on to us. I know you loved her, but you don't really know how horrible she was to Phoebe and me."

Mike opened his arms to include Phoebe. "Come here my darlings, there is only one person to blame, and that's me. I now realise how stupid I was to encourage such a relationship. It would not have been fair to Gina, her parents, and above all to the two of you, if we'd continued. I was attracted by her beauty, her youth, and ashamed to say was flattered that she found me attractive."

"She's a lovely girl and I'm sorry if I have brought her too much misery. I thought I loved her, but knew in the depth of my heart that I was never in love with her. There's a difference you know."

With an extra big squeeze drawing his children closer to him, Mike concluded. "My darlings, will you forgive me for being such a silly old fool? I should have known better."

Kate and Phoebe both nodded in acknowledgment and gently eased themselves from the deep embrace. Feeling a little embarrassed, but more cheerful, they made a hasty exit. Mike felt instant relief. Somehow the intensity that his passionate love affair had brought was gone and he felt no remorse.

# CHAPTER 23

Just to add to Mike's recent chagrin, the Labour Party was again returned at the 1950 General Election, albeit by a tiny majority of only five seats.

"I find this almost unbelievable," he expounded to Mrs. Honeywell. "I think the British people have been brainwashed into accepting that this malaise is now part of everyday life and they seem to have lost the will to want to do anything about it. The state is controlling more and more of our lives, and this is what the man in the street appears to want. What do you think Mrs. Honeywell?"

"I don't really understand any of it Mr. Pinkerton. I certainly voted for Mr. Churchill, but some of my friends think that the Conservatives are not interested in what happens in this country - only abroad. They feel they're better looked after by a party who is interested in every day life here, in this country, and the working man."

"Well all I can say Mrs. Honeywell is they've had five bloody years in which to do something about it and have done nothing. If anything, we're even worse off. Anyway, I'd better get off my soapbox as if I'm not prepared to take an active part in politics, I should not complain, but I do feel that so many gave their all during the war, with the loss of so many lives, and this country of ours is still deep in a quagmire with no prospect of getting out."

Mrs. Honeywell not wishing to get embroiled, was quick to say, "Well, Mr. Pinkerton, I must be on my way, Biddy and Paddy will be home from school wanting their tea. I believe Annie's coming home next week for half term. Brendan tells me she is doing very well at school and is enjoying it as much as ever. I can't wait to see the dear girl. She's coming over on the ferry on her own."

"If Brendan lets me know the day and time I will do my best to take him to meet her.

"I'll tell him Mr. Pinkerton. Bye for now."

Brendan was now working about 30 hours a week at The Bugle, and 10 hours a week odd-jobbing and gardening. "Well, it's keeping the wolf from the door. They're a really good crowd down at that pub and we have a lot of laughs," he told Mrs. Honeywell. "I would like to work a few more hours a week so if you hear of anyone wanting an odd job man let me know."

\*     \*     \*     \*     \*

"Hello, is that you Mike? It's Maisie." A surprised Mike was quick to reply. "Yes, Maisie, it's me. I thought I had been written out of your life. It's great to hear you. Why should I be so honoured to receive this call?"

"I'm phoning to ask a favour. I'm wondering whether you would mind picking up Lucy and Tilly from the Godolphin when you fetch Kate for half term. Sorry but I think my car is terminally ill and I have no other transport."

"Of course Maisie I would be delighted, and if you like I will take them back to school next week."

"You're an angel, thanks a lot. How are you anyway? Married yet?"

"Yes Maisie, I'm married with a new born baby." There was a prolonged silence.

Finally Maisie answered "So congratulations are in order. I'm staggered that as we have so many mutual friends that no one has told me."

"They probably didn't want to upset you and make you jealous." Another prolonged silence.

"Congratulations Mike, I hope you will both be very happy. I see you're still as modest as ever. Tell me is it a boy or girl, and what have you called him or her."

"We've called him Johnnie. Guess who after?"

"I know Johnnie would have been very honoured Mike."

"Shall I tell you something else Maisie?"

"Yes, go ahead."

"OK. What I've just told you is a load of bullshit. I'm not married. I have not had a baby, and what is more, my relationship with Gina finished a long way back. The woman I really love turned me down, so I am once again footloose and fancy free."

"Oh for God's sake you're incorrigible! Shall I tell you something? You managed to make me feel a teeny weeny bit jealous. Anyway, I cannot go on waffling to you all evening Mike, some of us you know have to work."

"I'll see you on Friday Maisie when I drop off the kids. Perhaps you can spare me a little of your valuable time and have a drink - or two - together. Bye for now."

"Goodbye Mike, I look forward to it."

As Maisie replaced the receiver a shiver of excitement surged through her veins. How pleased she was that Mike had seen common sense. 'How am I going to play this one?' she wondered. She did not wish to lose Mike for a third time, but on the other hand she did not want to catch him on the rebound after his love affair with Gina. Then, she thought 'some other young dalliance may take his fancy.' Deep down she felt Mike had strong morals, but was still not quite convinced whether he was emotionally ready to settle down into marriage for a second time. There was no doubt he had been deeply hurt by Virginia.

Maisie had now been on her own for seven years. Since then she had worked indefatigably to provide a secure home for Lucy and Tilly. She had done her grieving. It was now only happy memories she held for Johnnie. The nerve-racking days of his wild exploits had faded with time, and the danger of Mike's job was now not so apparent to her. Mike was a special man and maybe the agony of being married to a test pilot would be less traumatic the second time round. At least the war did not come into the equation. 'I must stop analysing every hypothetical situation, and start to live' she firmly told herself.

It was now some months since she had seen Mike, so with eager anticipation she decided to really smarten herself up for the occasion. Having had a beautifully cut new 'hairdo' and a manicure she luxuriated in a bath before trying on numerous dresses that had been hanging idly in her wardrobe for years. One by one, she discarded them.

"Oh God, what am I going to do? I look an absolute frump in them all. Why have I let myself go like this?" she said aloud, hardly daring to look in the mirror.   Looking eagerly at her watch she realised she had to stop dithering around. A decision was vital. Reluctantly she chose an old emerald green tailored dress that Johnnie always told her looked particularly stunning.

Maisie actually was a beautiful woman. Her naturalness, her warm sympathetic blue eyes and smiling face were her outstanding features. Her ability to make people laugh made everyone love her.

"My goodness Mum, you look glamorous," were Lucy's opening remarks, as Maisie gave her and Tilly a big welcoming hug. "Whe're you going?"

Blushing profusely she answered "I'm going nowhere my darlings, I just thought I would make myself presentable for your homecoming." She really did not want Mike to know she had spruced herself up for his benefit.

"Hello Mike, it seems an age since I last saw you" she said giving him a kiss. "Have you time to stay and have a drink?" Why, she asked herself, did she have to act so formally?

"That would be great Maisie." She turned to the children who were noisily chatting nineteen to the dozen. "OK kids, Uncle Mike and I would like to have a quiet drink together without all of your noisy chatter. I'm longing to hear all your news but it can wait a bit longer." They filed reluctantly out of the door.

"What are you having Mike?"

"I would love a G and T. Come on, let me pour them for you. What's yours."

"I'll have the same."

They sat down gazing at each other. Neither spoke. Their eye contact said it all, but neither made a move – Mike in fear of a third rebuff, and Maisie with her in bred reticence. . . .

Eventually, he got up, took Maisie by both hands, and pulling her out of her chair, "Come here my darling, I can stand it no longer." She fell limp into his arms. Surrendering herself to him. "Oh Mike, you rake, I don't know why, but I am in love with you."

"Maisie, my love, you have no idea what it does to me hearing those words coming from your lips. I have loved you from afar for a long time – many years before dear Johnnie died. I was always telling him how fortunate he was to have such a fantastic woman by his side. He knew how lucky he was Maisie. I realise you resented his reckless way of life that caused his untimely death, and the financial mess he left for you, but behind his bravado was a deeply caring man who worshipped you and adored his children. Always remember that."

"Yes, thanks Mike, You know how much I loved Johnnie – he was a great guy. Please now say no more. Let's just savour these few precious moments together. They remained silently locked in each other's arms. Their mutual love reverberating throughout their bodies.

All too soon their passionate embrace was interrupted by the chatter of children drawing nearer.

By the time the door opened Mike and Maisie had returned to reality and were demurely sipping their gin and tonics.

"Are you ready Kate?" asked Mike. "I've suddenly remembered I've invited Brendan and the gang round for supper. And as I am the resident chef, I'll have to get my culinary talents into swift action as soon as we get home. What the hell can I give them?"

"Don't worry Dad, I'll give you a hand. We'll soon rustle up something that will be fit for a king" Kate obliged.

Rubbing his hands together as he got out of his chair Mike confirmed "I'll collect Lucy and Tilly on Monday afternoon, but will give you a ring over the weekend to make the final arrangements."

As they clambered into the car Mike squeezed Maisie's hand firmly and gazed lovingly into her eyes. Then with a peck on her cheek, he whispered,

"Bye for now darling, look after yourself. I'll give you a ring tomorrow."

# CHAPTER 24

An elated Mike patiently listened to Kate's enthusiastic update of life at the Godolphin – She was in the school Under XV lacrosse team. Mary Winterton had chickenpox. Miss Williams had thrown chalk at her for not paying attention in French. She was taking nine 'O' levels, but was certain she wouldn't pass any of them . . She hardly drew breath.

Normally, Mike would hang on her every word, but on this occasion his mind was elsewhere. He was still transfixed by the close intimacy that he and Maisie had enjoyed in the past hour. He was so happy to think that at long last the love he felt for her was being reciprocated.

A flashing neon sign above a fish and chip shop caught Mike's eye. "How about fish and chips for supper Kate? How does that grab you?" Mike asked as he slammed his foot on the brakes and brought the car to a juddering halt.

"That's a brilliant idea Daddy, I'll go and get them." Within a few minutes she came out laden with two large bundles of fish and chips wrapped in newspaper. "OK, I've bought ten portions of cod and ten portions of chips. That should keep us going."

"That's fine, I think they're nine of us in all for supper. I've asked Inga to make a large apple crumble and some custard."

"You're culinary skills are certainly improving Daddy," quipped Kate sarcastically.

"Yes, I know, I'm learning fast. Mrs. Honeywell has been busy cooking too for the weekend, so it's quite a team effort – I have to admit though I'm only the 12th Man. Kate chuckled.

What a joyful supper reunion that turned out to be. In the last four weeks Annie had made surprising progress. She had some degree of hearing and had been fitted with a hearing aid. It was a cumbersome looking device, hanging conspicuously in a bag on her chest from which ran two wires which connected to an ear mould in each ear. To Annie it accentuated her difference to other children and she disliked wearing it. She did, however, admit it was bringing a new dimension into her life, so with reluctance she was persevering with it and loved listening to the radio.

Unknown to Brendan, Mike was also providing for Annie to have private elocution lessons from a student studying Speech Therapy. These two factors seemed to be giving her progress a noticeable boost.

The five children got on well together. None seemed to miss the absence of their respective mothers. Mrs. Honeywell's presence did introduce a maternal ambience to the proceedings as she sat thoroughly immersed in their incessant animated conversation.

\* \* \* \*

Mike was impatient to phone Maisie the next morning. Overnight he had been planning his next move.

"Morning Maisie, I loved our short time together last evening - thank you my darling. I hope you still feel the same."

"Yes Mike I do," she replied with no hesitation."

"I have a proposition to put to you. I'd like to take you away somewhere for a long weekend. What do you say?"

"That sounds exciting. When and where have you in mind?"

Mike was quick with an answer, as in his mind he had been fantasizing about this little pre-honeymoon most of the night.

"No time like the present. How about next Friday, returning on Tuesday? I want it to be a surprise, so I won't tell you where."

"Mike. It all sounds great. I'd love to come, but I cannot commit myself until I have found someone to hold the fort here and ensure I have enough staff to cover my absence. Leave it to me I'll work on it over the weekend and give you a 'yea' or 'nay' on Monday when you collect Lucy and Tilly."

"That's great news – we'll have a wonderful time. Oh, by the way is your passport up to date?"

"Heavens, you're not thinking of going abroad?" What's wrong with Bournemouth?" she said a little tongue in cheek.

"There's nothing wrong with Bournemouth - that's a good idea! Maisie will you please leave it to me. At this moment I haven't a clue where I'm taking you. I want to surprise you. Just let me know whether you have a valid passport to give me more scope to work with, and I will get cracking straight away. As we haven't much time, I'll speak to you tomorrow. Lots of love to you – I can't stop thinking about you."

"Me too Mike, I don't know what you've done to me. I thought I was in complete control of my emotions."

"Glad you're not. Bye for now."

Replacing the receiver, a shiver of excitement ran through her veins. "I thought I had my emotions under control, "Maisie repeated aloud. "That's a joke. Oh God, where's my passport?"

It was no easy task sorting herself out. Relief to find her passport and better still that it still had a few more months to run. Two things she crossed off her list of jobs to be done.

Fortunately, Nancy, the cook, put Maisie's mind at rest. "You go away and enjoy yourself my dear. You certainly deserve a rest. I can manage to look after everything here and even come and live in. Perhaps I could bring Bill, my old man, for moral support."

After going through her daily routine with Nancy, and writing down a detailed rota of staff duties, Maisie felt confident the club would be in safe hands. She awaited Mike's call with excitement.

"It's all systems go Mike. Have passport – will travel."

"That's wonderful news, I'll now go ahead with the booking. I want us to have a holiday darling we'll never forget."

"Please, please Mike don't go to too much trouble. We'll have fun wherever we go. I love Bournemouth."

"We'll probably settle for that. It's all in my hands now so I can do without your interference. I'll pick your kids up about four tomorrow afternoon if that's OK. I'm afraid I can't get there before as I have so much work on, but I will phone you every evening."

'What on earth am I going to wear?' This thought suddenly filled her with panic. Maisie's sad looking wardrobe was mainly pre-war, shabby, and unsuitable for a middle-aged woman. As for her underwear – well that certainly was something to be desired. Her only redemption, was a pair of unworn sexy cami-knickers and some silk stockings that had been a gift from an American GI in an unsuccessful attempt to lure her into bed.

She then remembered a glamorous fox fur cape that had laid in a box for years at the bottom of her wardrobe. If the mice hadn't taken up residence she would bring it out for an airing. In the past few years most of the family's clothing coupons had been used up on Lucy and Tilly, so as Maisie counted them up she exclaimed to herself, "bad luck kids, it's time Mum pampered herself a little."

With that she gathered up every coupon she could lay her hands on and went off on a shopping spree. That in itself boosted her self esteem. She could not recall when she last had such a selection of exciting clothes and felt she could ably cope if Mike decided to take her anywhere smart, which she thought was his intention.

"Bournemouth – here I come!" she said excitedly.

# CHAPTER 25

The sun was just breaking through the early morning mist when Mike arrived to collect Maisie. As he put the suitcases in the car, she suddenly felt apprehensive. Where was he taking her, she wondered. Wherever it was, she imagined he had booked a double bedded room. That in itself made her feel vulnerable and that he was taking her for granted.

Still with a feeling of bewildered excitement and deep in thought, Maisie realised Mike was driving through the gates of Eastleigh Aerodrome. "Why are we coming here Mike? Have you forgotten something?" she enquired.

"No, my darling, I've arranged for us to have our own aerobuzzer for the weekend." Her heart sank. Visions of the hair-raising flights she had suffered with Johnnie came flooding back.

"Mike, I cannot believe you would do this to me. You know better than anyone the fear that Johnnie subjected me to. I have told you many times that I never wanted to get involved with another pilot, and here I am with another one trying to frighten the wits out of me. It beggar's belief. How could you?"

"Please Maisie, just calm down. Please trust me. I take my flying seriously, am particularly safety conscious, and with such a valuable cargo on board, I will be ultra cautious." Squeezing her hand tightly he said "Please have faith in me."

Maisie was not amused. She recounted the nerve shattering flight she once took with Johnnie. He had become so irritated with her nagging him to be careful that he snapped and told her that if she knew better to get on and take over the controls. The minutes that followed had frightened her rigid.

"I assure you, it will all be plain sailing. The mist has lifted, I'll check the weather on our route and the landing conditions the other end. All you have to do is sit back and relax."

Reluctantly, with Mike's assistance, Maisie climbed into the cockpit of the Auster, and then once he was sitting by her side he gave her a big kiss. After double checking that all systems were in order, he patted her gently on the knee, "Right, we're off sweetheart, please don't worry, you're in good hands," his voice now shouting over the roar of the engine. Maisie gave him a sickly grin.

Once air bound and crossing the English Channel, Maisie bravely muttered, "Am I allowed to ask you where we're going Mike?"

"I'll tell you when we land," he replied. For most of the journey they sat in silence, and then to Maisie's surprise soon over the French coastline she saw Mike referring to a road map in order to pin point the aerodrome of their destination. Maisie couldn't resist saying "I trust you won't be stopping at the traffic lights?" This broke the tension. Mike laughed, "No, I'll jump all the lights – you're not still feeling nervous?"

"No, of course not" she sarcastically replied.

"NOW, tell me where we are Mike," Maisie asked when the Auster came to a halt and he had switched off the engine. "We are at Le Bourget Aerodrome, a few miles from Paris my darling. Sorry, it's not Bournemouth. After we've been through customs, we'll take a taxi to our hotel in the Latin Quarter of Paris."

"That sounds wonderful Mike," she said as she pecked him on the cheek. "Do you mean I can now actually relax?"

"No, no, not yet, the taxi ride will most likely be far more hair raising than your air trip." They laughed. "Sorry I'm such a wimp Mike," she said as he helped her out of the aircraft and she purposely fell into his arms.

"Let's get our bags into the customs shed and then I'll come back and put the Auster to bed for the weekend. It won't take many minutes."

Although Maisie had been initially shocked and annoyed at Mike's insensitivity at flying her himself knowing the fear Johnnie had instilled into her with his erratic flying antics, she felt this trip had given her a sense of accomplishment. Mike had given her confidence. Only the return journey would tell whether she was overcoming her fear of flying.

As the taxi recklessly wove its way through the frenzy of Paris traffic, Mike and Maisie sat in silence, contentedly holding hands and imbibing the atmosphere of the magical city.

Mike broke the silence. "I think we're nearly there. Not wanting to be presumptuous in any way Maisie, I have reserved separate rooms." He smiled.

"I should sincerely hope so, I wouldn't have expected anything else" she replied with a wry smile. "I wouldn't expect us to share a bed so early on in our relationship. I don't believe in sex before marriage." Keeping a deadpan face, she watched the expression on his face change instantly. His smile faded, only to be replaced by a look of alarm. He didn't quite know what to make of her last remarks. Maybe Bournemouth would have been a better option.

The taxi drew up outside the Hotel Christine in St. Germain-des-Pres. It was after 1pm as they walked through the attractive courtyard and into the foyer of what was once a mediaeval abbey. They checked in, dumped their cases and then head for a little bistro in St. Germain. As they walked along the boulevard they could feel the warmth of the spring sunshine on their backs. After Mike had pointed out that he had already booked a restaurant for dinner they shared a bouillabaisse and a bottle of Sancerre.

"What could be better than this? Sitting in the warm spring sunshine, sharing a bouillabaisse and a bottle of wine with the one you love. Cheers darling Maisie, here's to us!"

"It's just blissful Mike. Thank you for inviting me and going to so much trouble organising it all. I love you so much. Here's to us." They clinked glasses looking longingly into each other's eyes.

In Mike's view, a natural conclusion to this romantic lunch would be to saunter back to the hotel where an inviting and luxurious double bedded room beckoned, but remembering Maisie's earlier remarks he refrained from making such an immoral suggestion. Instead, they spent the rest of the afternoon wandering along the boulevards and discovering the little alleyways and side streets – their burning love kept on hold.

Back at the hotel Mike found himself reluctantly unpacking in the little single room he had booked, but not expected to use. Maisie, on the other hand was wallowing in the luxury of the sumptuous double room. She knew only too well she was keeping him on tenterhooks. She carefully hung up her new clothes in a cupboard, and then laid an alluring little number on the bed together with its accessories. She then put her sexy nightie provocatively on top of the pillow, and then slowly proceeded to prepare herself for the evening ahead. They had decided to meet for drinks downstairs at 7.30pm.

At 7pm there was a tap on the door. "Who is it?" Maisie called.

"Who the hell do you think it is?

"Hold on Mike while I just put on my dress." With her dress still unzipped, she opened the door. Mike came staggering in with a bottle of champagne in a bucket of ice and two glasses.

"Am I allowed into the ladies boudoir? I thought this would not go amiss to start the evening rolling," he said as he placed the bucket and glasses down on a table, and then put his arms out to give her a kiss.

"Mike I'm not properly dressed. Do you mind doing me up," she said turning her back to him. Seeing her beautiful back he could not resist slipping his hands inside and coupling her breasts and pulling her close to him." As her dress dropped to the floor, leaving her standing in her cami-knickers silk stockings and high heeled shoes. She wriggled around to face him. They kissed.

"Mike you're taking advantage" she said slowly easing herself away and bending down to pick up her dress from the floor.

"What do you expect? Coming in here and finding you in a state of undress. Leave your dress where it is I'll zip you up when we've had the champagne, you look absolutely ravishing like that."

Feeling embarrassed Maisie quickly pulled her dress up. "Please Mike will you zip me up without any more hanky panky."

Their bedroom frolics prevented them finishing the champagne. "We can finish this when we get back" Mike cunningly suggested, realising that at least that would get him over the threshold and with a bit of luck he would not be abandoned to his single room.

"I'm taking you somewhere Maize which you might find a little over the top, but it should be good."

Mike had booked a table in a quiet corner of Maxims. There they discussed their childhoods, their former lives and their children. Mike told Maisie about Annie. How, since he and Johnnie had rescued the O'Reilly family during the blitz, he had felt a moral responsibility towards the family, and that he was financially supporting Annie and was proposing to continue doing so.

It was then that Maisie realised that not only was she desperately in love with Mike, but she had the highest respect for him. She knew she wanted to spend the rest of her life with him. It was there that Mike's longstanding love for Maisie was confirmed. It was there they both knew their love was forever. It was a truly romantic evening.

Mike's rather half-hearted suggestion of going on to a night club was greeted with little enthusiasm. The lure of that inviting bed at the Hotel Christine was now too great a temptation for them both. Maisie had finished her 'hard to get' play-acting. Her love for Mike was so overpowering she just wanted to surrender to him.

It was only as they reached the bedroom door that Maisie managed to kiss Mike on the cheek and say "Thanks Mike for a wonderful evening. Sleep tight, see you in the morning." He looked askance for a moment and then seeing the smile on her face, unlocked the door and said, "Come here you little cock teaser." With that he picked her up and threw her on the bed and jumped on top of her.

"Mike, I can't ruin this dress, it's almost all I've got."

"I know how to get that off," he said unzipping her and almost wrenching it off. The cami knickers presented a bit more of a problem, but in no time, their clothes abandoned, and all their inhibitions thrown to the wind they were locked together in joyous lovemaking . . . .Exhausted, they relaxed in each other's arms.

It was Mike who made the first move. It was a warm night so he flung open the windows to the courtyard. "Do you feel like a little glass of champagne darling? We can't waste it."

Intimately, they sat sipping their champagne with only the light of the moon revealing their nakedness. There was no need to speak. The harmony between them said it all.

The silence of the night was soon interrupted by a plaintiff English voice from another open window in the courtyard. "Come on Ivy, give us a bit. Please Ivy, give us a bit." Mike and Maisie were highly amused at this coarse interruption to their passionate night. After about the seventh time of "Ivy, give us a bit" echoing into the night air, Mike walked to the window and impatiently shouted "Come on Ivy, for God sake give him a bit so we can all get some sleep."

Closing the window he said jokingly "that sexual titillation is just too much. Their laughter was soon overcome by their need for sleep. Two deliriously happy people, locked in each other's arms, slept like babies.

# CHAPTER 26

Following the grim days of the war and six years of austerity, Mike and Maisie's long weekend in Paris was something they never dreamed possible. There was gaiety, music, and a sense of freedom they had all but forgotten. The smells of garlic, coffee and Gaulloise cigarettes wafted from every cafe. The strains of the songs of Maurice Chevalier, heart throb Jean Sablon and Edith Piaff could be heard through the open windows. Artists, buskers, the colourful markets, the patiseries, and the enticing restaurants all blended together to make this wonderfully vibrant city a holiday they would never forget.

Mike and Maisie felt they had not left a stone unturned. They walked for miles visiting Montmartre, along the banks of the Seine, the Louvre, Notre Dame, Le Jardin des Tuileries, always making time for a relaxed lunch.

When daytime turned to night, and after a couple of hours in bed, they were ready for a romantic dinner and then to dance the night away, making sure not to miss out on the Folies Bergère.

All too soon Monday arrived and their thoughts turned to home and their children. Although not wanting to admit it, Maisie now had the return journey foremost in her mind. They decided to take it easy, to do nothing in particular except to have a leisurely lunch in one of the many little restaurants in St. Germain-des-Pres.

Out of the blue, as they sat in the warm sunshine with a kir royale watching the world go by, Mike took Maisie's hand.

"Darling Maisie, this has been the most wonderful weekend I could ever have imagined. I know I have asked you this question twice before, and am hoping if I try again it might be third time lucky. "I love you as I have never loved before – will you marry me?"

This came as a complete surprise. Maisie realised she was madly in love with Mike and  wanted to spend the rest of her life with him, but was not expecting him to pop the question so soon. She hesitated, quite taken aback . . .

"Please say something darling, the suspense is killing me."

"Mike, I too love you more than words can say. I wasn't expecting you to ask me so soon. My answer is; yes, my darling, I know I cannot live without you and I would be very proud to be your wife. I feel, however, we mustn't go headlong into marriage. Our children are of prime importance to us both, and we cannot just announce to them that the two of us have decided to get married. It must be handled gently and tactfully to avoid any resentment from them."

Mike got out of his chair, whisked Maisie out of hers, pulled her into his arms and oblivious to all around said,

"My darling, darling girl, you have made me the happiest man on earth." Even the bohemian Parisian lunch goers looked a little startled as the two of them became  enveloped together for many minutes, speechless - tears rolling down their cheeks.

Suddenly their  lives had suddenly taken on a new dimension, and Maisie realised only too well the path ahead had to be taken with a certain amount of caution.

"We mustn't leave our children in the dark for too long Mike. They would be mortified if they first heard the news from someone else. I also don't think it would be wise to suddenly tell them that the two of us had decided to get married. We must approach them gently, and sound them out first to test their reactions."

"I have to admit that makes good sense. Let's hope they don't object too much," said a rather disappointed Mike.

"I don't think they will. If they do . . . well, let's cross that bridge when we get to it. I think we must keep our engagement under wraps until our daughters are brought well and truly into the fold, and know there is a strong likelihood of us getting together."

Mike continued. "We may need a bigger house. I think it's important that each girl has her own bedroom."

During lunch Mike and Maisie got carried away with their future plans. Maisie thought it important they started their new life together afresh, and bought a matrimonial home together. To this end she was going to put Rose Cottage on the market and try to sell the lease on the club, or even perhaps put a manager in to run it. They were in another world and hadn't realised the time.

"Good lord! It's a quarter to four" said Mike looking at his watch. "Come on sweetheart, I want to buy you an engagement ring. We must find one here in Paris. It will always remind you, in fact both of us, of this unbelievably wonderful weekend."

Mike hailed a taxi "Rue du Faubourg Saint-Honoré, s'il vous plait," as he gave Maisie a helping hand. She seemed in a complete daze.

"Everything will work out for the best, you'll see. We've plenty of time to make our future plans. I know I'm a little impulsive darling. I want to shout the news from the rooftops and ask our friends and families to join us in our celebrations. Of course you're right – we must try to be a little patient. Perhaps we could go and take all the kids out for lunch next Sunday. That would be a start and just see how the land lies. They know you haven't a car, so they won't think it odd that the two of us are together."

"Do you call that being patient Mike"? Maisie enquired laughing as the taxi drew up in one of Paris's most fashionable streets.

As she stepped out on to the pavement she was taken aback by the ultra chic Parisian women, so slim and beautifully turned out, many of whom had a poodle or Yorkshire terrier on a lead. She wondered how they had recovered from the war so quickly while Britain was still in a state of austerity. As Mike pulled her by the hand to lead her into Cartier, she could not but help but feel a complete country bumpkin.

"Let's see what knuckle dusters they have on offer here" he quipped. She was dazzled by the display of rings. Mike had asked the salesman not to show her any prices making her choice even more difficult. Her hands too showed the wear and tear of eight years of hard work.

"I'm so embarrassed by my hands Mike. They don't warrant a lovely ring, so in no way do I want anything ostentatious." After much deliberation she chose an antique platinum ring, square with a flat square cut diamond in the middle surrounded by more diamonds. "I think this is just exquisite Mike. I wish you would let me know the cost, because I don't want you to spend the earth. I would love anything you chose so long as it isn't ostentatious."

"I assure you Maisie, in no way is it too expensive. In fact by choosing a second hand one you were very economical." She smiled and kissed him on the cheek. "Thank you darling, I'll treasure it for ever." Because of the currency restrictions, Mike arranged to pay for it through Cartier in London. "I'll take care of it for the time being," he said as he picked up the box and put it in his pocket.

"I think we had better do no more window shopping today and get back to the hotel. Don't forget we've a plane trip tomorrow."

Maisie's eyes looked up into the skies, "Don't think I've forgotten", she said with a smirk.

In the intimacy of their bedroom, and a glass of champagne, Mike actually got down on his bended knee and taking her hand said, "Maisie, my darling will you marry me?"

Maisie couldn't resist replying "It would be funny if I turned you down now."

"Oh really funny! After all the teasing you have put me through, I would expect nothing less."

She flung her arms around his neck - "Mike, Mike darling of course I'll marry you. This, darling, is for ever, and not until some young slip of a thing comes along and takes your fancy."

"Maisie, that is an assassination of my character. I'm not like that at all. You must trust me." As he slipped the ring on her finger he said slowly and clearly. "L-o-v-e is T-r-u-s-t, T-r-u-s-t is L-o-v-e. I will never let you down." "I too Mike will be faithful, will love and honour you, but not too sure about the 'obey' bit." Their sense of humour in itself was a strong bonding force.

It would have been inappropriate for Maisie to suggest that she took the ferry home. That might stretch his sense of humour too far. She must grit her teeth, tighten her seat belt and think of England, have trust and not look nervous. 'Oh to be back in England,' she thought.

# CHAPTER 27

The landing at Eastleigh seemed easy compared with the sudden coming back down to earth at the club. Maisie looked at the old familiar surroundings in a new light. They were dark, gloomy and decidedly shabby. She wondered how she had come to accept such a depressing environment. 'Just like me', she thought, 'dark and shabby.'

She then remembered the dire straits she had been in over seven years' ago when, as a grief-stricken widow, without any experience, she had taken over the reins of this residential club.

She should not be downcast, it had kept herself, Lucy and Tilly in good stead, providing them with a home, a good income, the opportunity of making friends and given Maisie no time to feel lonely. She must not now look at it with disdain. Her trip to Paris had momentarily made her feel blasé.

For Mike's sake, and for her own self-esteem, she must, however, take a firm grip of herself and smarten up her image. As she gave her beautiful ring a last glance before hiding it away, she made a resolution to get rid of her 'mumsy' image once and for all.

\* \* \* \*

As Mike swung into the drive of Creek House he was surprised to see a racing green Triumph Herald parked outside the front door, 'Who the hell's that?' he wondered.

To his horror, there sitting at the kitchen table talking to Inga was Gina.

"What on earth are you doing here Gina?" he enquired.

As Inga hastily disappeared, Gina got up to kiss him. Mike politely turned his cheek.

"Mike, I've come to see whether we can make amends. As hard as I've tried, I find I can't live without you. Can we please try again?"

Feeling exceedingly uncomfortable, Mike replied. "I'm so sorry Gina, but the answer is emphatically "no."

"Gina, I'm to blame for letting our affair go so far. The last thing I want to do is hurt you, but you must realise that our relationship had no future. I'm far too old for you. You deserve someone younger and better than me. It would be unfair to you, your parents and my children if we got together. You will want your own children."

"Mike, I want to have your babies."

"Dear Gina, I already have two children, and would never agree to have more. I'm now going to be brutally honest with you. When I met you I was in love with someone else. This love was not reciprocated, so I sought solace elsewhere. Gina, I loved you, but was never in love with you. I behaved very badly and was, I know, a complete rake. I ask you for your forgiveness."

By this time tears were rolling down Gina's cheeks. Mike knew he must not put his arm around her for comfort. Instead he produced a large handkerchief from his pocket. "Here take this."

Mike continued. "I am still in love with that person, and she with me, and all being well we hope to get together in the near future. I hope I have not upset you too much Gina, but I know you would prefer me to be completely honest."

"You're a great girl, and I know you will soon find the man of your dreams,  then you will wonder what you saw in me."

She tried to smile. "Off you go now and good luck." Picking up her clutch bag, she left. Mike closed the door, not wanting to watch her drive away.

'Phew, what a homecoming!' he thought, 'I richly deserved it.'

How he wondered would Maisie take his little rendez-vous with the woman she disapproved of. Should he in fact tell her at all knowing her sensitivity. He felt he had not yet won her complete trust.

It didn't take him many minutes to come to a definite conclusion. With a little trepidation he picked up the telephone.

"Hello darling, have you settled in OK? How was everything there while we were away? Did they manage without you?"

"Everything seemed to have gone very smoothly, probably better than if I had been here." Was all well with you?"

"Well, not really, I had a bit of a shock. I found Gina here when I got home. Inga had let her into the house. She wanted to give our relationship another try. I told her that it was out of the question. I confessed to her that during our relationship I had really been in love with someone else, and that same person had now come back into my life. I'm afraid I was unkind to her and sent her packing pretty swiftly."

There was a long pause. "Maisie, are you there?"

"Yes Mike, I'm here hearing you loud and clear, and don't know what to say."

"Maisie, you know why I did it. I wanted you and couldn't have you, and like a stupid idiot was flattered that someone so young could find me attractive. I very much regret it as I feel I used her. Quite unforgivable, although I did kid myself for a short time that I loved her". . .another long pause. .

"Maisie darling, I hope I haven't upset you. Maisie, please say something." . . . . . . "You would have been upset if I hadn't told you."

"Are there any more skeletons in your cupboard that are going to come rattling out?"

"There are no skeletons in my cupboard darling, and Gina was no skeleton. You knew all about her, and I've hidden nothing from you. Until this afternoon I had not seen or heard from her since she walked out on me months and months ago. Why she suddenly thought she could come back into my life I do not know, but I have certainly crushed any ideas she may have had.

"Darling Maisie, my slate is clean. I love you more than words can say. I've done nothing to doubt your trust in me."

"No Mike, you haven't, it's just my jealous streak coming out. Of course, I love you. I'm glad you told me – thank you for that."

"Can we go and take the kids out to lunch next Sunday, and perhaps drop a little hint that the two of us are becoming really good friends?"

"I will phone their house mistress and ask her if it is possible?"

"Great, I'll wait to hear from you. Sleep tight darling. I'm missing you already. Remember 'Love is Trust, and Trust is Love.'"

"I will Mike, God bless darling."

As Mike was leaving for work the following morning he was waylaid by Brendan.

"How was your weekend Mike?" he asked.

"Magnificent thanks. Is all well with you and the family?"

"Yes, everything's fine. You seem in a bit of a hurry now. Would it be OK if I call round to see you this evening – it's nothing that can't wait."

"By all means old boy. I may not be back much before seven – I have a lot of back log to make up. Are you working at the pub tonight?" Brendan shook his head.

"I'll tell you what I'll do I'll come down to you as soon as I get back. I must rush now." He jumped into the Talbot, revved up the engine and sped off in a cloud of dust.

# CHAPTER 28

Brendan was having a few qualms about sending Paddy off to Ireland. He had grown to love the boy and knew his departure would leave a vacuum in their lives. As for Paddy, he was ticking off the days on a calendar. He couldn't wait. To him it was one big adventure and he appeared to have no concern whatsoever.

Brendan had now become a Jack of all trades, what with his gardening, pub management, and his latest project had been attending a book-keeping course. He was desperately looking for more part-time work as he was hoping to accompany Paddy to Ireland when he went to live with Rory and Biddy in the summer. He also wanted to give Biddy and Annie a holiday.

He first told Mike of his intentions.

"I think that's a cracking idea Brendan. I know you are now doing the books at the pub, paying the wages, as well as working in the bar. How many more hours a week do you feel you could work? Don't forget Biddy, she'll want to see something of you."

"Ideally Mike, I would like ten. My worry is that I would like to go to Ireland for the last week in July and the first week in August. An unfortunate time, as grass and weeds are still growing in abundance in the gardens, and of course , the busiest period at the pub."

"That can't be helped. At least you will be giving everyone plenty of notice to make alternative arrangements. Why don't you visit some of the small boat builders along the Hamble river. I'm sure there must be one or two of them who could do with their books being kept regularly up to date. Go for it Brendan."

Mike was always so positive. He had given Brendan the incentive to realise that his trip to Ireland need not be a pipe dream, and that with some forethought and determination it was a feasible proposition.

On her return from Paris, Maisie had wasted no time in setting the wheels in motion on how best to sell her business. She had also written to the tenants of Rose Cottage informing them that it was her intention to put the cottage on the market and so their lease would not be renewed.

As they drove to Salisbury that wet Sunday morning, Mike and Maisie discussed how they were going to tactfully approach the children about their relationship. Their conversation seemed to get nowhere. Exasperated and impatiently Mike brought it to an end.

"Oh for God's sake darling let's just play it by ear – que sera, sera. Don't let's pussyfoot around too much. The fact is the two of us love each other and have decided to get married. We've made this decision. It is our decision. Of course, we want our kids to be happy for us, but we don't have to ask their permission."

Soaking wet from their walk from a service in the cathedral, Kate, Tilly and Phoebe excitedly clambered into the car. "Don't worry about Lucy, she's going to meet us at The White Hart. She didn't think there would be room in the car, and as she's a prefect she's allowed to go down to the town alone."

As they all sat round having a pre-lunch drink and listening to all the school girl chatter, Mike couldn't help thinking what a bunch of super kids they were – a great family. Lucy, 17, was deputy head girl, in her last term at the Godolphin and going on to read modern languages at St. Andrews University. An attractive and unassuming girl, with the vivaciousness of her father and naturalness of her mother.

Then his eyes moved to Kate – to Mike she could do no wrong. Kate possessed the looks of her mother but not the character. Her warm and smiling personality and sympathetic nature were paramount. Her love for sport overshadowed her academic inclinations.

Tilly was only a month younger than Kate. Again an attractive girl with blonde curly hair and beautiful blue eyes – a splitting image of her father, except Johnnie's mass of blonde curls had been tamed with Brylcreme, to conform with his macho image. Her life revolved round horses and animals, with an ambition to become a vet.

Phoebe was the quiet one whose sensitive nature, Mike felt, had suffered most with the break-up of his marriage to Virginia. She had not settled into boarding school as easily as the others, but it was still early days, and Mike was sure that if she were not overwhelmed by the other girls her artistic talents would come to the fore. He was sure that Maisie's presence in her life would be a great asset.

As he listened to the gabble of their voices and surveyed his soon to be enlarged family, Mike wondered, what he had let himself in for?

Mike and Maisie kept exchanging glances across the table. The conversation was so concentrated on the children's school activities, they were beginning to wonder whether the object of the lunch party was in vain.

Suddenly in the middle of their desserts Kate piped up, "Well, how's your love life Dad?"

Mike look startled. Not daring to catch Maisie's eye he replied, "What may I ask do you mean by that Kate?"

"I just wondered whether you had replaced Gina."

"Would you mind if I told you I had?"

"Yes, if it were someone like Gina. She . . . ."

Phoebe interjected, "She was horrid Daddy. She really hated us and we hated her.

"Surely, you wouldn't want me to spend the rest of my life alone."

Kate replied, "No not really, but we wouldn't want someone like

Gina. With all due respect Daddy you need someone older."

"What about Mrs. Honeywell?" Mike joked causing raucous laughter.

"Well at least we'd get some decent food and not have fish and chips every night. Actually, she'd be ideal Daddy. Come to think of it you'd make a perfect couple! Perhaps all four of us could be your bridesmaids."

Amid laughter Mike continued, "Auntie Maisie's on her own, perhaps she would have me."

"Oh yes, that really would be good, especially as our father and uncle Mike were such good friends," Lucy chipped in. Tilly endorsed Lucy's enthusiasm. "You .. ."

Maisie butted in at this point.

"Excuse me, don't I have a say in all this?"

Kate was in full flow "No, not yet auntie Maisie, we'll come back to you if Mrs. Honeywell turns Dad down."

"I'm duly flattered."

"OK kids, let me just tell you something." Looking at Lucy and Tilly he continued," Joking aside, I do love your mother. We have always been close friends, and there is no one with whom I would rather spend the rest of my life with. . except, of course, Mrs. Honeywell." The laugh was still on the unfortunate Mrs. Honeywell, whose ears must now be burnt to a cinder.

All eyes fell on Maisie waiting for her to say something. She was on the spot.

"Don't all look at me – I'm lost for words. I have to admit I adore Mike, so who knows what the future may hold. I certainly wouldn't want to push Mrs. Honeywell out of the running. I agree with you kids, the two of them would make a perfect couple."

The seeds had now been sown, and all four girls were returned to school, none of whom seemingly disapproved of this, to them, hypothetical match.

The road ahead for Mike and Maisie now seemed clear. The felt they could  really make plans for their life together. So much so that on their return journey from Salisbury they had decided to announce their engagement during the summer holidays before Kate and Phoebe flew off to join Virginia in Boston. They would have a quiet wedding, family only, as soon as the children broke up for Christmas, and then have a big party to celebrate over the Christmas period.

Mike's parting remarks as he left the club that night were "Oh God Maisie, July seems a long way off, and December seems an eternity."

"I feel the same darling. Surely we can spend at least one night a week together."

"I'm going to make bloody sure of that," he said as he sped off.

# CHAPTER 29

Mike felt himself blushing as he encountered Mrs. Honeywell the next morning. How could they all have been so cruel to laugh at her expense? She had been a stalwart to them all in the traumatic and stressful days gone by. "And all we could do was to take the piss out of her." He felt ashamed, realising how much he owed her.

He didn't think he could look at her in the same light again. It also crossed his mind that if he and Maisie bought a house between them what would happen to Mrs. Honeywell. She'd be lost without them. He wondered, in the light of yesterday's conversation, what Maisie's reaction would be if he suggested that Mrs. Honeywell came too! For that matter, what would happen to Brendan and family? He felt morally responsible for so many.

He was still chuckling to himself when Mrs. Honeywell interrupted his thoughts. "Mr. Pinkerton, while I was feeding the chickens last evening, I heard your telephone ringing. I think Inga must have been out, so I answered it. It was Mrs. Pinkerton. Her mother, Mrs. Bellingham Smythe, has died, and she would like you to phone her. She is staying at The Grovesnor Hotel in London - here's her telephone and room number," she said handing him a scrappy bit of paper.

"Oh dear, thanks, Mrs. Honeywell, I'd better get on with that straight away."

Having told Virginia how sorry he was to hear of the death of her mother and asked how she was keeping, her response was terse.

"The funeral is to be held a week today at St. Mary The Boltons, Kensington at 11am. Could you collect Kate and Phoebe from school and take them straight there. After the funeral everyone will be invited back here, to the Grovesnor, for the wake. I would like the children to come to that, so perhaps you could drop them off at the Grovesnor and pick them up about two hours later."

Mike could hardly believe what he was hearing. "Excuse me Virginia, am I understanding you correctly? You expect me to collect the children from the Godolphin, ferry them up to London, take them to the funeral, deliver them to the Grovesnor and then disappear for two hours or so, before collecting them and returning them to school. Who do you think I am?

"Firstly, I would like to point out that I had great respect for your mother. I would even go so far as saying I got on with her far better than you and spent a great deal of my married life trying to shore up chasms in your relationship with her.

"I resent you trying to exclude me from the wake, and know Kate and Phoebe would want me to be there. What's the matter with you Virginia? Who pissed on your cornflakes this morning?

"I see you're as vulgar as ever Mike. I would have thought you would have grown up by now. You're out of my life and I don't want to have the ordeal of meeting you, especially at my mother's funeral."

"I should think your mother would turn in her coffin if she could hear your views. You must chose. Either you make all the arrangements for Kate and Phoebe to attend the funeral, or if you want me to bring them, the three of us will go to the funeral and then to the wake together.

"I can assure you, Virginia, I will keep my distance from you, and save you the embarrassment of having to meet your vulgar ex-husband, or having to introduce him to your hoity-toity friends"

He slammed down the phone. "The bitch, the bitch, the selfish bitch. Thank God, I'm out of that one."

Mike felt so irritated that it crossed his mind to ask Maisie to come with him to the funeral but having slept on it decided not to pursue the idea. He had too much respect for Mrs. Bellingham Smythe, and it would be unfair on Maisie to put her through such an ordeal.

\* \* \* \*

Constance Bentley had married an Indian Army Officer, Harold Bellingham-Smythe in 1913, giving birth to Virginia the following year. Three months' later, Harold was severely injured while on active service in Mesopotamia (now Iraq) while fighting against the Ottoman Empire. He was invalided out of the army and he, Constance and Virginia returned to England. They moved into a wing of Harold's parents' home, Helmsley Hall, in Yorkshire.

Harold lived for a further ten years, but his life was confined to a wheelchair. Virginia, an only child was spoiled by both her parents, and waited on hand and foot by servants. Anything Virginia wanted, Virginia had. It was no wonder she had grown up with such a selfish attitude to life. Maybe she should have been more pitied than blamed.

However, this indolent lifestyle was not inherent in Constance who voluntarily helped to look after wounded troops returning from France. She became a JP and devoted most of her life to charity work, perhaps to the detriment of her daughter. After Harold died, the relationship between Constance and Virginia became increasingly antagonistic, Virginia building up resentment towards her mother.

A lifelong friend, Sir Henry Bouverie gave a most touching eulogy at the funeral. Mike, Kate and Phoebe had no idea of the noble work she had done, right up to the time of her death. She had come to live in London in 1945, where not only did she devote much of her time helping the war wounded of the second World War, but continued her work as a magistrate, and right up to the time of her death was working three nights a week with London's 'down and outs.'

'Queen of the Soup Kitchen' she had been nicknamed. Sir Henry also revealed the lighter side of Constance's life, from which he had obviously benefited. She had been quite a party animal, loved entertaining and going to the theatre. All in all, she had been quite a woman; a woman that both Kate and Phoebe announced were proud to have as a grandmother and only wished they had known her better.

Virginia had not succeeded in demoralising Mike, and with head held high, he, together with Kate and Phoebe entered the private function room at the Grovesnor. A formidable Virginia stood by the door, and seeing her two daughters, and ignoring Mike, superficially flung her arms around them. "My darlings, it's just wonderful to see you . . . . ." Mike cringed and launched himself quickly into a sea of unknown faces, his eyes mainly focused on a waitress with a tray of wine. Looking around, he recognized no one. He was just thinking of downing his glass of wine and retreating to the bar, when he felt a tap on his shoulder. It was Hanson.

"Hi there Mike, in case you' don't recognise me, I'm Joe Hanson."

Mike shook his hand "It's good to see you again Joe. How long are you over for?"

"I wish I knew. I want to get back to the States soon as possible as I have a lot on, but Virginia wants me to stay until she's sorted everything out."

"I expect you've heard that Mrs. Bellingham Smythe has left Virginia out of her will. Her whole estate bar bequests to various charities has been left in trust to Kate and Phoebe until they're twenty one. As you can imagine, Ginny is seething and wants to contest the will. Please don't let her know that I've told you. I think you ought to prepare yourself. Since she heard the news she's been impossible."

Mike was flabbergasted. "Oh my God Joe, I can't believe it. Is it necessary for Kate and Phoebe to be told? The last thing I want them to know is that they will inherit money at such an early age.

"It will give them no incentive to get on and find decent jobs. I've been trying to keep them on a strict allowance, and teach them the value of money. As yet not very successfully."

"Well Mike, I have no idea of the procedure over here. Look. I'll introduce you to Henry Bouverie, who I believe is one of the trustees."

Sir Henry agreed with Mike's wishes not to tell the children about their inheritance until they were older. He wasn't sure whether the age of their inheritance could be altered to them attaining twenty five.

He took a card from his pocket. "Here's my phone number and address. Please contact me as soon as possible, and we can have a meeting with the solicitors drawing up the estate."

"Thanks Sir Henry, I'll be in touch." They shook hands.

Mike was worried that Virginia in a malicious moment may chastise the children for inheriting her mother's money, so he decided he must extricate them quickly before they were enlightened to the fact.

Mike returned to Creek House with mixed feelings that night. He was overjoyed to know that Kate and Phoebe would have a secure future, but disturbed to think of the consequences this could entail.

The red danger light flashing in his mind was the effect that over indulgence had had on their mother. Both Kate and Phoebe were natural, caring and appreciative girls at present, and Mike was determined these characteristics must be preserved at all costs. He also realised how important it was to keep a financial equilibrium with all four children. In no circumstances must Lucy and Tilly be made to feel like poor relations coming into the family. He must bear this in mind at all times he told himself.

# CHAPTER 30

On July 19th 1951 the sun was beating down on a perfect English summer's day. Maisie, now the proud owner of a smart second-hand shooting brake collected the four girls from school for the summer holidays. Piling their trunks, all their clobber and four high-spirited teenagers into this newly acquired car was no easy task. Lucy was momentarily a little downcast saying a final farewell to her friends at the Godolphin, but this was soon replaced by exhilaration for her new life ahead.

Driving along, the chatter was unceasing, but as soon as Maisie noticed a lull in their loud crescendo voices she made herself known.

"Please kids, can I say something? Uncle Mike is having a small party at his home this evening and so I'm taking you all back to the club to drop off Lucy and Tilly's luggage, and for the three of us to change before taking Kate and Phoebe home. I hope that's OK. I suppose your trunks are all full of dirty clothes, but if you can dig out something reasonably smart, and not take too long dithering about choosing what you're going to wear, it would help."

"Why is Uncle Mike having a party tonight, Mum?" asked Lucy

"Because Kate and Phoebe are flying off to America the day after tomorrow, and there is no other time. Kate and Phoebe can you try to decide what you're going to wear too so you don't cause too much chaos when you get back to your home?"

Maisie might just as well have kept her mouth shut because chaos ensued, not only at the club, but also at Creek House. Mrs. Honeywell had been meticulously preparing all sorts of nibbles and canapés, and everything had been organised until the onslaught of the four garrulous girls and the contents of Kate and Phoebe's trunks were scattered everywhere. Inga tried, rather unsuccessfully, to keep most things confined to their bedrooms.

Fortunately, by six o'clock they had all scrubbed up really well and were looking more than presentable to greet Mike on his return from work. Maisie had decided to wear the same dress as she wore in Paris – that wonderful evening at Maxims, and the first night she and Mike had slept together. A night she would never forget.

"My word, what a bevvy of beauty!" he exclaimed as he got out of his car and kissed them all one by one, and a special hug and squeeze for Maisie. "I thought we would have a party to celebrate the beginning of the holidays before Kate and Phoebe fly off to Boston. I 'd better get cracking on my barman's duties."

"Kate, would you go and ask Brendan, if they would all like to join our party at a quarter to seven. They're going off to Ireland in a few days' time, so we can drink to their holiday, and wish Paddy good luck. He's going to stay there to see how he likes it. I've already invited Mrs. Honeywell to join us."

He caught Maisie's eye. She was smiling ear to ear, and then he saw the four girls sniggering away.

"Oh, very funny," he remarked as he disappeared to attend to the liquid refreshments.

Soon he came out armed with jugs of iced Pimms infused with lemon, cucumber and mint. With the temperature still over 75% F, the supply could not keep up with the demand, so he anchored Inga in the pantry refilling the empty jugs and ensuring the children had a weaker version.

Annie, too, had just returned from Seaview, her boarding school on the Isle of Wight. She looked a picture of happiness, and was now going out of her way to communicate with all and sundry. She and Biddy were both growing up to be attractive young ladies, although now looking less alike. Gone was the sibling rivalry that had hampered their early days. Mike looked at Annie with pride. He could see the money he had invested in her education and extra therapy reaping its rewards.

As the Pimms began to dry up, Mrs. Honeywell carried out a tray of champagne glasses, followed by Mike with bottles of champagne. After ensuring everyone had a glass and Maisie was close to his side he said, "Please may I say a few words?"

"I consider I'm the luckiest man on this planet. I want you to be the first ones to know that I have asked Maisie to marry me and she has accepted. She's the most wonderful woman I've ever known. I can't tell you how much I love her. We are both so fortunate to have our four gorgeous children and hope, as the years go by, they will share in our happiness." Mike fetched the ring out of his pocket and (for the third time) placed it on Maisie's finger.

As it slipped down over her knuckle Maisie with a twinkle in her eye said, "Mike, I shall have to give this some serious thought."

"You would say that," he muttered as he kissed her on the hand.

Lucy, Kate, Tilly and Phoebe immediately came rushing up to them amidst repeated "congratulations" and all four of them went into a big emotional clinch. Eventually, Lucy extricating herself and lifting her glass -

"Congratulations Mum and Mike. I for one am absolutely thrilled. I hope you will both be very happy."

"Maisie and Mike." Everyone lifted their glasses.

Kate then chipped in "Before I get too excited about this union, I would like to ask Auntie Maisie what her cooking credentials are, because for the last seven or so years, apart from Mrs. Honeywell's lovely meals, we've been living on fish and chips. I'm just wondering if we can look forward to more variety to our diet?"

Amid laughter Maisie quipped "Well I may be able to rustle you up a rabbit pie. I lived on rabbit the previous seven years."

Without exception everyone seemed happy for the two of them. Amazingly enough, the announcement had taken everyone by surprise. Even the four girls, said they weren't expecting it, but were really pleased for them. Brendan was delighted and Annie with her lovely smile congratulated them both.

Mike concluded his toasts by wishing the O'Reillys a wonderful holiday, and a special toast to Paddy "Good Luck Paddy," they all raised their glasses: "Good Luck Paddy." Paddy was nonplussed and showed no emotion. He was too excited at what lay ahead.

As Mrs. Honeywell was clearing up, Maisie noticed she seemed to be crying.

"What's up Mrs. Honeywell?" Maisie enquired. "You look upset."

"Oh no Mrs. Kershaw, I'm so happy for you both I can't stop crying. Mr. Pinkerton, you know, has been lonely for a long time now, and I'm so pleased he has chosen you. He's such a gentleman, and you are such a lady. You're perfect for each other. I can't tell too how much I'll miss Paddy and his devilish ways. Still sobbing she continued with her chores.

The six of them were still sitting in the garden reminiscing way after the sun had set and the chill of the evening had set in.

"Right then, who's for fish and chips?" They all winced.

"Actually there's ham, salad, and potatoes in their jackets all ready on the kitchen table."

"Goodness, things are already looking up," said Kate, looking at Maisie. "You've seen nothing yet girl" was Maisie's instant reply.

# CHAPTER 31

Even with Inga's and Mrs. Honeywell's invaluable help it was a mad scramble to get Kate and Phoebe off to America. Kate had entered some tennis tournaments over there and needed her racquet restringing, a tennis dress and tennis shoes, and one or two other things. Lucy met her in Southampton and they went shopping together, as she was going on a back packing holiday with a school friend to France. They did not meet with much success.

"I don't know what I'm going to do Mrs. Honeywell, I won't be allowed on the court unless I'm suitably dressed, and I don't want to wear my awful navy blue school shorts." She continued her moaning to Mike when he returned from work.

"I'm sorry Kate, you knew you were going to the States, you should have thought about it before. It's too late now, what you haven't got, you will have to go without. I'm sure your mother will soon kit you out. There's bound to be more choice in Boston than Southampton. I don't want to hear any more about it. You are even putting Mrs. Honeywell on edge with your grumbling."

Mrs. Honeywell had the added aggravation of helping Brendan and his brood get packed up for Ireland. After a frenzied rush from both households, they were gone. There was tranquillity at last.

Handing Mike a cup of tea Mrs. Honeywell wearily said, "As much as I love them Mr. Pinkerton, I can't say I'm sorry to see the back of them. I was really beginning to wonder whether the girls would ever sort themselves out, and even with my help Brendan was beginning to lose his patience with his children. But I know, give it a day or two we'll miss them and wish they were all back. It's very sad to think that Paddy won't be coming back with them. So much seems to have happened over the last few years."

"It certainly has. I'm sorry too Mrs. Honeywell that Paddy won't be returning with them. He's a grand kid, but I'm sure it's better for him to be with his own parents, who are also younger, to keep him in check. He has such a happy disposition he'll settle down quickly, and I think Rory has found him a good school."

Mike had so much on his mind, he wondered what he was doing sitting down drinking tea with Mrs. Honeywell. She was obviously pleased to have him for a few minutes on her own without a lot of demanding children.

She continued, "If you don't mind me saying so, I think you have made a good choice in choosing Mrs. Pinkerton. She is such a lovely lady and I know Kate and Phoebe are really pleased about it. Will she come and live here?"

That was a question he did not want her to ask, because he knew Maisie was keen for them to buy a house jointly, and he didn't want Mrs. Honeywell to worry about her future. "We haven't thought that far ahead. At the moment we are just relieved that our four children are happy with the idea. We'll go slowly from there."

"This won't do Mrs. Honeywell I must get a move on I've got so much to do. Thanks for putting up with my unruly kids and sorting them out. Mrs. Pinkerton is coming over this evening, and I'm hoping she'll come and stay here for a night or two while the children are away."

An animated Maisie arrived much earlier than expected. Lucy had gone off on her back packing holiday and Tilly was staying the night with a friend. She had some good news.

"Mike, I think I have got rid of the club. My landlords have offered me a good price to buy the lease. I have a feeling they will knock it down for redevelopment, which after all the hard work I have put in will be a bit sad. I think I would be silly not to accept it."

After weighing up the pros and cons, Mike concluded, "Darling, I think you must go ahead. That will be one problem off your back, and you can then concentrate on selling the cottage."

"That makes me feel sad too Mike. It holds so many happy memories of Johnnie and the children growing up. Mind you some pretty nightmarish ones as well. How's your divorce going?"

"Keeping fingers crossed, I have my divorce nisi, and hopefully it should be made absolute fairly soon. I know Virginia was so keen to get shot of me and eager to get her grips on Joe, that she has pushed things through at a spanking rate. However, two things concern me. Firstly, she feels bitter that her mother has excluded her from her will, and secondly, I am wondering what her reaction will be when she hears that you and I are engaged.

"She has made it clear that she doesn't want me, or indeed, anything to do with me, but I fear she probably doesn't want anyone else to have me either – especially you. As I am still feeling enraged at her behaviour at her mother's funeral I am probably maligning the woman, so I shouldn't pre-empt a situation that probably won't happen. Let's change the subject."

He continued, "Well, what's for supper, Maisie?"

"You must be kidding – YOU invited me! Don't tell me – 'you'll just pop down to get some fish and chips.' How many times have you said that?"

"Come on fuss pot, grab a cardigan, I'll take you to The Jolly Sailor at Bursledon . Now that is pretty enterprising, I didn't even suggest The Bugle here in Hamble." Maisie smiled and gave him a peck on the cheek. "I don't know what I'm letting myself in for."

\* \* \* \*

Sad news greeted the O'Reillys on their arrival to Pallas Green. Molly O'Shea had died of tuberculosis. Unknown to Brendan she had spent the last four weeks of her life in a sanatorium. Bryony had deep remorse.

"My dear Mammy, Brendan, led a life she did not deserve. She suffered from cruelty, poverty and sickness since she was a wee child. The 'Faith' dominated her early life, and then she met Jimmy, our Dad. Even before he became a drunk, he treated her like dirt. She waited on him hand and foot, and never got so much as a thank you. He used her as a breeding machine, sexually, physically and verbally abusing her. No animal would behave like that."

Tears came to her eyes. "And do you know she was so loyal to him, for many years, refusing to hear a word said against him, and she stuck by him till the end. How did she manage that?'"

She continued, "I know, it was 'The Faith'. The fear of being burned in hell was perhaps greater than the living terror she suffered with our, cheating, cruel and lying Dad. 'Dear sweet gentle Mammy happiness passed you by. I'm sure we children could have done more. We let you down.'" Copious tears followed.

Rory was at work, taking Annie, Biddy and Paddy with him so was not there to witness Bryony's misery. The ever-empathetic Brendan put his arm around her. "Bryony dear, I knew your Mammy well. She was a kind sweet lady, but like Mary nothing would have moved her from the rigid belief she had in the 'Faith.' I too am a Catholic, but I fervently believe that 'The Faith' was responsible for Mary's early death, as well as Molly's. I respect the Catholic religion, but at the moment have cut myself off. Please rest assured Bryony, nothing you could have done would have changed the situation."

Comforted by these remarks Bryony continued. "Thank you for saying that Brendan. I must now pull myself together. What a terrible welcome I've given you. I have been so excited about Paddy coming to live with us – he seems to be taking it all in his stride."

"I can't tell you Bryony how much he's being looking forward to coming. I think he's invited nearly all his school friends to come and stay with you, so watchit."

Bryony couldn't get over the progress Annie had made since she last saw her. "It's quite staggering, she seems a different girl. You must be thrilled Brendan"

"I certainly am. You know if it hadn't been for Mike I would have done nothing. You know Mike is paying for Annie to go to this special school, and for extra elocution lessons? Even then, with everything being paid for I was still reluctant to send her away. Mike eventually persuaded me. I am so grateful to that guy, he pulled us right out of the mire."

Brendan decided to accompany Bryony to Molly O'Shea's funeral. Rory had said he would never dare put his head inside a church again, and Brendan was not in favour of Annie and Biddy attending, and therefore Paddy too was let off the hook. The sparsely attended funeral rather depicted the sadness of her life. Bryony's brother, Seamus was there with his wife, Beefy the Butcher, the lady from the corner shop, and last but not least Jimmy O'Shea came staggering in ten minutes late. He stayed until the end of the service, and then staggered out again. It appeared he had not even recognised Bryony or Seamus. If he had he certainly did not acknowledge either of them. It was the end of a tragedy. Brendan was thankful that Mary had been spared such an ordeal.

Rory and Brendan were enjoying a glass of Guinness in Chaser O'Brian's pub one day when they met some of the workers from the newly opened zinc mine. It appeared there were lots of vacant jobs going.

"Have you ever thought of coming back to Ireland Brendan?" enquired Rory.

"Not really, although I was made redundant a few months back, and now I am doing all sorts of odd jobs – it is not very satisfactory but I like living in England."

"Why don't you see what they've got on offer down at the mine. You don't have to take it. Wouldn't you like to come and live near Paddy?"

"Rory, it's not just Paddy, I have Biddy and Annie to think of. Biddy is doing well at school and I couldn't even think of taking Annie away, she making such good progress and loves it there."

At Rory's instigation, and just for the fun of it Brendan applied for a job as a Ledger Clerk, and to his amazement was offered the position. The salary was not great but the cost of living was much lower in Ireland. The other added incentive was the house attached to Rory and Bryony's had become vacant.

"Rory and I have decided it would not be fair on Paddy for us to have any more children. Instead, I shall work part time, and we hope to buy this house and the one next door. It went through our minds that you might like to come and live next door."

Brendan was quick to reply, "That indeed is a lovely idea Bryony, Rory has already mentioned it. To uproot myself from England now would be madness, not only for me but Biddy and Annie. One thing is certain I would not contemplate taking Annie away from her school now. I'm told that education for girls here in Ireland is inferior to that in England, so I want to do the best I can for Biddy. She is a bright girl. Dear Bryony, as much as I would love to live close to you it is a no-go. Maybe one day, I could come and retire out here."

"I quite understand. You know you would always be welcome."

Their two weeks in Ireland went by in a flash, and soon it was time to leave. It was a sad 'goodbye', and the first time Paddy had shown any emotion. As he gave Brendan a last hug, he had tears in his eyes. He was unable to speak. It was heart rending too for Brendan who had nurtured the boy for nearly twelve years.

As Rory drove the truck down the hill, Annie and Biddy waved tearfully, until Bryony with her arm round Paddy were out of sight. Paddy's new life was about to begin.

# CHAPTER 32

With just four weeks in the States, Kate and Phoebe had grown up.
Mike was staggered how much in such a short time two typical English
schoolgirls had changed into two American glitzy teenagers even down
to their accents. They were both wearing earrings, and Kate had fallen
madly in love. Mike showed his disapproval.

"Oh, don't be silly Daddy, everyone of our age wears earrings out
there." Changing the subject. "You should be really proud of me I did
really well in the two tennis tournaments I played in. I got through to
the quarterfinals of the singles in both tournaments, and guess what?
My mixed doubles partner, Chet, and I got through to the final in the
under 18 in one tournament. He's a fantastic player."

"Tell me more about this young man Kate." Mike asked.

"He's gorgeous Daddy. Very good looking, blond hair, blue eyes,
very sun tanned and legs to die for." There was a pause . . .

"Is that all you've got to say about him?"

"I don't know much more, except he's just left high school, hoping
to go to university, and was lovely to play tennis with. He really carried
me through the matches as he was so much better than me. He asked
me for my address, Daddy, so I'm hoping to hear from him."

Mike said no more. 'Oh dear', he thought, 'sex is beginning to rear
its ugly head. At least Phoebe hasn't found an 'amour' on this holiday –
well he hoped not'.

He did not like to question Kate and Phoebe on their mother's reaction to his engagement to Maisie. He hoped they would volunteer that
information sometime.

A letter addressed to Mike in Virginia's handwriting, postmarked
'Boston' arrived the next day. It read:-

*I might have guessed, you sneaky bastard – I always thought there was something going on between you and Maisie. Your engagement now rather confirms the fact.*

*I hope you will both be happy – Virginia.*


Mike could feel his anger swelling up inside. He thought Virginia would probably be upset to know he was to marry Maisie, but he never anticipated that she would suspect they may have had a previous affair. 'Just judging me by her own standards' he thought.

He wondered what action, if any, he should take. He would wait and discuss it with Maisie. Virginia would have bound to have filled Kate and Phoebe's minds with the necessary poison, and this he should rectify as soon as possible.

Mike realised that his marriage to Maisie was not going to be straight forward. There was so much that needed sorting, but he was determined not to allow Virginia to make his plans go awry.

Straight after work he called at the club to see Maisie. She was expecting him and already had two G and T's poured out. Mike showed her Virginia's note.

"How could she Mike? She's quite outrageous. What are you going to do?"

"Well, I've really come to ask you're advice. I know I must first ensure that Kate and Phoebe know the truth, and also that Lucy and Tilly have not heard the rumour.

I intend to write an abrupt note back to Virginia telling her that her note was outrageous, and we were not romantically involved until after I had received my divorce nisi. Something to that effect. What do you think?"

"I think that's OK? How about if I come back with you now and talk to Kate and Phoebe? That will be one load off our minds. We can also find out whether they've told Lucy and Tilly."

"Thanks Maisie darling, we want to nip it in the bud." Downing their drinks, Maisie continued,

"Mike you go on ahead, and I'll see you at your house shortly."

Fortunately, fish and chips were off the menu that night, and Mrs. Honeywell had prepared a lamb stew with pearl barley and carrots, so all Mike had to do was to throw some potatoes in the oven. If the children had been told of Mike and Maisie's supposed affair, they were showing no resentment.

The meal began with Kate asking what had happened to the fish and chips, and the usual banter continued until Mike asked "What was your mother's reaction when you told her that Auntie Maisie and I were engaged."

"Oh surely, you don't want to hear that" began Kate. "Yes, we do", said Mike.

Kate continued, "Well, she was really upset, and completely flew off the handle. She said she always suspected that the two of you were having an affair, and . . ."

"Just stop there Kate. Today she has sent me a note to that effect. I want you to know that it's a lie. Auntie Maisie and I have always been great friends, but never, never in the past did we have an affair. It has only been in the last two months, a long time after I received my divorce nisi that our romance has really blossomed. When your mother left me, I admit I did make advances towards auntie Maisie, but she regrettably rejected me. In desperation along came Gina."

Maisie intervened. "I can assure you everything your father has said is true. I hope you believe us. Have you by any chance told Lucy, Tilly or anyone else about our supposed torrid affair?"

"No we haven't auntie Maisie, and we won't. We're so thrilled that you and Daddy are together. We love you both and want it to last forever. The sooner you can come and live with Daddy the better. He's so much happier with you around."

The next day Mike wrote to Virginia.

*I was astounded to receive your accusation that Maisie and I had a previous affair.*

*This is totally untrue, and for you to tell our children this lie is unforgiveable. It is libellous. Our romance did not begin until after I had received my divorce nisi.   Please ensure you inform Joe of this fact and anyone else you may have told. Remember you should not judge other people by your own standards. Thank you for your congratulations – Mike*


As he posted it he wondered whether it would antagonize her further, or make her realise she had gone too far. Whatever, a few weeks' later Mike's divorce absolute was granted. This he hoped would get the spiteful Virginia off his back forever.

The wedding plans could now go ahead. Mike and Maisie both decided on it being low key with just family at the ceremony in Southampton followed by a reception for the family and a few close friends at the Polygon Hotel. Maisie had shied off going back to Creek House afterwards.

"I would feel the presence of Virginia there looking over my shoulder." As it was, after a couple of nights of honeymoon in London, she was to move into Creek House until such a time they would be able to buy a house together. This, Maisie knew, would take some time, as Brendan and family still occupied the Boathouse, and Mike had a conscience about leaving Mrs. Honeywell.

Mike was well aware of Maisie's reluctance to move into Creek

House and knew he must not delay some awkward decisions. At least he had the beautiful spare room redecorated, so they could move in there and Maisie would not have to feel that she was sharing her bed with Virginia.

The problem of Mrs. Honeywell was sorted without too much difficulty. Her sister, Mavis, who lived in Devon had just been widowed, and she had agreed to come and live with Mrs. Honeywell. This was good news and gave Mike confidence to warn her of their impending move. To lessen the blow Mike gave her a cheque for £500. In appreciation for all the wonderful help and support she had given not only to his family but also to the O'Reilly's over the years. He also gave her the reassurance that they would not lose touch. She was very moved although a little tearful, but said she fully understood.

Now to tackle Brendan. This was indeed a problem. He knew he now had to do this immediately before he heard it from Mrs. Honeywell.

"This Maisie, I hate to do – I feel I'm letting him down badly."

"That's rubbish darling. Let's invite him round for supper" Maisie suggested. "It's much easier to discuss things over a few drinks and a meal."

As Mike guessed, the news came like a bolt out of the blue. Brendan went quite pale.

"Look Brendan, there is no need for you to worry. I'll make sure you're not homeless. It will probably take us a few months to sell this house anyway. You know I have been investing in property and have built up a small portfolio of tenanted properties. What I'm proposing to do is to see if I can find a three bed roomed vacant house to purchase locally, so you can live there on the same terms as you now live in the Boathouse."

A little colour came back in to his cheeks, and in his soft Irish brogue he said, "Oh my word Mike, this has come as a bit of a shock. I don't see why you should buy a house for us. You know we could go back to live in Ireland with Rory and Bryony. They're keen for us to do so."

"Brendan. I consider you a close friend. I feel privileged to be in a position to help not only Annie, but all of you. Please don't think of going back to Ireland, your children need you here. They need a good education to help them along life's road. Please don't feel downhearted. I will make  the transition is painless, and Brendan your friendship means a lot to Maisie and me. In no way will we let that dwindle. We must also remember the strong bond between Annie and Kate."

After a long pause Mike got up from the table and gently patted Brendan on the back. "Come on, let me get you another beer. It'll all work out well, fear not."

Brendan was not so sure. He felt vulnerable, but was overwhelmed by Mike's generosity.

# CHAPTER 33

The sale of Rose Cottage was completed early in 1952, and although it was possible to put the entire proceeds into Mike and Maisie's new house, Mike insisted on half of it going into a separate trust for Lucy and Tilly.

He bought an attractive three-bedroomed brick and flint cottage down near the hard at Hamble, conveniently a few minutes walk from the Bugle. It was in desperate need of restoration but he wasted no time in getting in a reliable builder to modernise it. Apart from reassuring Brendan that he had everything under control, he decided to keep his new acquisition under wraps until it was nearly finished. Creek House went on the market and Mike and Maisie started house hunting in earnest. Maisie was looking forward to putting her own imprint on a home of their own and to stop living in the shadow of Virginia. Mike felt this too.

On 6th February. It was Maisie's fortieth birthday. The day had begun on such a happy note as she opened her numerous cards and presents. To her delight all four children had remembered, and Mike had bought her a Triumph Herald Estate car to replace her clapped out car she used to ferry the children around.

Mike had left for the day, and as was her custom Maisie turned on the wireless. With Inga now back in Sweden, the four girls away, and the absence of Paddy shattering the peace of the neighbourhood, there was an ominous silence. She found the wireless was company and was inclined to keep it on most of the day as a background, listening mostly to music. Suddenly her ears were alerted.

"This is London. It is with the greatest sorrow that we make the following announcement:- It was announced from Sandringham at

10.45am today February 6th 1952 that the king, who retired to rest last night in his usual health passed peacefully away in his sleep earlier this morning."

"The BBC offers profound sympathy to Her Majesty the Queen and the Royal Family. The BBC is now closing down for the rest of the day . . . ."

This really tugged at Maisie's heartstring, almost as much as if he had been a member of her own family.

George VI had become king on the abdication of his playboy brother Edward VIII, who gave up the throne to marry his American mistress, Wallis Simpson. George, or 'Bertie' as he was affectionately called was completely unprepared to take on this momentous job. He was shy and suffered from a serious speech impediment. With the unceasing support of his wife Elizabeth and regular speech therapy he soon won the heart of the nation. They agonized with him, and he won their love and respect.

At the outbreak of World War II the admiration for this unassuming and gentle man who had unexpectedly been launched in to the role of monarch of the greatest empire in history was plain to see. Throughout the war, both he and Queen Elizabeth remained at Buckingham Palace. During the blitz – 'wherever they suffered he was there'. It was known he had a lung disease, but his death was sudden and had a tremendous impact on his subjects.

"The king takes his rest and Britain mourns." And mourn they did. He was a great loss.

It was an exciting time in aviation with the development of the jet engine. Mike felt fortunate to witness this new concept in aeroplane history. However, Supermarine's new baby, the Swift, was a problem child from the outset.

Mike Lithgow had flown it on its maiden flight in December 1948, and from then on it had undergone massive modifications to improve its performance at high speeds and altitude. Also greater stability was needed.

Although Mike found flying the Swift stimulating – indeed it was the first swept-wing jet to land and take-off from an aircraft carrier - to him it was nothing compared to his beloved Spitfire. In spite of the radical modifications made, Mike believed, it was overshadowed by its rival, the Hawker Hunter. The Swift did, however, in 1953, again with Mike Lithgow at the controls, break the world speed record by going 735 mph, beating Neville Duke's record of 727mph in a Hawker Hunter.

Days later America's Skyray pushed it up to over 753 miles per hour. It would only be three years later that this record was smashed by Peter Twiss flying a Fairey Delta. As the first man to reach a speed of 1000 mph he broke the world speed record by reaching 1,132 mph. These were exciting times, and Mike would have liked to have been centre stage in this speed race. Alas, he was now nearly fifty and his testing days were drawing to a close.

With this in mind, and the imminent house move, Mike thought that this would be a good time for a career change. He had already declined a job with BAC as it would have meant he would have to move to Singapore, and thought this would have been too much of an upheaval for Kate and Phoebe, especially with Virginia living in America.

He decided to put an idea he had in mind to Maisie. "Darling, I'm thinking of applying to BOAC as a pilot. I have a commercial flying licence, and as my testing days are virtually over, I thought this could be the way to go. I thought maybe we should sort out my future career before we actually buy our new home. What do you think? I don't want to do anything that doesn't have your full backing."

"Not only is that considerate of you Mike, but amazingly practical. What alternatives do you have?"

"That's a good question. I don't have training for anything else, I'm afraid. The commercial air industry is growing fast, and it shouldn't be too difficult for me to get a job based at London Airport. I love flying, and would like to continue to do so for a little while yet, but it would mean I would be away quite a bit. If you rather I didn't I will look elsewhere. Perhaps I could become a bus driver, or even better a train driver."

"I know it would be curtains on our marriage if I were responsible for severing your connection with your beloved aeroplanes. By the way I would prefer you being a bus driver to a train driver. I wouldn't fancy you always coming home dirty and grimy from those filthy steam trains. You would soon lose all your appeal." He smiled and gave her a kiss on her head. "I love you darling."

While working out his month's notice with Vickers Supermarine, Mike put the finishing touches to Brendan's new home and the day arrived for Mike to show it to him. It was a Saturday morning, and he and Maisie decided to go down to the Bugle for a pub lunch where they knew Brendan was working. They had asked Biddy to join them after her morning at school.

"To be sure Mike, this is far too good for us – it's just lovely." Biddy just smiled from ear to ear.

"It's unbelievable, and so convenient for you Dad being so near the pub." There was a large courtyard at the back, with a brick building at the bottom. It was the old outside loo. Brendan quite expected to open the door into an old toilet, but to his surprise found a sink. Both hot and cold water and electricity had been installed and a wooden clothes rack hung from the ceiling.

"I thought this would be a good place for you to do the washing Brendan, or should I say, Biddy, rather than cluttering up your small kitchen." Biddy quick to intervene - "You must be joking."

"We'll probably be able to give you our old washing machine when we move, and that would fit in there a treat." Mike added.

The cottage was quite tiny, but it had three bedrooms and a bathroom upstairs, and a large living room/diner with an attractive fireplace and a kitchen. It had all been newly painted in white, which gave a feeling of freshness, light and spaciousness.

"I know Mike, this will be an ideal home for us all. Thanks again and again, you're a great guy, and we know how lucky we are."

"It's really super uncle Mike and auntie Maisie. Thank you. When can we move in? I just can't wait. Annie will love it."

"It's all ready now, so whenever you like. Just take your time and take whatever you like from the Boathouse. The furniture should fit in really well down here. Give us a shout when you're comfortably in."

Maisie volunteered to give Brendan a hand on moving and perhaps, if he liked, to give it the finishing touches. "That dear Maisie would be gratefully accepted."

# CHAPTER 34

"Mike, you look amazing. My goodness you have scrubbed up well." This is how Maisie greeted him as he stood in front of her in his uniform before leaving for his first day on duty in his new job with BOAC. He had just finished a month's intensive training on the Comet, and now was to take his first passengers to Johannesburg which would take over twenty-three hours. He would be making five stops – Rome, Beirut, Khartoum, Entebbe and Livingstone, and would be away for nearly a week. This was quicker by over four hours compared with the piston-engined Hermes. This was the beginning of a new era in commercial flying history, and Mike felt, he was now really part of it.

Everything in Mike and Maisie's life seemed to be coming together. The sale of Creek house was going through. Brendan and Biddy were happily ensconced in their new home and Annie was making a special visit from school to come and see it.

Mike could not hide his excitement – he felt like a schoolboy going out to bat in a cricket match for the first time. The only blot on the horizon was the thought of leaving Maisie for a week. That was a wrench. Fortunately, Maisie had plenty on her plate to be getting on with, and she knew she must try not to dwell on either his absence or his job too much. She must keep herself busy.

Maisie was to concentrate her house search to either Stockbridge or Alresford areas so as to be a bit nearer London Airport. She was ideally looking for a family house on either of the rivers Itchen or Test. Well aware of Mike's love for fly fishing, and although he had not mentioned it to her, Maisie thought that if she could find something with a few hundred yards of fishing, it would help to keep him occupied in his retirement. It might, she thought, even give him the incentive to retire early. She knew, otherwise, he would never retire.

Having collected property particulars from estate agents within a ten-mile radius of her two search areas, Maisie divided them into three days, and then made the appointments to view.

Before Annie returned for the weekend to view the house, Maisie went round Creek House, boxing up things, including pictures she thought would give Tumbledown Cottage, as Mike had called it, some extra touches. She hoped she wasn't giving away any of Mike's heirlooms, but would mention to Brendan that she may have to take something back if he protested too much.

Maisie went to collect Annie from the ferry so was there to feel the impact of her reactions. It all looked so inviting as she walked through the door. There was no question, she was enthralled by it all, and couldn't wait to get busy to organise her bedroom the way she wanted. Maisie also offered Brendan her old car.

"Brendan, I'm wondering whether you would like my old car. I quite understand if you say 'no'. It's getting on a bit, not very reliable, but most of the time gets one from A to B. I know you're interested in car engines, and you might find it of use. On the other hand you might think it's yet another problem and added expense you could do without, in which case I would try and sell it."

"Maisie, that would be a wonderful. I would very much like to have it. The problem would be where to keep it? With no garage, and no road to leave it on, I shall have to do a little thinking. Can you give me a day or two to make up my mind and I will see what I can organise?"

"Sure Brendan, we have no completion date on Creek House yet, as we want to find something first. If we have to complete before we buy we'll probably come and move in with you."

"Dear Maisie, you would be welcome at anytime. You know that. I would always give up my bed for you both."

"I know you would Brendan. I'll see you soon." She began to walk away, and then turned round. "How about Mrs. Honeywell's old shed up at the back of her garden – it might fit in there."

"That's certainly one idea" he replied.

The house hunting continued apace. Maisie had thought it would be a tall order to find something with river frontage, but in fact she found three family sized properties that fitted the bill. One made her feel quite spellbound, but as it had a large acreage with double bank fishing on the river Test, it was, she decided out of the question.

One had potential, but needed renovating, which she knew Mike would revel in, and the third one was too enclosed by trees and hardly ever saw the sun. That one was out. There were one or two others which were worth a second visit, so Maisie put aside a short list to await Mike's homecoming.

Mike had been away for four days, and having spent most of the time in his absence tearing around she suddenly felt tired and a little nauseous. Waking up the following morning more waves of nausea hit her.

"Oh God, don't tell me I'm pregnant." The thought flashed through her mind. "That's all I need," she said aloud.

The idea haunted her, so without delay she marched herself off to the doctor. Dr. Robinson, after enquiring after Brendan and family, asked Maisie what was her problem.

"Dr. Robinson I think I may be pregnant."

"What makes you think that?" he asked.

"Well, it's only that I have waves of nausea that keep coming over me, and alarm bells started ringing in my head, and I want to be put out of my agony."

"Do I take it that this would not be good news?"

"You are correct Dr. Robinson. I'm nearly 41, and Mike nearly 50, both far too old to have any more children. We already have four daughters between us who I think would be horrified."

Dr. Robinson examined her and then gave her a pregnancy test. He then told her that he thought she could very well be right, but would not know for sure until he received the results of her test. He would contact her immediately he received it." With a rather curt 'thank you' Maisie fled from the surgery in a state of panic.

She felt she could not wait for Mike's return. She had to talk to someone. Without thinking too hard she arrived on Mrs. Honeywell's doorstep. "What is it dear Mrs. Pinkerton?" sensing something was wrong. "Come on in."

"What am I to do Mrs. Honeywell, I think I'm probably pregnant." Putting the kettle on – Mrs. Honeywell's cure for most things, she said "What makes you think that my dear?"

"Well, I have been feeling nauseous for a few days, and now have just returned from seeing Dr. Robinson, who gave me an internal and a pregnancy test. He thinks it could be on the cards and will phone me as soon as the surgery receives the results. Mike and I are too old to become parents again, and what would our children think?"

"Don't fret dear girl. I'm loath to give any advice after the bad advice I gave to Mary, but I think you are panicking unnecessarily. I think it would be wonderful for two lovely people like you to have a child between you. I believe, after the initial shock, your children would accept it without too much of a to do. When does Mr. Pinkerton return?"

"The day after tomorrow. I won't even have the results by then. I think it will come as a complete bombshell to him."

"Will you tell him what you think before you get the results?" asked Mrs. Honeywell.

"I don't think I could keep it to myself. He can read me like a book and would know something was up."

"You know neither of you are too old. Many women have children in their 40's, and although there is a greater risk of something going wrong, it is unlikely. You cannot do anything until you know officially, you then have to talk to Mr. Pinkerton and know what he thinks – it is after all his baby as well. Finally, if you both agree it would threaten your relationship, the problem can be overcome. There are ways of having a legal abortion. Get used to the idea, you may change your mind, and of course it may be just your imagination."

"You're an angel Mrs. Honeywell, I am less suicidal now and feel I can perhaps tackle the situation. Thank you again. You're such a wonderful agony aunt. We'll miss you. Thank you. Goodnight."

# CHAPTER 35

Mike was so excited describing his trip to Johannesburg, that Maisie thought she would never be able impart her dreaded news to him. Just as he finished one story, off he went on to the next. Maisie found it difficult to concentrate. Eventually, he said, "Well, how's everything been here? How are you my darling, have you missed me?"

"Mike, I think I'm pregnant?"

"Good God Maisie, I've only been away a week, you haven't wasted much time."

"That's not funny darling. You've no idea how worried I am. I've been desperate to talk to you about it. I won't know definitely for a few days, but I'm suffering from morning sickness and fear the worst. We're both too old to have any more children, and I think our four girls would be horrified."

Mike went to sit by her side and put her arm round her. "Darling, we'll sort this out. I would love us to have a baby together. To me it would be the ultimate climax to our love. But if you feel you couldn't face going through with it, I'll quite understand. As for our children, they may initially be a little stunned, but am sure they would accept it in no time at all."

After a moment Mike continued, "We don't even know yet anyway, it may just be a phantom of your imagination. If the tests come back positive, we don't want to rush into a hasty decision we might regret. Let's live with it for a few days, and talk through all the pros and cons – a decision will evolve. After all the precautions we have taken, it is beyond belief how the wee mite got there in the first place."

Maisie laughed. Feeling a little more cheerful. "OK Mike, I'll snap myself out of my doom and gloom. I think I'm just suffering from shock. I know things could be worse." All the excitement she had generated in her house hunting expeditions had now been put on a back burner.

"Have you found us a house Maisie? We may now need a bloody great mansion."

"Well it's funny you should say that as I actually found you a bloody great mansion with bloody miles of fishing rights and bloody acres of land. I've kept the particulars but put it on the bottom of the pile. Right up your street Mike, but too much for you take on with a full-time career. I have found quite a few houses that are worth you looking at?"

"OK let's get started. I'm home for over ten days, so with a bit of luck we ought to come up with something by then. We have some big decisions to make – let's look upon them as exciting challenges."

"Yes Mike." As Maisie expected, the pregnancy test was positive. She knew deep down that Mike was really keen for her to have this baby, so gradually came to the conclusion it would not be fair to consider an abortion.

"Right!" she said over breakfast a couple of days after receiving her results. "The first exciting decision has been made. If you're happy Mike, I would like to go ahead with this pregnancy."

"Maisie, that's wonderful news. I can't tell you how happy I am. You never know I might have another man in the house to help me keep you gaggle of women under control."

"A boy would be great, but I think we must assume its another girl, so you will then be completely dominated. That'll teach you for making me pregnant."

They decided, just in case Maisie were to lose the baby in the first few weeks to wait a little before disclosing the news to the children. Maisie admitted to Mike that she had already been to cry on Mrs. Honeywell's shoulder, so they must go straight away to tell her their decision, and ask her to keep the news under wraps, because they didn't want anyone else to know before their four daughters.

Maisie was now able to focus on the next project – to find somewhere to live. If they didn't get a move on they would be homeless as the purchasers of Creek House were pressing to complete. Maisie's flippant remark about moving in with Brendan seemed not so way out as she had thought only a week ago.

Maisie's description of the large house with double bank fishing had spoiled Mile from considering anything else. This was a beautiful Georgian house near Stockbridge overlooking one of the chalk streams that flow into the river Test. He fell for it, almost literally, hook, line and sinker.

The adrenalin had set in. He and Maisie would buy the house and he would acquire the double bank fishing and land as a business. As it was already let commercially for another three years, this would bring in an income, and he hoped would give him a good insight into fly fishing and running a business.

"What do you think Maisie?"

"I think it is magnificent Mike. What worries me is that you might overstretch yourself, and that would be a nightmare. You're so bowled over by it that I am frightened you'll go rushing in without considering all the implications. I think you'd agree that impulsiveness is one of your traits. Please stand back and think it all through carefully, make sure you can comfortably afford it, not forgetting you have another big expense on the way."

"Yes ma'm," he answered smiling. "It's a good job one of us has their feet on the ground. I shall of course go and speak to my financial advisers, and also go and see Giles Baker, an old friend of mine who lets out rods on the Test, to see whether it is a viable proposition. It doesn't have to be a big money spinner, but I would like it to be profitable. It would be a wonderful occupation to take up when I retire."

Maisie was now getting caught up in Mike's enthusiasm. "Well the big bonus, so far as I'm concerned, is that it would keep your feet on 'terra firma', help wean you off your addiction to flying, and give you a challenge connected with something you enjoy doing. Even I think it makes sense, if you're sure you have the where-with-all to finance it comfortably, taking into account your other financial commitments."

"Thanks to dear old Dad, I feel confident it's well within our budget, and I have taken into account the baby and Annie and any unforeseen circumstances that may arise. We'll probably have four weddings on our hands to finance as well. Worry you not Maisie, your husband has it all under control. I imagine you won't be wanting any more children?"

"Is that meant to be a joke, because it's not funny? Maisie continued. "I adore the house, and I think with all your beautiful antique furniture and with my contribution – I have some nice little pieces too - we can make it into a lovely home. But Mike, I have modest taste and would be as happy in a small cottage."

"What with our enormous brood?"

The rest of Mike's leave was taken up by looking into buying this dream house. Feeling confident with his research, and knowing it had been on the market for a few months he put in a low offer, realising the likelihood of it being accepted was remote. He then left for his next trip.

At least Maisie's preoccupation with the house diluted the stress about her forthcoming baby. She had now come to terms with the fact, and the idea of an abortion was thrown out of the window. The more she thought about it the happier she became. She would, however, be relieved when they had broken the news to the children, but they had decided to leave that until the Christmas holidays.

It would be a May baby, so it would still give the four of them plenty of time to become accustomed to the idea before its arrival.

Not expecting the first offer on the house to be accepted, Maisie was surprised when the telephone rang and the estate agent told her it had been accepted. She told him that Mike would deal with it immediately on his return in three days' time. She was amazed, and immediately began to think there must be something radically wrong for them to accept, what Maisie had considered an almost insulting offer.. At least it was subject to a survey so that should pick up any major problems.

She longed to tell Mike, but that was impossible. She knew she would patiently have to wait for his return.

This news galvanized Maisie into action. She met the new purchasers of Creek House to find out what furniture and fittings they might be interested in buying, and then went for another viewing of Half Water House, to get a better feel of the place – the agents even gave her a plan of the house which was a great help.

By the time Mike returned home, in her mind, Maisie had already moved in. She had mentally arranged all the furniture, and knew who was sleeping where. She had also discovered that Mike's offer had included carpets and curtains. That was an added bonus, as they could move in, live in comfort while becoming accustomed to their surroundings, before deciding what alterations to make.

Maisie greeted her husband,

"Mike darling, I'm so glad you're back. It's all happening this end. You'll never guess what? Your meagre offer for the house has been accepted."

"It has? You're not kidding me?"

"Oh God, there must be something seriously wrong with it. We must get a surveyor's report done immediately and ensure that thorough searches are carried out. I suppose planning permission for a tower block has been granted to ruin our views of the river, or more likely it has subsidence." He picked Maisie off the ground and swivelled her round.

"My darling I'm so thrilled. I've now not only got the perfect wife, but crossed fingers, we have got our perfect home. I still can't believe they accepted my offer. We must do a little detective work in the area to see what we can find out. Maybe it's haunted."

"That would be an advantage. I would quite fancy a knight in shining armour to keep me company while you're away."

"At least he wouldn't make you pregnant – I hope. How have you been?"

"Thanks for asking. I notice you seemed more interested in the house than your poor suffering wife carrying your child."

"Absolute bollocks Maisie. It was you who was bursting with the news before you had even given me a kiss.

" She went up to him and gave him a big hug and kiss.

"It's wonderful to have you home darling. I think a drink to celebrate is called for."

# CHAPTER 36

Mike was determined not to let his house of dreams slip through his fingers, giving his solicitors and surveyor no peace until the legal formalities had been dealt with. By the time his leave was up he had been given assurance that the contracts would be ready for signing on his return, and as the vendors were keen to complete, there should be no delays.

"All being well Maisie, we should be able to move straight from here to Half Water House on or before 10th December, which will give us ample time to get a little ship-shape before the kids return home for Christmas."

"You are the eternal optimist Mike – that's what I love about you, your glass is always half full" Maisie replied. "I just hope you're right my darling, because the novelty of the house will certainly soften the news to the girls that little 'Jemima', as the baby was now nicknamed, is on the way."

For once in their lives things ran smoothly. At 7.30 am on the 5th December the large removal lorry drew up outside Creek House. Both Brendan and Mrs. Honeywell were there to give them a hand. Maisie had managed to soften the blow of their departure by asking Mrs. Honeywell whether she would be prepared to come and live in for a few weeks when she came out of hospital to give her a hand with the baby.

"You know it will be fourteen years since the birth of my last baby Mrs. Honeywell, so I'll need your expert guidance. I didn't expect to have to go through all that again - sleepless nights and dirty nappies. The very thought - Mike's got a lot to answer for."

Mrs. Honeywell plumped up like a mother hen.

"Nothing would give me more pleasure than coming to help you look after the wee bairn. I will get her, or you never know it may be a him, into a good routine, and by the time I leave, you will find it a complete doddle – believe me. I expect Mr. Pinkerton will need a little looking after too."

Her sad face had now turned to smiles as Maisie gave her a weak grin. Mrs. Honeywell now had something to really look forward to.

This was also a big day for Brendan. Mike, his mentor, had been by his side and sustained him all through the terrible traumas that had beset him during the blitz in 1941 and after. He knew Mike would keep in constant touch, and would continue to financially support Annie and to a lesser degree himself, but somehow he felt as if a rug was being pulled from under his feet. How he would miss their chats over a glass of beer in Mike's snug, their jaunts down to the Bugle, the fish and chip suppers round the kitchen table at Creek House, and all the Christmases the families had shared. Out of misery, so much happiness and comradeship had evolved.

Brendan would look back on those years with nostalgia as would Maisie and Mike.

Even Mike had a tear in his eye as he bade farewell to his loyal friends. As he drove away for the last time, through his mirror he could see Brendan with his arms around Biddy and Mrs. Honeywell waving until they turned the corner.

Maisie put her hand on Mike's knee. "Cheer up my darling, one door closes and another opens. It's not goodbye, you know, we'll keep in close contact with Mrs. Honeywell and the O'Reilly family.

We now have such an exciting life ahead to look forward to, and it's up to us to make a go of it."

Mike squeezed, then lifted her hand and kissed it. "That we will certainly do."

\*   \*   \*   \*   \*

Lucy was the first to arrive after her first term at St. Andrews. Maisie collected her from Winchester Station. She looked radiant. Obviously university life was suiting her, and she couldn't wait to see Half Water House.

"Wow, this is fab!" she remarked as she walked into the spacious entrance hall, dominated by a large Christmas tree twinkling with fairy lights and covered with a mass of red baubles.

Maisie was thrilled with her immediate reaction, and was quick to show her round the rest of the house.

"This is magnificent Mum, I'm so happy for you, but it is no more than you deserve. I know better than anyone the hell you went through when Dad was killed, how hard you've worked since then, and now for you to marry the wonderful Mike, Dad's great soul mate, is too good to be true. Tilly, I know, is also happy that you have found someone like Mike to look after you."

Although they intended to break the news when all the girls were gathered together, Maisie considered this a perfect time to tell Lucy, her eldest daughter, in the hope she could rely on her support.

"Lucy, I have something really important to tell you, and I want you to be the first to know." Lucy looked wide-eyed at her mother.

"Mike and I are expecting a baby."

Even wider eyed now an astonished Lucy replied, "You're what? Did I hear you right Mum? An old couple like you?

"Oh Lucy please don't be too shocked, we're as amazed as you are, but now we've had a few weeks to get used to the idea, we're really please and hope you will be too and give us your blessing. You know we are not all that old."

Lucy was lost for words and it was a few seconds before she was able to reply.

"I'm not shocked Mum, I'm just staggered. It's the most exciting news I've heard for a long time. Congratulations, where's Mike? I must go and congratulate him."

"He won't be back until tomorrow evening, when we intended to tell you all together."

"I just can't believe that I'll soon have another sister or even a brother. That is so exciting. I'm glad you have told me first. I can then be on hand to help resuscitate the others when they keel over from shock. Well done Mum!

"Well I don't think much skill was required. We're naturally worried about telling Tilly, Kate and Phoebe, so it'll be great to have your support. Whatever you do don't tell them beforehand. The news must come from us."

"My lips are sealed."

Kate, Tilly and Phoebe too, were wildly excited with their new home and by the time Mike returned home that evening, they had explored every nook and cranny in the house, trampled across the water meadows, sorted out their bedrooms, and were all lolling about in the drawing room in front of the fire. They had all made themselves feel at home.

None of the children had seen Mike in his uniform before, and as he walked in to welcome them to their new home, Phoebe greeted him with, "My goodness Dad you look really handsome in that uniform," and Kate followed it up with

"Auntie Maisie has really taken you in hand and smartened you up at long last."

"Thanks kids and its great to see you too." He gave them all a big hug and after listening to them gabbling all at the same time about how wonderful the house was, he interrupted them,

"Where's Maisie?" he inquired.

"I think she gone out to get some fish and chips for supper," answered Kate facetiously.

"You've only been home five minutes, and I get this abuse," Mike said as he walked out to find Maisie. There she was in the utility room amid a mountain of washing.

"How are you my darling?" he said holding her in his arms.

"All the better for seeing you. Have you ever seen anything like all this she said," pointing to the pile of dirty clothes on the floor. You would have thought between them they could have brought something home clean."

"Would you like me to bring mine down as well?"

"Oh God no, I really don't know what the hell I've taken on, and to think before long I'll have horrible dirty nappies to add to this unsavoury collection."

"Come on, close the door on it tonight. It's after six and I'm about to open the bar." As Maisie followed him out he inquired, "What's for supper Maisie? Kate says she fancies fish and chips."

"Kate's going to have what she's given. I should think, thanks to you Mike, the poor kid's addicted to them by now. I've actually prepared quite a tasty supper. Are you going to break the news to them or am I?"

Maisie then told him that she had already told Lucy and she had taken it really well.

"That's a relief. OK, I'll tell them shortly while we're sitting round the fire, then we'll have the rest of the evening to relax – let's hope."

Amid the joyous chatter, Mike tapped his glass. "I have an announcement to make. I want you four to be the first to know that Maisie and I are going to have a baby."

That brought instant silence to the proceedings. Kate Tilly and Phoebe were dumbstruck. Lucy, fortunately on cue flung her arms around

Mike and Maisie.

"That's wonderful, many congratulations Mum and to you uncle Mike. Well there's life in the old dog yet," she teased.

"That's quite enough from you young lady, and will you drop the 'uncle' bit – both you and Tilly please now call me Mike, and I know Maisie would like Kate and Phoebe to drop the auntie bit. Following Lucy's lead, the other three, perhaps a little more formally added their congratulations. "I just can't believe it," said Kate, and Tilly added "It's going to take some getting used to, but I think it's really exciting. To think we're all going to have a half brother or sister."

Phoebe was a little more reticent, and just gave them both a peck on the cheek and said 'congratulations'.

Although a variety of subjects were discussed that night, somehow it always reverted back to baby 'Jemima' and by the end there seemed a general acceptance of this great event.

Mike and Maisie soon noticed that the two of them became the butt of most of their jokes, which they interpreted as a sign of approval.

# CHAPTER 37

Half Water House buzzed with activity in the first few months of 1953. When Mike was at home he spent most of his time learning all aspects of fly fishing from Tom Fleming, or better known as Tommy Trout, to whom Mike leased his part of the river. Mike was surprised how much there was to learn, and as the weeks went by he became quite obsessed by it all.

"It's a funny thing Maisie. I can liken flying alone in the blue skies and soft gentle clouds in a Spitfire, with only the sound of the Merlin engine for company, to that of standing alone on the river bank, with only the sound of the stream rippling by. From there, I can look up and marvel at the skies and nostalgic memories they hold, in the same way as I used to look down at the awe-inspiring beautiful lush country-side with its rivers meandering their way through the valleys. That in itself gives me a continuity. You know I don't get that feeling with the Comet."

It gave Maisie peace of mind that Mike was getting such satisfaction which seemed to bode well for life after his retirement.

With the help of a hard working daily help Maisie had made the house into a lovely home. It exuded an ambience of love and warmth, and within just a few months they felt they had been welcomed into the neighbourhood, making many new friends.

Maisie's pregnancy was passing by without a glitch, and she appeared to have unending energy. All four girls were keen to be sent a regular progress report. By the beginning of April, Jemima was beginning to make her presence known. Mike loved to place his hand on Maisie's stomach and feel the baby kicking. Their excitement was mounting.

"It's an awful thought Mike to think that only seven months ago I was seriously thinking of having the pregnancy terminated. I'm so glad I did not make a hasty decision."

"That's thanks to dear old Mrs. Honeywell," said Mike. "I think she has had her suitcase packed waiting for the call for weeks now - you would think it was her having the baby. If I'm away when you go into labour, and I'm unable to go and collect her, Brendan has offered to bring her over.

"She is hoping to come over while you are in hospital to look after me. I could do with a little tender loving care."

"How you dare say that Michael Pinkerton. I think we should get this straight. It's me having the baby, not you, and Mrs. Honeywell is coming to look after Jemima and me. You're a grown up boy now and can fend for yourself.

"Mrs. Honeywell assures me she can get Jemima into a strict routine before she leaves us. That is vital in my view. If she is able to do that it will save you, Mike, getting up too many times in the night."

"Oh very funny, Mrs. Comic Cuts!"

Pressure was being put on Mike and Maisie from Kate and Tilly. They had both decided they had had enough of school and did not wish to stay for the Upper VIth. They both had good 'O' level results, but had no desire to go to university. What they had in mind was to get to London as soon as possible and share a flat with some of their school-mates and have a bit of fun.

A useful career seemed far from their minds. They had had enough of being penned up in a strict boarding school, and were seeking freedom.

"What do you think Mike?" asked Maisie.

"Well I can't see any point paying vast school fees for another year at school when they have no ambition to go to university. In fact they seem to be lacking any ambition at all. A secretarial course would not go amiss and would give them a good grounding for anything they chose to do later. They don't have to go to London to do that.

"Supposing you suggest, that there is a good secretarial college in Winchester, then they could live at home. That'll call their bluff. I know what kind of reaction you'll get to that idea, but it will be an interesting exercise."

"You are cruel Mike. I'll do just that. We mustn't beat about the bush for too long as we have to give a whole term's notice, and that should have been handed in a few weeks' ago."

Wherever they decided to go Mike realised there was no point keeping them on at school, so handed in their notices that same day.

With so much on their plates Mike and Maisie weakened. Bearing in mind the sensitivity their forthcoming child may be having on their two girls. Kate and Tilly were given a place at St. James Secretarial College in London, together with their two school friends who had been accomplices in this devious plot. They were all to share a flat together in London.

\* \* \* \* \*

Maisie had almost reached her due date. Mike was away on a flight and Mrs. Honeywell had moved in. Maisie was driving Mrs. Honeywell home after buying provisions to tie them over while Maisie was in hospital. Mrs. Honeywell was all set for a cooking session to keep the 'master of the house' from feeling neglected.

As they drove past the newsagents, Maisie spied a hoarding.

COMET CRASH - 43 DEAD

"Oh my God, no."

"What's up dear?" inquired Mrs. Honeywell.

"I've just seen a poster saying a Comet's crashed and they're 43 dead. I know it's Mike."

Tears were rolling down her face. She'd been through all this before. Everything flashed through her mind – Johnnie's terrible flying accident, Johnnie's motorcycling accident that killed him. Being bereft with two small children and no money, and here she was again.

"Oh God," she said aloud "This time it's five children . . .Mrs. Honeywell do you think he's died intestate, leaving me with five children. I can't go through it all again."

The ever-calm Mrs. Honeywell put her hand on her knee. "Calm down, calm down Maisie my dear and just drive carefully, we don't want another accident. You're jumping to conclusions. You don't know whether it's Mike. Let's find that out first before you let your imagination run riot. Take deep breaths and try not to panic.

While Mrs. Honeywell staggered in with all the shopping, Maisie ran on ahead to phone BOAC. Her address book, which she said she always left by the telephone, was not there. By this time Maisie was shaking all over and Mrs. Honeywell became concerned the shock would cause her to go into labour.

Having quickly put the kettle on the Aga, Mrs. Honeywell gently took Maisie by the arm. "Please try not to panic dear. Sit down a second and try to think when you last used your address book."

"I can't think. It's always there by the phone."

"You look downstairs, and I will go and look in every room upstairs. It can't be far away." As Mrs. Honeywell was foraging around upstairs, Maisie's voice called out "Got it. Mrs. Honeywell I've found it."

"Thank goodness for that. Where was it?" Mrs. Honeywell asked as she came trundling down the stairs.

"In my bag." She tried to force a smile.

"I'll make us a nice cup of tea" - Mrs. Honeywell's answer to every problem. More frustration followed – the line was incessantly engaged. Maisie by this time was almost literally tearing her hair out .

"This is just terrible. Bloody aeroplanes they have been the bane of my life, and I swore I would never never become involved with anyone again connected with those lethal machines." She broke down sobbing her heart out.

The door opened. It was Mike.

# CHAPTER 38

Putting down his baggage Mike saw Maisie was distressed.

"Maisie, darling what's the matter?"

Maisie got up and fell into his arms "I thought you were dead Mike," she continued still sobbing and unable to speak for a minute or two.

"Darling girl, I was hoping I would arrive home before you heard the news. I was just leaving the airport when I heard that another Comet had crashed. It didn't cross my mind you'd have thought it was me – why I don't know. I guessed you'd be a bit disturbed when you heard it was a Comet." He turned to Mrs. Honeywell.

"Thank goodness you were here Mrs. Honeywell."

"Maisie, this may surprise you but I'm going to quit this job. I've had enough. This, I think is the third or fourth Comet crash. I know each one has been justified – this one was taking off in a severe tropical storm from Dum Dum Airport in India, but I think there could be a structural problem that needs investigating.

"Being a commercial pilot just doesn't grab me in the same way as being a test pilot. I can't wait to be able to get to grips on my fly fishing venture."

"Are you being honest Mike? I hope you're not doing this just for my sake. I'm sorry I completely over reacted. I was certain it was you in that Comet, and that was followed by a severe 'deja vu' attack. The past came flooding back – then the thought of being left with five children was no joke. Then I had visions that you had died intestate – oh Mike I had an hour of going to hell and back. By the way, have you made a will?"

"I'm being honest Maisie. I'm not doing it for your sake, although I took you into consideration when I made my decision, and thought you would approve. Yes, of course, I've made a will, and if by any chance I'm run over by a bus, you will, I assure you, be well looked after."

Mike would have to give a month's notice. He was intending to keep his flying licence going as a back up . . just in case! "I've a few ideas incubating in my mind to prevent me getting under your feet." He looked at her and smiled.

"I'm sure you have. Tell me what you're scheming."

"Well, I don't think golf is my scene, but you never know. I would like to learn how to glide, and the other thing at the very very back of my mind, would be to have a go at power boat racing. But Maisie I won't even think about anything until I have my fly fishing business running as a going concern."

Mrs. Honeywell was busy in the kitchen busily preparing some 'good and honest' comfort food as she described it. She thought Mike could do with something really nourishing after all his hard work. Maisie was convinced she was more concerned with Mike's welfare than she was for either hers or Jemima's.

"You really mustn't spoil him too much while I'm in hospital Mrs. Honeywell. He'll expect me to wait on him hand and foot. How about teaching him to cook, wash and iron, that might be more to the point?" Mrs. Honeywell laughed, "You are a tease Mrs. Pinkerton."

It was early evening and Mike had gone to see Tommy Trout. Suddenly without warning Maisie's waters broke, and within a very short time she was having regular labour pains. It looked as if Jemima would not hang about for too long.

"Are you ready to go my dear?" asked Mrs. Honeywell.

"Yes, my case is packed. I've just got to put in my wash things. I'll go and do that straight away. You know Jemima's not due for at least another week."

"That's no worry. You get your things and I'll go and find Mr. Pinkerton."

*  *  *  *

Mike wasted no time driving to Winchester Hospital, and Maisie was soon ensconced in a single ward surrounded by nurses asking her numerous questions.

"Look darling, I feel a bit of a spare part standing here. You're now in safe hands. I think I will go and find a pub and have a beer and come back in a short while"

"Don't be too long please Mike."

"Of course I won't. I think I need a drink to steady my nerves," he quipped. "Good luck Maisie my darling. I'll be back in no time at all."

Although he did have a quick beer he sprinted to the nearest florists and had them make up a beautiful arrangement of flowers. Puffing and panting he arrived back to the hospital, and as he was walking along the corridor towards the labour ward, he was met by a smiling maternity nurse.

"Mr. Pinkerton, you are the proud father of a lovely daughter. Mother and baby are  fine and ready to see you."

Sheer relief. Mike, although he had tried not to show it, he had been concerned for both her and Jemima throughout her pregnancy.

He walked into the ward, festooned with flowers beaming from ear to ear. "You amazing woman you. I'm so thrilled, and so relieved it's all gone well."

With a tear in his eye he bent down and gave Maisie a passionate kiss. He then looked at his tiny new baby.

"She's just lovely Maisie, can I hold her?" As Maisie gave Mike the baby, she folded back the shawl exposing its bare body. Baby Jemima had a willy!"

"Well I be jiggered. She's a boy! Mike exclaimed. "That really is the icing on the cake. You wretch, how could you, and even the nurse, pull my leg on something so important. Actually I wasn't in the slightest bit disappointed when she told me it was another girl. But a boy, you and I have given birth to a boy.

"He cradled the baby in his arms at the same time bending over to give Maisie another kiss. "He's a handsome chap – just like his father."

"Before you get too carried away my darling, can I just correct you. I was the one who actually gave birth to this miracle baby. I gave birth to him while you imbibed beer in the pub. Your contribution to this event was a complete doddle, if not significant."

They both laughed as Mike handed the tiny scrap back to his mother and pulled up a chair to sit close to them both. As he affectionately trailed his finger gently across the baby's forehead he said, "Right, now for a name – 'Jemima' must not be mentioned again. That would not be good for his macho image." They thought for a minute or two then Mike made a suggestion.

"How about 'John Richard Kershaw Pinkerton'? The 'Richard' part is after my father who I loved and respected and to whom I owe so much, and the other two names after a phenomenal man we both adored."

"Darling Mike, that makes me want to cry. If you're really happy with that, so am I, and I know my children will be over the moon. I haven't checked yet to see whether Johnnie has been born with wings, but I suppose if he hasn't you won't take long to implant them. Before you go off to the pub to celebrate could you go home and telephone all the family and friends and tell them our thrilling news. I've left a list of names and telephone numbers by the phone."

Mike nodded and again congratulating Maisie he said "I think visiting hours are from 2pm, so I'll see you tomorrow soon after two. God bless darling, take care of Johnnie"

Maisie laid back and closed her eyes with a feeling of euphoria. 'There's no greater feeling of achievement for a woman having just given birth,' she thought. After another glance to see Johnnie snugly wrapped in his shawl sleeping peacefully, she fell into a deep and contented sleep.

# CHAPTER 39

Maisie's easy confinement, and the fact she had a nurse at home meant she was discharged from hospital much earlier than had been anticipated, much to Mrs. Honeywell's delight.

Mike had invited Brendan and Biddy over to meet Johnnie shortly before he went off on his next trip. He was keen to know how they were all getting on and catch up with Annie's progress.

It was obvious they had all settled happily into their new home and Brendan was finding it much easier to make ends meet. His bookkeeping skills had come into their own and he now had quite a few part time jobs on the go as well as playing a large part in the running of The Bugle. In just a few months Biddy had changed in looks and ways. She was looking grown up and thriving at her grammar school.

"How's Annie getting along Brendan. Is she still making noticeable progress?" Mike asked.

"That she is Mike. She loves Seaview and has many many friends there. They are preparing her to take a few 'O' levels, but I'm a little worried what kind of work she will be capable of doing when she leaves Seaview next year. Mrs. Lovelock has already warned me that this will not be easy. Annie has quite a good mathematical brain. In fact, like Biddy, her school reports indicate she has a good all round brain but her hearing impairment will limit her in her choice of career."

Maisie entered the conversation. "This is just a thought Brendan. I haven't even mentioned it to Mike, but I'm wondering when she breaks up whether she would like a holiday job here for a short while, to help with Johnnie."

Mike emphasised his approval to this idea. "I think she might enjoy that and would be earning some money. We could ask Mrs. Honeywell to come back for a week or two to teach Annie baby husbandry. It would give her an insight into working with babies which she may like to follow up."

Thanks Mike and Maisie. I think it's a cracking idea. I will put it to Annie and let you know her reactions."

Mike had a new toy. He had bought a television set to watch the Coronation of Princess Elizabeth. There was to be a national holiday, and Mike in his enthusiasm thought not only would the girls meet their new brother for the first time, but would have the enjoyment of being able to watch the Coronation in the comfort of their own home. Few homes possessed a television, so it was a real novelty "that's if I can get the bloody thing working," he added.

Before Brendan and Biddy left Mike had included them in their Coronation Party starting at 9.30 am with a slap up breakfast . . .

"To be prepared by Mike" Maisie chipped in, as Mike was getting carried away with it all. She continued. "Then we'll have a slap up lunch, also prepared by Mike." She looked at him smiling.

Kate and Tilly had other ideas. They, with four other school friends had decided to go and line the route, and travelled up by train the night before straight from school in order to secure a good position. They eventually marked their territory outside Kodak in Regent Street. It was the 1st June, nearly mid summer but the weather was atrocious. The heavens opened, as the four of them dossed down on the pavement for the night. The atmosphere was electric – everyone sharing their food and drink and singing patriotic songs. It was an experience they would remember for the rest of their days.

The rain persisted most of the following day, but it did not quell their enthusiasm. After seeing the procession going to and from West-minster Abbey they fought their way to Buckingham Palace to watch

Queen Elizabeth II come on the balcony accompanied by The Duke of Edinburgh, Queen Elizabeth the Queen Mother and Princess Margaret and a young Prince Charles.

After just a bird's eye view of this spectacle, they wearily made their way back to Waterloo, and still with flags flying and saying 'Long Live the Queen' they caught a train back to Winchester where Mike met them.

Lucy and Phoebe seemed genuinely pleased to meet baby Johnnie. Lucy in particular couldn't put him down. "Oh Mum he's so cute, can I have him?" she asked.

"Not likely, not after all I've been through." Phoebe in her quiet way couldn't take her eyes of him. She asked Maisie whether during the holidays she might be allowed to paint a mural in his nursery. "That would be lovely Phoebe, you're so good at art."

Mike did actually produce the 'slap up' breakfast and Coronation Day at Half Water House was a great success. It didn't seem to matter that the weather had interfered with the, already, poor reception of the television. To see a television was, in itself, an experience, and to actually watch all the ceremony rather than listen to a wireless broadcast was an exciting experience for them all.

Annie seemed excited at the prospect of coming to help look after Johnnie for a few weeks during the summer holidays. Mrs. Honeywell had already taken her under her wing during the day showing her how to change nappies and she watched him having his bath. By the end of the day she was even holding him, a little nervously it must be said.

Unfortunately, the O'Reilly's had to leave before the arrival of Kate and Tilly, but it was a wonderful reunion when the two wet and bedraggled girls arrived home. They couldn't wait to meet their little brother. Johnnie was awake and happily gurgling away in his carrycot, appearing as if he were aware of his appreciative audience.

Mike came in with glasses and a bottle of champagne. "I think we must wet the baby's head," he announced. "Not again Mike, you'll drown the little fellow soon." Maisie added.

They all raised their glasses . "To Johnnie." "Johnnie" they all followed in unison.

# CHAPTER 40

It was a relief to Maisie when Mike arrived home after his last trip with BOAC. After a further crash of a Comet in Rome it was discovered they had a structural weakness and had to be withdrawn from service.

Half Water House was now a hive of activity. Mike was getting to grips with everything there was to know about fly fishing, river management and had even become an expert on the sex life of the trout.

Maisie had originally thought the house to be unnecessarily large but now with the four girls at home, Johnnie, Annie and Mrs. Honeywell, together with various friends coming to stay, there was hardly room to swing a cat. Talking about a cat, they still had Timo and a newly acquired kitten called Shenko, including Mike's new black Labrador Jet (he always called his dog Jet). The house was bulging at the seams.

Then there was the menagerie out in the garden – chickens, ducks, geese and in the dovecote two fantail pigeons Mike had called Forni and Kate, because they spent their lives fornicating not only with each other but every other pigeon that passed by.

The huge kitchen with its long table and its five oven Aga was the hub of the house. Maisie had Johnnie's precious cuckoo clock hanging in prominence on the wall with the quail chirping every half an hour and then on every hour 'Cuckoo, cuckoo' according to the time. The open door and the absence of a cuckoo was particularly significant to Maisie, Kate and Tilly who could remember Johnnie knocking the cuckoo off its perch with a bread roll, after a morning session at the pub.

For the first two weeks of the summer holidays Mike had seven women living at Half Water House. His tiny hut on the river was a handy haven to escape, and when things were a bit boisterous at home he would quietly take himself off to the pub. Stockbridge had many pubs, so he thought he would visit them all to find out which was his favourite.

Kate and Phoebe were soon off to Boston to see Virginia, and Lucy with some university friends, again went off back-packing through France, Spain and Portugal. Suddenly, there was relative peace, and Mike and Maisie were able to spend quality time together.

Mrs. Honeywell put Annie through her paces and she was soon hands on - bathing, changing nappies, doing the washing and taking Johnnie for long walks. Mrs. Honeywell was impressed with the way she handled Johnnie and her natural maternal instinct but told Maisie "of course, regrettably, her deafness would hamper her from becoming a nanny because she is unable to hear a baby cry. The tone of baby's cry is such a good indicator on whether he is in pain or just wants attention. However, Mrs. Pinkerton she is learning a great deal and seems to really love Johnnie. I know she'll be sorry to leave him. This is a wonderful experience for her and she's gaining more confidence every day.

The young student, Jamie Fairchild, who had been giving her extra elocution during term time, lived in Winchester and had volunteered to give Annie six more lessons while she was staying at Half Way House. The sessions of concentrated speaking were of mutual benefit to the two of them, and Annie's eyes lit up in his presence. Either this was because she enjoyed his lessons, or because he was good looking.

Jamie was about to begin his final year before qualifying as a Speech Therapist and would not be returning to Seaview for Annie's last year.

As in the previous year Kate returned from Boston madly in love. This time it was a short encounter with a man she had sat next to on the aeroplane.

"Daddy we chatted non stop throughout the flight. He lives in London and is going to take me out in a few weeks' time."

"It was a tennis player last year, and this time it's a man you picked up on an aeroplane. Dear Kate it must be the American air that has this effect on you. You are not safe to be let out of our sight.

"What does this young man do?"

"I've no idea what kind of job he's got, if any, but he's hoping to become a Member of Parliament and is standing at the next election."

"How old is he then, and in which constituency is he standing?" Mike asked becoming a trifle concerned.

"Oh Dad, I wish I hadn't told you now. I didn't expect you to interrogate me. I've forgotten what constituency but I know it's got a large Conservative majority and I think he's about thirty."

"OK, I won't ask you any more questions, tell me about your holiday."

Phoebe remained discreet about Kate's new acquaintance, and Mike thought it was more than he dared ask to question her about it. She was longing to get down to her mural in Johnnie's nursery and had already designed it. She had decided she wanted to paint it on to the ceiling instead of a Spitfire flying through the clouds. That was no surprise.

Mike and Maisie had been to London to vet the flat that the four schoolmates were to share while they were attending St. James Secretarial College. The Secretarial Course did not seem to hold much allure for either of them. It was the London scene that was the magnetic draw.

Mike asked them whether they were looking forward to the course. Kate replied, "Well, I can't wait to get up to London with all our friends, and at least doing a secretarial course is one better than domestic science which lots of our friends are doing."

Mike was quick to reply, "I really don't like your half-hearted attitude. You know it costs a lot of money to send the two of you there, and you've jolly well got to knuckle down and work and make a success of it. If you do well there will be so many interesting jobs open to you. It's up to you both. If after the first term you are making no progress, you're coming straight back here."

"Yes Dad."

"Yes Mike," they said smiling at each other before making a hasty retreat.

All too soon it was just Ma, Pa and baby Johnnie left rattling around in Half Water House. Maisie was pleased, and for that matter so was Mike, that Mrs. Honeywell and Annie had left. She now had her baby to herself and could enjoy looking after him and Mike had no reason to shy off to the pub so readily. They were fortunate enough to have found an obliging daily help who would always come and baby sit when required, so it would generally be the two of them who would go out together for a pub meal. Life was good.

\* \* \* \*

The London scene had obviously panned out as Kate and Tilly had anticipated. They were enjoying themselves so much that their visits home became less and less frequent. Fortunately, they did not seem to be neglecting their lessons as they both seemed to pass their relevant tests and examinations with flying colours. Whereas, it appeared that Tilly was a lively participant in the social scene, Kate's love life with her prospective parliament candidate was far more intense.

Mike became concerned. His fun-loving daughter had suddenly become serious and Mike somehow felt this man was controlling her every move.

It wasn't until January 1955 that Kate eventually asked whether she could bring Alan Beale down for the weekend the first time Mike had heard his full name.

"Thank God for that Maisie. We're at long last going to be allowed to meet the man who has taken over my daughter's life. He must be quite an up and coming politician to have been chosen for such a safe seat as Richmond."

Mike met them at Winchester Station. Alan was nothing how he had imagined. Kate had described him as good looking. Well that was open for interpretation – his overall spivish appearance rather dispelled that image. Thirty? Mike wondered. He must give the chap a chance.

The look on Maisie's face said it all. She gave Kate a warm hug and then held out her hand to greet Alan. "How do you do Alan – it's great to meet you at long last."

"Hi there, he replied."

To break the ice Mike ushered them into the drawing room, and offered them a drink. "Dad I would love a gin and tonic please." "How about you Alan what can I get you?"

"I'll have a beer – a brown ale please."

"Sorry, we've only got bitter or light ale, but I can easily nip down to the pub and pick up some brown ales," offered Mike, quite pleased for an excuse to go to the pub.

"No, a bitter will do."

Maisie came in with some crisps and nuts, "Kate it's lovely to see you, how's Tilly? Is she behaving herself?"

"Yes, of course Maisie. She's in fine form, having a whale of a time and is busy looking for a job, as I am. You're soon going to have two wage earners in the family – hopefully. Of course, there will be a General Election soon and I want to be available to canvas for Alan and help him with his secretarial work."

This was a cue for Mike to come in, but knew he mustn't put Alan under too much interrogation or Kate would chastise him. "Kate tells me you're standing for Richmond Alan. That's quite something. What made you decide to go into politics?"

Alan then told Mike and Maisie that it was the influence of two of the lecturers at the London School of Economics that spurred him on. He told them that he had been a councillor in Islington for a few years and was hoping eventually to become an M.P.

The penny was beginning to drop. Mike had assumed that any friend of Kate's would be a Conservative and Kate's political leaning would be towards the right. It suddenly dawned on him that Alan must be a Socialist and was the Labour Candidate for Richmond.

He realised that he must tread ultra cautiously and avoid getting into a headstrong political debate with his daughter's loved one. He wondered whether Maisie had realised or whether she was going to jump in with both feet and upset a volatile situation.

"What kind of work to you do Alan?" asked Mike, simultaneously receiving daggered looks from Kate.

"I am in between jobs at the moment. I give the odd lecture here and there, but am aiming to make politics a full time career.

It was plain that Kate did not wish Mike to question Alan at any length on any subject. He felt stymied.

Maisie tried to come to the rescue by asking Kate how her job hunting was going.

"Surprisingly enough Maisie, I have been offered one or two really interesting positions, but feel I can't accept a full-time job until after the election."

"Dear Kate, if you've been offered a good and interesting job I would have thought it important to take it so you can to start helping to pay the rent on your flat. I have told Tilly that everyone has supported her long enough and it's time she became financially independent. Why not get a job while the going's good and help Alan in your spare time."

Alan intervened. "I need Kate's backing now and for her to put a job on hold. If you're not willing to support her, she can come and live with us."

That was a bombshell. "Who do you mean by 'us'?"

"Kate can come and live with me and my family. Looking around at all this opulence makes me sick enough, then when you tell her you cannot continue to support her is beyond my comprehension. That's why there's so much poverty in this country. It's greedy people like you who hold on to all your wealth while the working man in the street is near starvation."

Mike was fuming.

"That's enough Alan. I don't want to hear any more socialist propaganda. I have worked hard all my life, and hope I've put more in to life than I have taken out. I have given my children a good education and feel it is now up to them to start repaying some of the benefits they have received. The world does not owe them a living. And if I may say, the same goes for you. I know little about you, but I don't like your attitude. You seem to resent success or anyone having more than you.

"I suggest you make a success of your own life, before you start trying to put the country to rights. You might find some of those chips on your shoulder will disappear."

He turned to Kate, "I'm sorry Kate for my out burst, but I'm not prepared for your friend to come into our house and start criticising. I hope you understand."

"Daddy, I don't know why you have to be so rude. I was so hoping you would get on well together and understand each other's opposing views."

Alan stood up. "Come on Kate it's best we go now."

Maisie tried to defuse the situation. "Please don't leave yet. Kate you've no idea how much your father has been looking forward to seeing you. It's been a long time, and I can't see he has done anything to upset you. Why are you suddenly rebelling against your home and family? We all love you. Please stay at least until tomorrow – it wouldn't be good to leave now."

Alan again insisted on leaving. Maisie continued "Please Kate will you stay? If Alan insists on leaving, I will take him to the station,"

"No, you come with me Kate," insisted a gruff Alan

Mike deeply upset gave Kate a big hug. "My darling I'm sorry it's worked out like this. Please come and see us soon. I'm here if you need me. God Bless."

An emotional Kate was unable to speak. She followed Alan out of the door - it appeared with a certain amount of reluctance. Mike went to shake hands with Alan but was spurned.

While Maisie ran them to Winchester, Mike sat mortified, wondering what had got into his warm and effervescent daughter. He could not believe how she could have been influenced so radically in such a short time. He was exceedingly concerned, and at a loss to know how to rectify the situation. He felt helpless.

"I have to say I don't think I have ever met such an objectionable young man in all my life," said Maisie on her return. "I noticed Kate even carried the suitcases into the station. An intelligent girl like Kate wasting her life on someone like that is beyond my comprehension. Don't worry Mike, I'm sure common sense will prevail."

"Come and sit here Maisie. Tell me what I can do about it. She's just not the Kate I know."

Maisie went and cuddled up to him. "Mike I think you must now keep well out of it, leave her to learn by her own mistakes. She'll see the light, but it may take time."

* * * *

Kate's sudden rebuttal to the family preyed on Mike's mind during the following months. He was mystified by her sudden change. Maisie was a pillar of strength throughout, and the joy that Johnnie brought to them compensated for the gaping hole Kate had left.

Mike worked endlessly to improve his fly fishing project, and having sought planning permission constructed a large lake in his water meadows and formed The Half Water Fishing Club. The membership was growing fast.

# CHAPTER 41

Tilly was quick to notify Mike and Maisie that Kate had left their flat and had moved into a tenement building in Bermondsey, with Alan's family.

May 26th the 1955 General Election. To Mike's delight Alan was trounced, but unfortunately failed to lose his deposit. It was now more than three months since Kate had contacted Mike and Maisie. Tilly had met her briefly a couple of times in that period and according to her she looked thin and unhappy. Mike avoided the temptation to try to confront Alan and meet up with her, only managing to get a message through to Kate to say he would love to hear from her.

Then came the distressing news that Virginia had let it be known to Kate that she would inherit money when she was twenty-one. Because of this, and at Alan's instigation, Kate was trying to borrow money from the bank on the security of her inheritance. Mike was appalled. He immediately alerted Virginia and the Trustees that they must take action to prevent this.

While wrangling over this latest move was in progress Mike took a telephone call. It was late one night.

"Hello, who's there?"

Very faintly he managed to decipher "It's me, Kate."

"Kate, where are you, Are you OK?"

"No. Dad please help me."

"Kate, have you had an accident. Are you hurt?" Amid her sobs she said, "Alan has beaten me up and thrown me out of the house."

"Kate, if you can, quickly jump into a taxi and take yourself over to Tilly's flat."

"I haven't got any money," she replied.

"That doesn't matter, just get away from there immediately. Find a taxi, and I'll phone Tilly to tell her you're on your way. She or one of her flatmates will be there to meet you with the taxi fare. Whatever you do don't hang around there for long. Do you feel you can manage that? I'll wait here until we know you are safely at Tilly's flat."

Mike turned to Maisie "That shit has beaten up Kate. I'll tell you about it after I've phoned Tilly."

"Tilly, sorry to phone you so late. It's Mike. Don't panic, Mum's OK. It's Kate. Alan's chucked her out of his flat. She's getting a taxi to you. As she hasn't any money for the fare. Can you find enough to pay off the taxi?"

"Oh poor Kate. Don't worry I can sort out the fare and will keep my eyes open for the taxi to arrive."

"Thanks Tilly. She's very distraught. As he's beaten her up she will need a little consoling. Phone us as soon as she arrives and let us know how she is. I 'll be ready to get in the car and come up to London if needs be."

"Don't worry Mike, we'll look after her. I'll phone later."

Hearing the telephone conversation Maisie was fully aware of Kate's dilemma.

"I think Kate needs me Maisie. I think I must go up to London. Will you be all right? asked Mike.

"I wish I could come with you but it's too late to get someone in to look after Johnnie. I'll go and get the first aid kit and anything else I think may be useful."

Although he was concerned for Kate, there was an element of relief in his feelings. At least there was a chance to extricate her from the claws of this controlling man.

The telephone rang. "Hello Mike. Kate's arrived safely. She's very shaken up and quite badly bruised, but not bad enough to go to hospital. Alan evidently punched her in the face, opened his door and pushed her down the stone steps."

"Will you tell her Tilly that I'm on the way up and should be with you in about two and a half hours. Look after her until I get there, and Tilly be sure to lock your door. Alan may come looking for her and I feel your flat may be the first place he would come to. Don't let anyone in – you must avoid any confrontation with him. I'm on my way now."

Kate looked a shadow of her former self – painfully thin, sporting a black eye and badly bruised down one side of her right leg. Tilly and her other two flatmates had listened intently while Kate had poured out all her woes, she had calmed down considerably by the time of Mike's arrival.

"I'm so pleased to see you Kate. How are you feeling?"

Kate looked at Mike, "I'm sorry Dad."

"Don't worry about anything. I'm so pleased that you're not too badly hurt, and that nothing but a little tender care won't put right. Are you feeling a little more relaxed now, because I think you ought to get some sleep, and then tomorrow I hope you'll come home for a bit so we can get you well again."

"Thank you. I know I don't deserve it."

"Come on Kate, my bed is all ready for you. I'll get you a hot drink to help you sleep. Which would you prefer Ovaltine or Horlicks?" said Tilly helping Kate to her feet.

"Ovaltine would be great thanks Tilly."

Mike got up and kissed Kate goodnight. "Try and get some sleep. We'll sort everything out tomorrow. God bless."

Mike was soon wrapped up in blankets and eiderdowns trying to sleep in an armchair in the small sitting room, while Tilly happily dossed down on the floor.

Before anyone stirred the next morning Mike, looking decidedly unkempt having slept in all his clothes and unshaven, had been out and returned with pints of milk, and bacon butties for everyone. It was breakfast on the hoof as the four girls tore round in an attempt not to be late for work, Mike was eager to get Kate home.

It was a lengthy business getting Kate back on her feet again. Her bruises and grazes were the least of her worries, and to begin with she was reluctant to pour out her miserable story. She was profusely apologetic to Mike and admitted how she had hung on Alan's every word and how he'd poisoned her against her family.

"Dad and Maisie will you ever forgive me?" she asked. "I stupidly fell in love with him, and it's taken me quite some time to realise that he's a complete nut case. He has a mental problem and has recently been accused of causing grievous bodily harm, probably putting an end to his political career. I think anyway, deep down he was a communist, because he holds such extreme views. He's a bitter man, with violence always bubbling under the surface, to which I was regularly subjected."

"My God Kate, if I'd known he was attacking my daughter I would have been up and shot the bastard."

"That's what I was afraid of. I was too frightened to come to you for help sooner because I couldn't account for your actions. I thought you would only make matters worse. Dad, I've brought this whole sorry saga on to myself, I've only myself to blame."

Tears now pouring down her face, she fell into Mike's arms.

"I'm so so sorry will you ever forgive me, I know I've caused you so much unhappiness." She then hugged Maisie. "Maisie, I must have put you through a lot of stress too. Please forgive me. It's such a comfort to know that the two of you are together. Thank you Maisie for looking after him. He's so useless on his own."

"That sounds like my old Kate coming back to form. Like some fish and chips for lunch just for old time's sake?" suggested Mike laughing.

"Kate, we've all done equally stupid things in our lives that we live to regret. Put it all behind you now and move on. Don't give that little Hitler another thought. There's a wonderful life out there ready to welcome you with open arms. Don't look back, look forward."

"Thank you for being so understanding. Where are these fish and chips any way, I'm beginning to get my appetite back again?"

*　*　*　*　*

There was a new spring in her step as Kate settled down to finding herself a job. At the same time she had regular driving lessons and passed her driving test first time. She found herself interesting work as secretary to the Conservative MP for Winchester, David Johnson Smith, so she would be dividing her time between his home in the constituency and the House of Commons.

Mike was delighted with this appointment, as it would enable he and Maisie to see more of her. He did, however, query her choice. "My God girl, haven't you had enough of politics. Kate replied "Actually, I find it quite fascinating, and it will be interesting seeing it from the other side of the fence."

# CHAPTER 42

By September 1956 Kate was back sharing her flat with Tilly and when parliament wasn't sitting, she based herself with Maisie and Mike. She was back in the fold – the same caring Kate everyone knew, and seemingly not getting too carried away with the opposite sex.

Tilly had an interesting job at Sothebys, still living life to the full, and now, according to Kate, a regular boyfriend in tow. Lucy was living in Paris working at the British Embassy and Phoebe was studying Art in Bournemouth.

"Fingers crossed, all our kids seem settled for the time being, thank God" Mike mentioned to Maisie, "I am, however, concerned about Annie."

Annie was trying to do a typing and book keeping course, but was finding it difficult due to her lack of hearing. She had been so used to having children around all suffering from similar disabilities, and now she was finding herself in a hostile environment, being laughed at and bullied, because she couldn't keep up.

"I find it incomprehensible that the other kids don't recognise she has a problem, and be kind to her. I don't quite know what to do about it."

Maisie replied, "I'd be inclined to find out whether she can stick it out. If so, see how she does in her final exams, and then go from there. Kate will be able to find out how unhappy she really is. It would be a good idea to speak to her teachers too.

"You know Mike, she's going to have to integrate back into the real world. It's cruel I know, but the sooner she can adapt to it, the better. Let her finish the course, and then go from there." As an afterthought Maisie continued. "Another one to ask Mike is Jamie Fairchild. They have such a great relationship. He's her guru and I think she confides in him a great deal."

"Thanks darling, that's a great help. I'll act on all those suggestions."

Mike and Maisie frequently checked up on their own offspring, and those to whom Mike felt he had a moral responsibility. It was like a roll call, ticking them off one by one.

"We haven't mentioned Biddy, Mike. Do you know how she's doing?" asked Maisie.

"She's fine. She just seems to get on with life without causing a stir. She obtained good 'A' level results and is now doing radiography in Southampton – at the South Hants. That's good for Brendan as she's still living at home."

Mike continued. "I spoke to Mrs. Honeywell today. Do you know she's seventy-eight? She and Mavis seem to be managing well – we must go over and see them shortly and take Johnnie. She'll be amazed at his progress."

As they were talking, Johnnie now running around, was playing hide and seek with Jet the Labrador. Johnnie would go and hide and then Jet would find him, causing him to squeal with laughter. Timo just looked on bemused. The terrible twos had arrived in no uncertain manner. He was into everything, and Maisie found she could not let him out of her sight.

"I reckon we're too old for this lark Mike," she said as she rushed to rescue a Dresden vase that he had managed to pull off the table.

"Nonsense darling, that's what's keeping us so young."

"He may be keeping you young. I feel a hundred."

\* \* \* \*

Before meeting Jamie Fairchild, Mike visited Brendan to discuss Annie's welfare.

"I know she's not enjoying the course Mike and finding it difficult to keep up. She hasn't told me she's actually being bullied, but tells me everyone ignores her."

Mike then told Brendan, that the last thing he wanted was for Annie to be unhappy, but it would be beneficial to her if she could stick it out. He continued to tell him that he thought he would seek Jamie Fairchild's opinion if Brendan approved."

"As she's half way through the course now, I think she'll be able to see it through. It breaks my heart to see her unhappy again after her days at Seaview. Annie's got grit Mike, she'll see it through, but I think it would be an excellent idea to talk to Jamie. Would you like me to come with you?"

"Just as you like?"

"I think it would be quicker if I leave it to you, if that's OK, Mike?"

"That's fine Brendan. I'll let you know what he thinks. Take care and give my love to Biddy and Annie."

Mike wasted no time in contacting Jamie. They met in The Wykham Arms in Winchester.

Jamie already seemed aware of Annie's lack of enthusiasm with her typing course and her feeling of isolation.

"It's a strange thing Mike, anyone with a disability nearly always finds they are an outcast in society. The man in the street appears to be embarrassed by them and shuns them. Why? It is hard to understand, somehow it seems instinctive, but to those who are having to learn to live with their disabilities it can be earth shattering and have an added profound effect on them."

Mike asked, "Both Annie's father and I wonder whether it's fair to ask her to finish her typing and book keeping course."

"As you probably know I have a soft spot for Annie. I have known her for quite a few years now and have been blown over by her strength of character. My boss is starting up a Speech Therapy practice based in Winchester with the idea that when I can afford it I can become a partner. I have already mentioned to him that if possible I would like us to employ Annie as I feel she would be a great asset in dealing with people with speech problems. He approved of this idea. It would, of course, be a tremendous asset if she were able to type and book keep."

"Jamie that sounds a wonderful idea. So judging by what you've just said you think she should soldier on with the course?"

"I think without a doubt she has the character to see it through. Also if she knows that if she does reasonably well, there'll be a job waiting for her at the end, it will give her an added incentive. If you like I will mention this idea to her in the next day or two."

Mike left with a feeling of euphoria. He remembered that terrible day Annie was pulled out of the ruins of her home during the blitz, her subsequent suffering, losing her mother at such a tender age, her perseverance, how she kept smiling through, and now another door seemed to be opening to a bright future for her. Mike felt perhaps his job was nearly done.

He couldn't wait to get home to tell Maisie the news and he knew Brendan would be over the moon when he heard.

Having told Maisie about his meeting with Jamie, Mike said, "Thanks Dad, without your legacy, I couldn't have done it."

# CHAPTER 43

Annie persevered through the remainder of her secretarial course. It was the knowledge of knowing that she had a job at the end of her training that spurred her on. There was no doubt it was a struggle, as she had been made to feel a leper. When she wasn't being ignored, she was being ridiculed. It was the same feeling of isolation she remembered before she went to Seaview.

However, being able to help look after Johnnie, and the unswerving support she received from Jamie gave her self assurance, and towards the end of her course her smiles slowly broke through again.

Annie adapted to her new job at the Speech Therapy Clinic amazingly quickly. Jamie had insisted that she was not there just to do the typing, accounts and filing, but must play an out front role. Working with people with speech problems brought a new dimension to Annie's life. She was her own person at last, and an inspiration to those she met, enriching both their and her own self-confidence.

The friendship between Annie and Kate that had lapsed during Kate's days in the wilderness was renewed, and they would meet on a regular basis when Kate was in the area. During one of these get togethers Annie confided in Kate.

"Kate, I want you to know that I have fallen in love with Jamie. He is always so kind to me and we get on so well together."

Kate was lost for words. It should have been predictable that Annie, now aged twenty would fall in love with the man who had brought her out of isolation and been there for her for the last six years. Was this love reciprocated Kate wondered?

Jamie had done more to improve Annie's speech than anyone, but was it just his conscientious interest in his work, or had he too developed a love for Annie? She did not want Annie to be hurt.

"Annie, I can quite see how you have fallen in love with him. He is a lovely man, a real gentleman. Do you think he loves you?" Kate slowly asked her.

Annie nodded. "I think so. I hope so."

Kate did not wish to prolong the conversation, or in any way disillusion Annie, but she feared that maybe Jamie had never thought that perhaps a situation like this would have arisen. If he did not love Annie, it could put her wonderful job in jeopardy.

Kate's fears were soon allayed as a few weeks later Jamie and Annie arrived uninvited at Half Water House. Mike was at the Fishing Club and Maisie was putting Johnnie to bed.

"Is Mike around Maisie?" Jamie inquired.

"He's somewhere up near the lake I think, Jamie. Would you like to go and find him? Annie would you rather stay here and help bath Johnnie?" Annie nodded.

Johnnie seeing Annie immediately ran to her and with an impish smile put his arms up for her to lift him up and cuddle him. A close bond between the two had built up. Since a tiny baby, Johnnie had responded to Annie's' warm hearted nature.

Being unable to converse was superfluous in this special relationship. As in her school days, her interaction with Flippet, her rabbit, had played an important but silent therapy in Annie's development. Now, although a rather ageing rabbit, Flippet would be given pride of place in the new matrimonial home.

Johnnie safely tucked up in bed, Mike and Jamie returned. As was his wont Mike made straightway to the drinks cupboard. He took out two beers, the bottle of gin, some tonic, and then asked Annie what she would like. She too asked for a G and T.

Jamie then spoke. "Annie and I have come to tell that we are to be married."

This was unexpected news. Mike look stunned. "That is just wonderful news. Jamie, I think you're a lucky man. Annie, I am so happy for you." He kissed Annie and shook Jamie by the hand. Maisie followed suit and told them how excited she was for them both, and wished them every happiness.

Jamie had already been to ask Brendan's permission, who according to him was delighted.

Biddy too was full of enthusiasm over the announcement and had already booked herself in as a bridesmaid.

\* \* \* \* \*

Both Biddy and Kate were bridesmaids at a small wedding, but one that meant so much to everyone there. For Brendan to know that his darling Annie had found someone she really loved and who, he was sure, would always be by her side, was something beyond his wildest dreams.

The presence of Bryony and Rory from Ireland added to the nostalgia. Annie's best friend Sophie was there with her mother Mrs. Lovelock, the head of Seaview. It was a particularly poignant occasion for them, as it was, of course, at Seaview that Annie and Jamie had met.

Annie seemed to have won over the hearts of Jamie's parents, his brother Tom and sister, Penny, which Mike considered would be an added bonus to the couple's future happiness.

At the reception, held at Half Water House, Brendan made a short but touching speech referring to his Irish roots and how proud he was of his beautiful twins. He only wished that 'dear Mary' their beloved mother could have been there to have seen them develop into such attractive and intelligent young women. Mrs. Honeywell's muffled sobs accompanied Brendan's closing sentences.

"To me the only other person missing here today is Rory and Bryony's son Paddy, who shared his early childhood with us in England." It was not without emotion that he concluded his speech by thanking Mike, who with his soul mate and fellow test pilot, Johnnie, had dug them out of the rubble of their blitzed home.

"Words do not suffice Mike to show my appreciation to you for the unswerving help and advice you have given to the O'Reilly family, and for giving Annie such a good education that now enables her to walk tall beside her lovely husband Jamie whom I'm so proud to have as a son-in-law." Brendan raised his glass "Annie and Jamie. God Bless them both."

Brendan continued, "May I make a special toast?

For those who do not know, Maisie was Johnnie's widow, now Mrs. Mike Pinkerton and they too helped us survive those days when we thought all was lost." He raised his glass again.

"Here's to Mike, Maisie, and their children. In this toast I would like to include absent friends – my dear late wife Mary and Johnnie."

As Mike was concluding his speech, portraying the lighter side of their wartime experiences, Kate spied a handsome young man standing in the doorway. She quietly walked towards him and whispered, "Hello, how can I help you?"

A gentle lilting Irish voice whispered back.

"Hello, I'm Patrick Kennedy." Kate looked confused.

"I think you must be Kate. Do you not recognise me?"

Kate was mesmerised by his stunningly good looks. She shook her head, then suddenly, the penny dropped. "Don't tell me, you're terrible Paddy?"

"I am he," he said as he bent over to kiss her. They waited silently for Mike to finish his speech, then Kate took him by the hand and led him over towards Brendan.

Kate began "May I conclude this wonderful day by introducing Patrick Kennedy."

She hesitated. . "or better known in this neck of the woods as 'Paddy, the terror,' O'Reilly." Brendan's face said it all. He was overjoyed. Mrs. Honeywell, having sobbed her way through the speeches, was quick to join in this tearful reunion.

A perfect climax to a memorable day.

The End

\*   \*   \*   \*   \*

To Mike this was more than a fairy tale ending. He could not help feeling a sense of significant pride to know how he, not forgetting his family, had helped, Annie and the O'Reilly family to literally rise up from the ashes.

\*   \*   \*   \*   \*

As to what happened between Kate and Patrick. Well that's for another day!